"Now, use my phone and text Vince as if you're me, telling him that's where we'll be overnight. Let him know I'm still concerned about the lack of backup before but want to keep him informed about how we're doing."

"You think he'll respond now?" Dane asked. "He didn't before, right?"

"Yes, and I don't know if he received my correspondence then. He didn't answer his phone or any texts for a while. But time has passed and we're in a different location, which might affect the phone's cell reception and all. Let's just give it a try."

"Whatever you say, Madam Protector."

When Alexa glanced at him this time, Dane's dark brows were raised and his smile was challenging, as if he figured her response would be an irritated one.

Instead, she said, "Glad you recognize I'm in charge, Mr. Protectee."

Dear Reader,

This is my fourth book in the wonderful, long-running Colton series.

Shielding Colton's Witness is book number ten in the twelve-book Coltons of Colorado miniseries, featuring a family of twelve siblings, most of whom are involved in attempting to atone for the illegal activities of their deceased father and also to live lives of their own, many in law enforcement.

In *Shielding Colton's Witness*, Alexa Colton is a US marshal who provides witness protection, mostly to women in danger. But she is assigned to protect vice detective Dane Beaulieu, relocating him from the Colorado location where he has been given a new identity to Arizona, where he must testify against the police chief who was previously his boss—and whom he saw murder his partner and friend. The very handsome and enticing witness also wants to protect her...

I hope you enjoy *Shielding Colton's Witness*. Please come visit me at my website, www.lindaojohnston.com, and at my weekly blog, killerhobbies.blogspot.com. And, yes, I'm on Facebook and Writerspace, too.

Linda O. Johnston

SHIELDING COLTON'S WITNESS

—

Linda O. Johnston

HARLEQUIN
ROMANTIC
SUSPENSE

Special thanks and acknowledgment are given to
Linda O. Johnston for her contribution to
The Coltons of Colorado miniseries.

Recycling programs
for this product may
not exist in your area.

ISBN-13: 978-1-335-73810-3

Shielding Colton's Witness

Copyright © 2022 by Harlequin Enterprises ULC

For questions and comments about the quality of this book, please contact us at CustomerService@Harlequin.com.

Harlequin Enterprises ULC
22 Adelaide St. West, 41st Floor
Toronto, Ontario M5H 4E3, Canada
www.Harlequin.com

Printed in U.S.A.

Linda O. Johnston loves to write. While honing her writing skills, she worked in advertising and public relations, then became a lawyer...and enjoyed writing contracts. Linda's first published fiction appeared in *Ellery Queen's Mystery Magazine* and won a Robert L. Fish Memorial Award for Best First Mystery Short Story of the Year. Linda now spends most of her time creating memorable tales of romance, romantic suspense and mystery. Visit her on the web at www.lindaojohnston.com.

Books by Linda O. Johnston

Harlequin Romantic Suspense

The Coltons of Colorado

Shielding Colton's Witness

Shelter of Secrets

Her Undercover Refuge
Guardian K-9 on Call

The Coltons of Grave Gulch

Uncovering Colton's Family Secret

The Coltons of Mustang Valley

Colton First Responder

K-9 Ranch Rescue

Second Chance Soldier
Trained to Protect

Visit the Author Profile page at Harlequin.com for more titles.

Yet again and as always, this story is dedicated to my dear husband, Fred. I also once more want to thank all the other authors in this enjoyable series, as well as Carly Silver, our wonderful editor for the Colton books.

Chapter 1

Alexa Colton sat down at her desk at the Blue Lark-spur, Colorado, office of the US Marshals Service. Before putting her purse into a drawer, she pulled out her phone and checked the time. It was not yet eight o'clock.

She smiled, stuck her phone on her desktop and swiped her short blond hair back from her face. Time to get busy.

Following her usual routine, she had arrived early that day, said good morning to the few other marshals, deputies and support staff she'd seen, then hurried up the stairs to her office on the third floor and shut the door behind her.

Her own office. This room, with space enough only for her desk, two chairs facing it and a couple of file cabinets off to the side, was an accomplishment. She'd shared a large space before when she was a deputy marshal. But now she was a marshal working in witness protection and had her own workplace at twenty-six.

She booted up her computer on the right side of her desk.

Her phone rang at the same time she saw she'd received an email from her boss, Marshal Vince Cudahy. He wanted to see her first thing.

She wasn't surprised that he was the person calling but was a bit concerned that he was both calling and emailing at the same time. What was on his mind? It had to be something important, with that kind of urgency.

Answering her phone, she said, "Hi, Vince. What's going on? I just sat down and saw your email."

"Good," said his deep, scratchy voice. "You're here. I'll be right there."

He hung up before she could offer to join him in his office instead. Whatever he wanted to talk to her about must be important.

She stood and took a quick look at herself. She wore what was standard around here—a black, long-sleeved shirt with metallic buttons and a badge on the front pocket, tucked into black pants. Her tied shoes were black, too, the thick tread on the soles for safety if she ever had to run while on the job.

She didn't have much time to make sure she appeared appropriate since her door was flung open almost immediately.

Vince must have headed over quickly, although it wouldn't have taken long to get here from his office at the end of the hall.

"Hi, Alexa," he said hurriedly. "Got an important assignment for you, starting tomorrow."

"Great," she said. "Tell me about it."

Fiftysomething Vince was at least twice Alexa's age. He had neither facial hair nor hair on his head, and his features were loose and wrinkled. But there was a shine to his light brown eyes beneath his pale brows that suggested he was passionate about what he said and did. Right now, he held a file folder in his thick hand.

"Sure," he said. "Sit down."

She obeyed, leaning forward in her chair as he took a seat at the other side of her desk.

He clasped his hands together and stared. "So are you ready to take on another assignment?" His voice remained scratchy but almost harsh, as if he expected her to say no—which was unlikely to happen. Alexa was proud of what she did.

Another person in trouble she could take care of, to help bring criminals to justice? *Bring it on*, she thought. "Absolutely," she replied. Over the past year, since she'd begun working in witness protection, she'd helped four women stay safe, shielding them from people they ultimately testified against in court. Every situation had gone well, and she loved helping victims in need. Her subjects had seemed relieved to have another woman in charge of guarding them. In her custody, none of the witnesses had been harmed; those they'd testified against had all been found guilty of the crimes they'd been charged with.

"Okay, here are the basics. I'll explain more, but to do this you'll be heading to Arizona tomorrow with the man under your protection, who is currently living here. He has had several of our marshals taking care of him over the past months. He'll be testifying against another law enforcement officer in Phoenix at the end of this week."

Wow, even with no details yet, Alexa was somewhat floored. She would be defending a man this time? If so, that would be a first. And another law enforcement officer?

Plus, Phoenix, Arizona, was a substantial drive from Blue Larkspur—at least a day away.

Oh yeah. This could be a real challenge.

Was she up for it? Especially since she'd be watching over a man, who might not feel a woman could handle it? Of course! Sure, the situation could feel uncomfortable, driving a distance alone with a guy needing protection, but so what? She'd handle it as well as she had the others.

She had questions but let Vince take the lead in describing more about the situation.

Her subject, who'd been given the name Daniel Brennan, had been in the program for a while. Alexa wondered why he'd had so many different marshals protecting him but didn't ask; she assumed the danger he was in was the reason. He would be testifying as the key witness against a police chief in a murder trial. "You're to take over watching him first thing tomorrow, so you'd better get ready today."

"Will do," she said earnestly. "Is it okay if I take the rest of the day off to get ready?"

She had something in mind to do that afternoon to bring any anxiety under control before it even began— ride her favorite horse at the nearby dude ranch owned by a couple of her siblings.

"Sure thing. You should get in touch with your subject soon to let him know your schedule, though. He'll be expecting your call. I've given him your phone number to confirm your identity when you contact him."

"Of course."

"And be sure to stay in touch with me and let me know any questions that come to mind and if you have any concerns." Her boss was standing now, regarding her with those intense eyes as if attempting to see inside her head to make sure she was okay with this new assignment. He shoved the file folder toward her, and she glanced inside as she accepted it. It contained at least a couple of printed pages. "It's highly classified," Vince said, "so be careful with it."

"Of course. And this sounds like one interesting and important assignment. Thanks for giving it to me." Alexa stood, too. She felt proud. She hadn't been in this job that long, and her boss was trusting her with something that sounded highly significant. But she worked hard and was glad to see her efforts were paying off.

"Yeah, I know it's a bit different," he said. "And it's definitely important." He leaned his large body toward her slightly and said, "Now make me happy that I decided to give it to you by succeeding at it. Got it?"

"I definitely do." This time Alexa gave her boss a genuine salute.

His grin turned the creases on his face upward. He saluted back, pivoted officially and, after opening the door again, stomped out of the office, closing the door behind him.

Wow. Alexa felt her heart race but took a deep breath and then another. First thing, she needed to learn as much as she could about Daniel Brennan.

She sat back down and opened the file, studied it for a few minutes, then researched the situation both in the secure department files and online. She'd heard of the underlying case since it had dominated the news a few months ago, but she hadn't heard of any local connection internally—like, having one of the victims and a witness, who remained alive, under witness protection. Those other marshals who'd taken care of him had apparently been appropriately discreet.

The police chief defendant at the upcoming trial, from Tempe, Arizona, was named Samuel Swanson. He was not only accused of murdering a cop who'd been a subordinate but also had been under investigation for running a prostitution ring.

That cop's partner, who'd also been working on the investigation, had also been shot, and had disappeared, according to the media—but Alexa knew he really was the one in protective custody, the man she was about to guard.

Daniel Brennan was that cop. His real name was Dane Beaulieu. His picture had been made public earlier, and Alexa suspected there'd be a lot more in the news about him, and the case, as the trial began.

Dane Beaulieu. Alexa couldn't help blinking when she saw his photos. As an important witness, and a victim of a shooting who'd survived and wanted to get justice for his brother officer, he sounded like a possible hero. And he certainly was one handsome guy.

But that was irrelevant.

She would call Daniel Brennan on the secure phone supplied to him by the department and let him know she would see him tomorrow.

Dane Beaulieu sat on the cheap sofa in the living room in the tiny apartment he'd called home for the past few months. No, the apartment *Daniel Brennan* had rented, he reminded himself.

The apartment rented for him by the US Marshals Service, of all things. Him. A law enforcement officer. Under witness protection.

Absurd. But necessary. His preference was to stay alive, and there were those who wanted to do away with him and had the knowledge and ability to accomplish that much too easily.

It was midmorning. He'd just gotten a text message from Marshal Vince Cudahy, letting him know he would soon be hearing from the marshal who was to take over his protection, and giving him a name and phone number to watch for.

The name Vince had texted him was Alexa Colton, which was interesting, too. Dane knew the name Colton. There were quite a few family members in law enforcement across the country.

Plus, here in Blue Larkspur, he'd heard that a member of the Colton family, a judge, had gotten into trouble with the law himself years ago by making extra money while convicting some innocent people, and that had led to other family members starting an organization to help other people, in an attempt to atone for it.

And a woman? Well, in his experience, it wasn't only men who did well in law enforcement. He hoped this one excelled, as the five marshals previously assigned his case had done.

Vince had also noted he'd sent an email. Dane checked it out on his secure laptop, also acquired from the Marshals Service. The email didn't include much information, but it did provide some background.

Not that there was much info there, though.

Well, it sounded like, over the next day or so, he'd have a lot of time to talk with Alexa Colton and find out more.

It was almost time to leave. To go home. To do what he'd wanted—no, needed—to, for his own peace of mind, as well as to now accomplish the very little he could for his dead friend and partner, Alvin O'Reilly.

And to do his own job, on hold now and maybe forever, as a vice detective for the Tempe Police Department. Which he missed. He didn't like being in hiding. He didn't like having to go against the man who'd been his chief. But it all had become necessary, thanks to that chief.

He rose and started pacing, glancing at himself in the mirror over the fireplace with false logs that glowed when a button was pushed. His mind had been working on jokes about that from the moment he'd first seen it.

He loved jokes; the cornier, the better. And these days, getting a laugh about anything was a good thing.

He made himself smile as he looked into that mirror, though he felt no humor at the moment.

He'd pretended to be a real human being named Daniel a few days ago when he'd left this apartment to get his dark hair trimmed into its usual conservative cut. He'd had Marshal Paul with him at the time, acting as a buddy but watching the world around them for Dane's protection. They'd also stopped at a grocery store before coming back here. Even knowing he would need to leave this place soon for the trial, he'd bought a bunch of stuff that shouldn't go bad—frozen food and otherwise. But he missed even being able to shop when he chose, along with everything else in a normal life.

So when would he hear from this Alexa? They

needed to head for Phoenix tomorrow to get him settled in and prepared to testify when the trial began in a couple of days.

The homicide had occurred in Tempe, which was in Maricopa County, Arizona. The trial would therefore be held at the Maricopa County Superior Court, which was located in Phoenix.

He wasn't clearing out this apartment yet, though. He'd wait till things were over, hopefully successfully, and then return to—

The burner phone he'd recently been given rang. He looked at the screen before answering, having already memorized the number with the Colorado area code Vince had sent, and this was it.

He swiped the screen to answer and made sure his voice was firm. "Hello?"

"Hello, Daniel," said an equally firm female voice— a bit deep and somehow sexy, though that didn't make any sense given the circumstances. "This is Alexa Colton. I believe Vince Cudahy let you know I'd be in touch."

"Yes," Dane confirmed, "he did." He waited for her to continue.

"You and I should have an interesting time ahead of us," she said. "We'll drive to our destination tomorrow. I'll pick you up at 8:00 a.m. Does that work for you?"

"Definitely. See you then."

She hung up immediately, which was fine with Dane. No need to draw things out now. They'd have a lot of time together to learn more about each other soon.

The drive to Phoenix should take around nine hours but, knowing the situation, he figured they would make some preplanned stops for security purposes. Worst case, they could figure out a locale to stay overnight since the trial didn't start till Thursday, three days from now.

How would it all work out? Would he need Alexa's protection? It was certainly likely.

He'd no doubt have opportunities to determine Alexa's competence after they met up tomorrow. He would protect himself as much as possible, too.

For now, he decided to chill as much as he could for the rest of the day, here in his small apartment. He'd make a sandwich for lunch, and have a dinner of leftovers later.

He checked his fridge. He had plenty of food.

Even better, he had a couple of bottles of beer.

He figured that, as he drank one, he'd ponder how things might go starting tomorrow as he hoped to get justice for his friend and partner. With the help of a US Marshal—with one sexy voice.

He wondered what she looked like…and knew he'd soon find out.

Alexa left the office a short while after the phone call. Her subject had sounded nice, professional, ready to proceed and, hopefully, to listen to her instructions as they headed for Phoenix.

She would find out how nice, and how respectful, starting early tomorrow.

Right now, as she headed for the Gemini Ranch, she called Kayla St. James. She'd rather bother one of the ranch hands than either of her twin siblings Jasper and Aubrey, who were four years older than her. As ranch owners, they tended to be fairly busy most of the time and would most likely refer her to Kayla anyway to saddle up her favorite horse, Reina. Sweet people that they were, the twins always tried to accommodate Alexa as long as Reina wasn't busy with dude ranch guests of the day.

Fortunately, according to Kayla, Reina was available, which made Alexa smile.

When she arrived, she parked her white SUV, an imported hybrid that served her well, in the open lot in front of the ranch's vast and attractive main lodge. She grabbed a backpack from the floor behind her seat and headed toward the door, calling Kayla again. "I'm here," Alexa said. "I'll go change then meet you at the barn, okay?"

"Sounds good."

The inside of the main lodge entry was crowded, filled with the buzz of a lot of conversations. Alexa smiled, glad for Aubrey and Jasper's success. They always seemed to be busy, and she was proud of them, even though she didn't see either of them in the large room lined with multipaned windows and decorated with a lot of dark-shaded wood.

It didn't take Alexa long to wind her way through the lobby to the restroom, where she changed into clothes a lot more amenable to horseback riding than a marshal's uniform. The long-sleeved denim shirt should be comfortable enough in the October coolness since it wasn't raining. Her dark blue jeans and Western-styled boots completed the outfit—along with her official weapon, a gun she always carried but kept hidden in a pocket.

Still not seeing anyone she knew, she returned outside to place her uniform in a secure area in her SUV, not visible from the outside, then locked it. Finally, it was time. She hurried back through the main lodge and out the rear door, then along the paved pathway to the barn.

The empty corral told her that any guests taking rides late this morning were already out on the trails. She was happy to find Kayla near the stall door, apparently finishing up with securing the saddle onto Reina's back. Reina was lovely and sweet, a pale bay horse with a white face. Jasper and Aubrey had indicated she was at least part Arabian.

At five foot seven, Alexa wasn't a particularly short woman, but the ranch hand was a couple of inches taller. The way Kayla handled horses and their feed made it clear that her muscular physique wasn't just for show. She wore casual clothes, too; jeans and a green sweatshirt this day. Her long, dark brown hair was in its usual ponytail down her back.

"Hi, Alexa," she said right away, her smile broad beneath her arched brows.

"Hi, Kayla." Alexa approached and ran her hand down Reina's face, enjoying the warmth and feel of the short coat and the way the mare snorted and nodded her head.

"Looks like your friend is glad to see you. So am I."

Alexa laughed. "Well, I don't think I have to tell you how glad I am to see both of you. I need a ride."

"Job giving you a hard time?" Kayla knew that Alexa was a US Marshal who protected people for a living. They'd talked about it often—or at least the generalities Alexa could discuss—whenever Kayla accompanied Alexa on her rides. Kayla also knew not to ask specific questions about what Alexa was up to.

Before Alexa could ask if she was going to have

human company that day as well as equine, Jasper came into the barn. Like the women here, he was dressed casually. He moseyed forward, smiling broadly. "Hi, sis," he said as he reached them. He wore his strawberry-blond hair on the long side and his dark blue eyes glittered as he shared a brief hug with Alexa.

But as he stepped back and looked at his ranch hand, Kayla moved away. "Sorry I won't be riding with you," she told Alexa. Holding her hand up in a wave goodbye, she headed for the door. Alexa had noticed that she seemed to walk away often whenever Jasper approached, and had always wondered why, though neither of them talked about it.

When Jasper offered to ride along with her, she decided that today she would use the opportunity to be pushy about it.

He rode beside her on Shadow, a gorgeous black horse with a somewhat aggressive personality. Few of their guests were permitted to ride on a steed so assertive, but he was one of Jasper's favorites.

This was far from the first time that Jasper had joined Alexa when she wasn't with Kayla. Sometimes Aubrey rode with her or she rode with both of them. But things appeared to be too busy for Aubrey to be her sister's company today. From what Alexa had heard, a TV show was recently shot on the ranch. Plus, Aubrey had to be planning her wedding. Yes, she'd met the right guy and was getting married. Alexa was even a teeny bit jealous.

"So what's going on, Alexa?" Jasper asked. "You've got some time off?"

"Only this afternoon. I'm starting a major project tomorrow."

Jasper knew better than to ask for details.

Alexa's own mind kept circling around what she would be doing the next day. The potential danger she'd face. How she'd handle protecting a fellow law enforcement officer who happened to be a man.

For this afternoon, she forced herself not to focus on it.

They rode across the narrow stream behind the barn and along a path into the woods, discussing how active the dude ranch was and future promotional plans.

Alexa loved this route. The woods contained mostly leafless trees, yet the brisk October air and crunching under the horses' hooves somehow made her feel happy. Even more enjoyable was the feel of Reina's wide, warm body walking slowly but determinedly ahead. This was a wonderful trail ride.

Still, the question always inside Alexa whenever she saw Jasper and Kayla's interactions, or lack thereof, surfaced once more.

"So," she blurted. "Tell me. At last. Why does Kayla act that way around you?"

She looked at her brother astride Shadow and he shrugged a broad shoulder. "Okay. I guess I should finally let you know. You can thank our dad for it."

"What!"

Ben Colton had been dead for many years. He'd been a judge—and, as it turned out, a corrupt one. To support his twelve children and their mother, he'd taken bribes and kickbacks from owners of private prisons and juvenile detention centers to sentence adults and kids, guilty or not, to their facilities. He had died before suffering any consequences.

And as a result of his misdeeds, their family had

begun a very special organization, The Truth Foundation, to help clear the innocent. Some had also gone into law enforcement—like Alexa.

"What do you mean?" Alexa prodded.

Jasper then told her that Kayla's dad had been one of the people their father had put away for life. "I've no idea if he was guilty or innocent. Kayla knows my issues with our dad, so she's at least civil to me as one of her bosses, and Aubrey, too. But we're definitely not friends, even though we're civil co-workers."

"Wow." Alexa shook her head slightly. "Another thing to blame our dad for." She felt a bit choked up, so she pressed her heels into Reina's side slightly harder. "Let's go!" she said, and Reina began galloping, with Jasper and Shadow following.

It wasn't long before Alexa decided to enjoy her time with Jasper more, so she slowed and started asking her brother questions about what was going on with their other siblings—anything he knew about all ten of them, including Aubrey and her engagement. And then the conversation turned to their mom, Isadora, who preferred being called Isa.

"Far as I can tell she's dating someone," Jasper said.

"Yeah, and if I'm right that person may be the local police chief," Alexa responded.

They talked and rode a short while longer, but Alexa recognized at last that it was time to go and start getting ready for the next day. Her mind had already begun to wander away from their conversation.

"This has been great, bro," she finally said to Jasper as they walked their horses side by side along a wider portion of the trail.

"I hear a 'but' in that. Time for you to leave?"

"Afraid so. But I'll want to do this again. Soon."

And that, she would look forward to, though she wasn't sure how long she'd be involved in her upcoming assignment.

They soon turned a corner in the path and headed back to the barn. On the way they saw several other sets of horses being ridden by visitors and led by mounted ranch hands—including, at one point, Kayla.

Alexa chose not to wave. She'd see Kayla again, maybe even have her join her on another ride sometime soon.

But at the moment, Alexa's thoughts had turned to wondering about how things would go tomorrow with the man she would be protecting. How much danger was he in? How perilous would it be for her?

But she hoped that her charge, who'd sounded okay, at least, in their brief phone call, would be cooperative.

Chapter 2

Several hours had passed since Dane had spoken with Alexa.

He would therefore soon be leaving this apartment. This small hangout he'd lived in for months. Would he remain safe? Who knew? But at least so far, no one had come after him here.

Not that he wasn't prepared for something, whether or not he was under protection. What mattered was that he would do all he could to get justice for Alvin and make sure his rat of a former boss paid.

He just wished his life hadn't changed so dramatically. But he would deal with it in the best way he could, danger or not.

He looked around the place yet again as he sat on the cheap blue-upholstered sofa, leaning back in his T-shirt and jeans and holding the bottle of beer he'd lifted from the coffee table in front of him.

He would work along with the marshal protecting him to ensure both of them remained safe and healthy. The sexy-sounding lady marshal who would be officially in charge of taking care of him.

Well, whatever it took for him to be able to return to his real life was a good thing.

Away from this tiny hellhole.

Oh, it was okay. The living room walls were smooth and white, and they contained a collection of photos of the Colorado Rockies, mostly in the winter, since the mountains were decorated with gleaming white snow.

The TV on the wall worked well with a remote control, and Dane used it often to try to keep from being bored. At least there was a cable system so he could watch anything from news to true crime to comedy, if he ever wanted to do that. And yeah, there were a few shows hosted by comedians who thrived on corny humor. His favorites.

But was he bored? Hell yes. A lot of the time. He wanted to be out there, working his job, checking out evidence, following leads, doing…something. Anything besides waiting.

And thinking. Overthinking. Again. Like now. About what had happened to drag him here. About being shot. And, worse, about the loss of his good friend and partner, Alvin.

But Dane wanted to survive, to testify at the murderer's trial. And so he'd do as he was told.

For now.

The kitchen had all the necessary amenities.

He wondered what that Alexa, his protector, had eaten to start preparing for their journey. Hopefully, something a lot better than he'd had.

His thoughts wandered now to what it would be like when she arrived tomorrow. She was picking him up here early in the morning. He couldn't stop thinking about her deep, sensual voice...

As a US Marshal on witness protection duty, she'd be armed. And him? Yes, he still had his gun. He'd wondered, when he'd first entered WITSEC, if they'd try to take it from him to ensure he wouldn't shoot the marshals assigned to him. But, considering he had been in law enforcement for years, too, they'd likely realized that he knew better. That he'd only attack to defend himself.

Although if the person assigned to protect him attacked him... Unlikely.

Putting his beer down, he settled back on the sofa and stared at the TV remote control on the table in front of him. He didn't necessarily want to watch anything. Not even silly humor.

How was he going to sleep tonight? He needed to be rested in the morning.

What might relax him now?

An idea occurred to him. Oh, it was unlikely to relax him, but it shouldn't hurt, and it worked well with his sense of humor.

He grabbed his burner phone and checked the screen for recent phone calls. The number he was looking for came up right away.

He pressed the number and was pleased when the call was answered immediately. "Daniel?" demanded a sexy female voice. "Is everything okay?"

Daniel of course. Dane hopefully wouldn't have to answer to Daniel Brennan much longer, but he did now. "Yes," he said, "with me. I'm ready to go. But I'm calling to confirm that all's okay from your end, too."

"Yes, of course." Her voice wasn't so sexy with that grumble in it. "I'd have let you know if there were any problems."

"I figured. I'm tickled to know there aren't any. In fact, I'm so tickled, I'm wiggling about it and laughing." Dane couldn't help smiling, even though that might be corny and it wasn't much of a joke.

Apparently, Alexa didn't think so, either. "Whatever. Don't call again, though, unless you do have a problem. We both need to get our rest now. See you in the morning."

Dane made himself calm down and drop any attempt at joking. "Right," he said. "See you in the morning. I assume we're both to eat breakfast first."

"Exactly. We'll want to get on our way fast."

"Fast it'll be," Dane said, wondering how it would be to ride in the car for a long period of time with this woman whose voice he enjoyed hearing, but who'd not given any indication she had a sense of humor.

Well, he'd find out tomorrow.

"Good night," he said and hung up.

It was morning, and Alexa was driving along the wide streets of Blue Larkspur toward the large apartment complex to pick up Daniel.

Daniel. She fortunately hadn't lost any sleep after their phone call last night. What had it really been about, though? she wondered for far from the first time as she stopped at a traffic light.

The witness who was now the subject of her protection duties had sounded a bit strange—and yet there

was something about him that she'd appreciated.
Maybe it was his attempt to keep things light as he'd
checked on the status of an outing that would be anything but light, even though she didn't think what he'd
said had been particularly funny.

She wondered what their conversation would be a
short while from now, as they drove to the city where
his life was likely to be in danger. Danger she would
handle.

The light changed, and Alexa drove the plain gray
SUV the Marshals Service had obtained for her for
this assignment, rented with a license that couldn't be
traced to her or her employer and shouldn't draw the
attention of anyone looking to stop Daniel from arriv-
ing in Phoenix. She'd had it washed, and the inside still
held the slight scent of a floral cleaner. She inhaled,
concentrating on the clean smell for a moment to get
her mind off what she was doing.

But then, she had to get back to it. As if she'd ever
really left.

Only another few blocks to go.

She could have stayed overnight in the extra apartment leased by the marshals in the complex where
they'd rented an apartment for Daniel, but she had decided to stay at home. From what she'd understood
from Vince, things seemed calm here in Blue Larkspur and although there were some criminal activities
in her hometown that her family wanted to stop, she
hadn't heard of anything going on lately.

While she drove, Alexa let her mind wander—for
now. She couldn't help thinking about the last tele-
phone call she'd had before dropping off to sleep last

night from the person she always spoke to at least once a day: her fraternal twin sister, Naomi.

They remained dear buddies, despite the fact they lived in different towns. They were the youngest of the dozen Colton kids, and they'd always been close to one another.

"Now, you be careful tomorrow," Naomi had said after they'd finished talking about what they would be doing for the rest of the week. Naomi was a reality TV show producer, of all things. And *she* thought it odd that Alexa had become a US Marshal, despite the fact that so many of their siblings were involved in law enforcement.

Alexa hadn't told her any details about her current assignment, only that she was off on a job for the next week or so, starting today.

And given the fact that she worked in witness protection, she wasn't surprised that her sister had warned her to stay safe.

There. Alexa saw the sign for The Village, the largest apartment complex in town. She drove along the wide entry with its pillars on both sides, and soon turned left. She pulled over and checked her phone. Vince had sent her a map of the area, indicating where Daniel's apartment was located. It was the last building on the left, and at the end of the ground floor.

Okay, it was time. She got out of the car and scrutinized the area. She noticed two women exit through a door in the next building over and kept her eyes on them. They headed the opposite direction from her and into the closest parking lot. Probably just residents leaving for the day. She'd glance at them often anyway.

She got to the door to the subject's building. It had small glass panes but was mostly thick wood. Good. A phone hung on the wall near the entrance, the apartment numbers listed.

Alexa chose Daniel's number from those programmed into her phone.

"Hello, Alexa," he answered immediately. "You here?"

"Yep. Buzz me in." She wanted to take a quick scan of his unit to ensure nothing looked wrong before they took off.

"Right," Daniel said, and she heard a buzz then a click at the door.

She turned briefly to reexamine the area. She no longer saw those women, or anyone else. Good. She pulled the door open and entered the hallway.

She'd entered through the door closest to Daniel's unit. Even so, she took a quick stroll down the corridor, passing half a dozen closed doors, watching and listening. Though she heard what might have been TVs or radios inside some of the units, she didn't find anything abnormal about the place.

She returned to Daniel's apartment and tapped on the door, which opened immediately. She hurried inside and shut it behind her.

And there he was, the man whose photo she'd looked at often during the past twenty-four hours. He was tall, maybe six feet, and definitely good-looking, although that didn't matter. He was the subject of her protection. That was all. But it didn't hurt to study him, to ensure she knew all she could about him.

Okay, dark brown hair, slightly long but in a conservative cut. Green eyes that stared at her, and she hoped she wasn't blushing. A handsome, angular face, with a well-shaped nose and slightly full lips.

Oh yeah. *Definitely* good-looking.

"Hello, Daniel," she said, nodding at him. "Are you ready to go?"

"Of course. I'm more than ready. I've been waiting for today for a long time."

Alexa understood what he was saying. And now she hoped to talk to him about what he'd gone through, what she had read about him and the events that had led to his being in witness protection.

She noticed a carryon suitcase on the floor behind him. "I assume that's coming with us?" She nodded toward it.

"Yeah. And I hope to return here for everything else that's mine really soon."

"In other words, you want the court decision to happen fast and well."

"Exactly. So— Let's go."

He couldn't help glancing at her often. Her hair was light blond. Short, with side bangs. Framing a face that was lovely, highlighted by gorgeous, intense blue eyes.

Dane wasn't biased professionally. He'd always liked women. Respected them. Knew they could excel at whatever men did, too. And he'd worked with some really skilled female cops and investigators in his own offices. No reason to think any less of them than the men he worked with.

But maybe he did have prejudices hidden so deep inside that he didn't really know about them. Till now, maybe, and he certainly wasn't proud of the way his mind was going.

Still— Could a woman do a great job at protecting him?

Well, sure. She had to—to keep him safe. He'd find out. He'd help to the extent he needed to, wanted to, but for her to have been picked for this particular assignment, making sure he got to testify against the guy who'd murdered his partner, who'd also injured him, who'd led to him feeling so damned sad and angry... Well, her superiors had to think a lot of her.

As Dane settled in the passenger seat of her car, watching Alexa start driving away from his apartment complex toward Interstate 70, he assumed she would head in the best direction toward Phoenix that he'd found online.

But she was a local. He wasn't. He'd leave the route determination to her.

Still— "Would you like me to drive?" he asked. She'd gotten right into the driver's seat while he'd loaded his suitcase, his laptop inside, into the rear portion of the vehicle, so he hadn't been able to ask her before.

She glanced at him, then turned her eyes back to the busy city road they were on. "Why? Are you one of those men who assumes women aren't capable of driving? Or maybe not capable of witness protection?"

"Hey, I'm one of those men who enjoys being taken care of well by whoever does it, and if it happens to be a woman, so much the better. I just thought, since you're supposed to coddle me, protect me, make sure I get to our destination alive, that as a US Marshal you would want to be able to check out the roads we're on, our surroundings, to ensure you take perfect care of me." He'd said it seriously.

"Okay, consider yourself my kid for now. Yes, I'll protect you. Get you to our destination safely, or at least as safely as possible. But I've done this before. I know how to scan our surroundings to make sure everything's okay. So, you can just sit back and enjoy the ride. For now, at least. It's a long drive, so I might ask you to take over some of it, although I've already scheduled a few stops along the way."

He figured she had. She seemed professional. Efficient. Prepared to do her job. Never mind how beautiful she was.

And she considered him her kid? No way. She was younger than he was, for one thing. He assumed she was around twenty-five or twenty-six, young to be in charge of a subject in witness protection, so that was something impressive about her, too. And he was thirty.

He looked out the window, figuring he'd start a conversation soon to help them enjoy the drive more than if they stayed silent…or argued. And he didn't only want to think about her skills or looks or anything else that was personal. Like her sexiness.

They had a professional relationship, after all. He was relying on her. And—

"Are you armed?" she asked.

"Yes," he said, and patted his side pocket where he'd placed his weapon.

"Good. Me, too. And soon, I'll want to hear your side of what happened."

"Sure." He'd planned to do that, if it made sense. Not quite yet, though. Once they got on the first highway, the first step toward their goal.

Only— They apparently were already there. As he'd been watching, they'd driven around several Blue Larkspur streets, sometimes even circling a block, he believed, before getting back onto a main drag.

She had evidently been maneuvering to make sure they weren't being followed. He'd been watching, too, and appreciated her professionalism as well.

She pulled onto a ramp that would head them northwest through Colorado, where they'd then turn south into Utah.

So he'd been right in his assumption. And she seemed right in having picked the best route.

He nodded to himself and settled his shoulders back on his seat. "Okay," he said. "Let's talk about what happened."

Chapter 3

Alexa was eager to hear it, but she had something to tell Daniel before she learned those details.

It was important that he knew the plans for this trip.

"Great," she said. "But first, I want to tell you how this journey to Phoenix will proceed. You're aware, aren't you, that the trial will take place there, even though the homicide occurred in Tempe?"

"Yeah," he said, "I am. The Maricopa County Superior Court is in Phoenix. But they're not that far apart."

"That's right."

"So, do you plan to drive us there right now, on this—what?—nine-hour trip, O Wonderful Chauffeur?"

She couldn't help glancing at him as the car ran smoothly over the current road. His tone was sarcastic enough that she had a desire to shout right back in his face, which she couldn't do.

He watched her with his dark brows raised and a hint of a grin on that face that shouldn't be so handsome, considering the irritating personality lying beneath.

"Nope," she finally said. "Yes, I'm starting us on this expedition, but you're going to help. Got it?"

"Got what? You haven't told me anything."

"I'm about to," she said.

"Hey," he said. "I want to hear all about those plans. How are we getting to Phoenix? And what are you going to do to keep me safe?"

Tie him up on the floor of the back seat, was the wish that circulated through her mind. Why was this guy so annoying?

And yet so darned sexy?

"I'm going to make several stops in towns along the way, at locations I already discussed with Vince. He'll have deputies or other law enforcement officers available at some, but not all, and I don't know which. But, of course, neither will anyone who might be after you."

And who did he think that would be? Not likely to be the ex-police chief he would be testifying against, who was in custody, but Alexa figured the guy might have hired others to help him. Daniel might know. And he'd already agreed to tell her more about what had happened to put him in the position of needing witness protection. Pointing at more specific enemies should be part of that, or at least she hoped so.

"Sounds good," he said. "What's our first stop—or should I guess?"

"Go ahead and guess," she said, shaking her head. This guy was a know-it-all on top of everything else...

although maybe he wasn't just a smart aleck. Maybe he did know a bit.

That would make him an interesting subject of her witness protection. An interesting assistant who could help take care of himself.

"Let's see. The first noteworthy place I saw on the map was... How about Moab?"

He was right. It was the first town of any substance they'd get to after turning south.

But she had to ask. "Was that the last town you got to when you were first brought to Blue Larkspur from Tempe by one of my predecessors?"

"No. We flew to Grand Junction with me in disguise, then drove to Blue Larkspur from there," he said. "And in case you're wondering, I felt fairly comfortable in witness protection that soon, even though that marshal had just taken over. I'd never been under anyone's guardianship like that before. I suspected the marshal had info on everyone on that plane, including the pilots and flight attendants. That's what you witness protectors do, right?"

Alexa couldn't help feeling a little proud as she answered him. "Yep, that's what we do. And more. In case you're wondering, I've spent some time checking out the route and places we'll be stopping, as well as the facilities we'll have in Phoenix. Am I sure you'll be completely safe? Well, I'll make certain of it."

"Hey," Daniel said. "You're my marshal now. Thanks."

She was cruising in the slow lane on the four-lane road and managed another glance at her passenger. He was smiling at her—and what a smile. Large and apparently serious and—well, it couldn't be grateful, could it?

"Yeah," she said in response. "I am." Should she demand that he tell her his underlying story right away? Maybe soon. To get started, and learn more, she asked, "Do you live in Tempe?"

"Yes. And I really appreciated my home until…until what happened. But with the local police chief involved in the shooting that killed my partner and wounded me, I was glad when some good cops showed up and prevented me from getting hurt any worse. Fortunately, they determined I needed federal help and called the FBI while I was being treated in the hospital. The FBI put me in touch with the marshals, and I was glad when they said they'd help me. And move me to safety in witness protection, at least temporarily."

She'd wondered about that. She'd wondered a lot about the details of his situation.

"So they're the ones who brought you to Blue Larkspur?" she asked.

"Exactly." Daniel's voice sounded grim, uncharacteristic during the short time she'd known him, and she glanced at him. He was looking at her and, yes, he appeared even more than grim. Furious, maybe. But that still didn't minimize his good looks. "I might as well tell you the whole story now," he said, "since you asked, and we'll be on this road for a while."

"Good," she said, and she really was glad she would hear his side of what had happened.

Still, she had to be careful. She scanned the highway around them and saw nothing out of the ordinary. There weren't many cars on the road, but a couple of semis drove the other direction. The barren land was fairly flat with a few rises here and there, probably no place anyone could lie in wait without being seen.

Not that anyone was likely to know where they were or how they were getting to their destination, although they might be able to guess the timing somewhat thanks to the upcoming trial.

Still, she glanced in the rearview and side mirrors as well. Nothing looked in the least menacing.

She would keep watch, nonetheless.

"So here it is," Daniel began. "And by the way, yes, I know I'm Daniel to the world right now. But I'd appreciate it if you'd call me Dane while we're alone. I'd like to be myself as much as possible. And I'm hoping once the trial is over, I can return to my real life."

"Got it," she said, and gave herself a strong mental reminder to be careful which name she used for him, at least when they were around other people. "Okay, Dane. Tell me everything."

"It all began a few months back when I was my regular self, a vice detective in Tempe, Arizona." His tone was strong yet husky, and came across well despite the hum of the car tires on the pavement beneath them. Alexa looked over at him. He was leaning against the seat, arms folded and hands behind his head, as if he wanted to appear relaxed, but he didn't. "My partner, Alvin O'Reilly, and I were close friends and were used to getting difficult assignments—and succeeding in solving whatever crime they involved."

So he'd been a successful cop, or at least he believed so. Why was Alexa not surprised? He exuded confidence and competence. "Sounds like a career all of us in law enforcement strive for," she said to encourage him to go on.

"Yeah, sounds that way," he said dryly. "Our assignment at that time was to uncover a major prostitution ring in Tempe. Sounded like an interesting task, even as we got right down to work and did our usual good job of researching the situation till we learned who all the major players were. And that was when the shock hit us."

He became silent, and Alexa glanced at him. His arms were down now, and his expression as he stared out the windshield suggested he was reliving the emotion he had just described. Or attempting to shove it out of his mind.

"Who were they?" she asked quietly even though she knew the answer from her research.

He turned his head to look at her, though she couldn't go on watching him. She planted her gaze back on the road in front of them.

"We didn't believe it at first. We didn't want to believe it, even though the evidence was solid. But the guy in charge of the prostitution ring was none other than our boss, Chief of Police Samuel Swanson."

"How awful," Alexa said. "And I suppose he thought that, considering his position, he'd be able to get away with it."

"Yeah, that's what he thought."

Dane just sat there for a few moments, still looking forward. Alexa wondered what he was thinking but didn't ask. Not yet. He'd surely continue.

"Alvin and I just collected all the evidence we could. In silence. Without telling anyone in the department since, with the chief so involved, we didn't know who we could trust."

"Got it." Alexa's mind started swirling about what

she would do if she ever found herself in a similar position.

She couldn't imagine Marshal Vince Cudahy running a prostitution ring, though Swanson had clearly proved anything was possible. But if anything like that ever happened, she knew she would do all she could to bring down whoever was committing such crimes, Vince or otherwise. Thanks to her own family situation, that was who she was.

Even more fortunate was the fact that as a Colton she had relatives she could trust who were also in law enforcement. At least she would have people to discuss the situation with, get their take on what she should do.

She didn't mention that to Dane.

Alexa had questions, though, about what had happened, but for the moment, she had to concentrate on her driving since a midsized green sedan was about to pass them, and she needed to make sure it didn't get too close. And that no one inside was paying any attention to Dane and her. That no one in the sedan was someone she needed to protect Dane from.

The car just rolled by in the passing lane. Only a driver inside, and though he glanced over, it seemed he only wanted to make sure he was passing safely. He didn't appear to try to look inside Alexa's vehicle.

Soon, he was ahead of them, and Alexa's breathing returned to normal.

"So what did you do?" she coaxed, wanting Dane to continue.

"We tried to stay discreet, although the chief, of course, knew what our assignment was. Maybe he thought we weren't smart enough, or brave enough, to out him even if we learned he was our target. Or maybe he thought we weren't even clever enough to figure out his connection, or would ask to become his ally. Well, he was wrong on all counts—and his revenge was to set us up.

"Alvin and I saw some things online about an upcoming evening of fun at an all-night club connected with a hotel. We also got a tip that some of the women there might be connected to a ring of exploited sex workers. So, of course, we had to go to the party undercover. And then, as we approached the door, the chief walked outside, hailed us, his left hand raised, smiling and calling out that we were invited, too, although since we'd come in disguise, he might not have recognized who we were at first."

"Really?" Alexa had to ask.

"That's what I figured, although we did have our phones out and were covertly taking pictures as part of our surveillance. Swanson, as he got closer, held his hand out, clearly wanting us to hand him our phones. And, no surprise, we refused. That was when he drew his gun. Maybe he knew by then who we were. Alvin was closer and...our boss shot him, grabbed his phone, then turned and fired at me. He hit me, but his shooting Alvin was enough of a warning and so I fled, bleeding and all.

"I was damned fortunate to get out of there. My wounds weren't exactly light, surface injuries, but I still managed to run and hide—and call 9-1-1."

He paused then, although he was breathing hard, and Alexa figured it was difficult for him to talk about it. "I'm glad you were okay enough to do that," she said.

"Me, too. And some uncorrupt cops arrived quickly, fortunately, so Swanson had to stand down. I learned later that he'd been smart enough to pretend to others that he'd had my back and that the shooter had run off. I didn't know where or how he'd hidden his gun, but I did know I was momentarily safe with the cops who'd showed up, and probably others."

Alexa could only nod, picturing the mayhem. Picturing a dying, or dead, cop on the ground. Picturing the handsome, strong, smart detective—currently off the job, but planning to return—beside her shot as well.

She shuddered, glad she was driving. Otherwise, she might want to hug him.

"Swanson visited me in the hospital," Dane continued. "Apparently at least some of the others in charge believed his story that he'd been helping rather than being the guilty party, so he was able to come see me. But my colleagues who knew the truth had already called the FBI for help and they'd sent some agents to keep an eye on me. Did they believe me? Apparently so, considering their getting me into witness protection, as soon as Swanson was arrested."

"Do you know if Swanson had any collaborators on the police force?"

"I assume so and so apparently did the FBI, since they put me in WITSEC, but so far no one else has been arrested, so there must not be sufficient evidence to point to any particular individuals, despite threats against me. Anyway, now you have the facts about why I'm in witness protection. My side of it, at least. And apparently others in law enforcement believe me, and whatever evidence there was, enough to have taken Swanson into custody for Alvin's murder and for heading the prostitution ring, too. I was the only other one outside at the crime scene at the time, so I'll be the main witness at his trial."

That didn't mean Swanson didn't have allies who would do all they could to prevent Alexa's charge from testifying.

Well, Alexa would do all she could to ensure he remained safe and able to testify at the police chief's murder trial. Not to mention running an illegal prostitution ring.

Why did some cops go bad like that? Especially one at the head of his department. He surely made enough money as chief of police.

But maybe he didn't think so.

Others who shouldn't went bad, too, like her father the judge...

Ugh. Alexa had to turn her mind in another direction. She had an idea of what Swanson's situation was, thanks to the police files she'd read.

She knew he'd been running the prostitution ring. He had to make money in commissions, or whatever. And maybe getting to enjoy the sex on the side. Or helping other men have sex anyway. Or—

Enough. She needed to keep her mind on her driving, not illegal acts.

And she had to watch the road and what was around them...

Her cell phone rang. Fortunately, this car had Bluetooth. She answered it. It was Naomi.

"Hi, sis," Naomi said.

"Hi back," replied Alexa. "How—"

"Are you on your road trip?" demanded her twin.

"It's my sister Naomi," Alexa told Dane, then said to Naomi, "Yes, I'm on my road trip and—"

"Just be careful, okay? I have a very bad feeling and need you to be extra cautious. Got it?"

The best Alexa could do under the circumstances, without revealing to Naomi what she was up to, was to assure her twin that all would be well.

But when she ended the call, she felt uneasy. Her sister sometimes got an eerily accurate sense of foreboding.

Well, that just meant Alexa had to keep a more watchful eye out.

For now, she'd already noticed that the earth around the road looked different. They were reaching the Colorado/Utah border and Arches National Park. That very special area where the natural red rock landscape appeared almost planned, in tall, carved-looking arches.

Amazing.

And it was a good way to hopefully distract Dane from his pain, and to distract her from her concern about her sister's call.

At least for a while.

"Hey, Dane, are you watching our surroundings?"

He hadn't been. Not really. He'd been too wrapped up in his thoughts, his recollections, his anger and what he hoped to accomplish in the next few days. Plus, he'd wondered why Alexa's sister had warned her to be extra cautious. Did she know where Alexa was, and who she was with? Alexa seemed very concerned, if her frown was any indication. But at least she didn't appear distracted.

At her question, he looked around at their surroundings. "Wow!" he couldn't help exclaiming. "I've heard of this kind of astonishing landscape, even saw photos, but I haven't seen anything like it in person before. Have you?"

"No, but it's definitely remarkable," Alexa said, her voice sounding awed. "It lives up to its reputation."

For the next part of the drive, Dane couldn't help smiling as they both gawked at the scenery surrounding them and talked about it. Dane had a passing thought that it would have been fun just to visit this location with the beautiful woman beside him whose company he enjoyed, view the landscape, discuss it as if they were merely sightseers, not a witness to a murder under witness protection and the marshal assigned to protect him.

They grew quiet for a while as they took in their surroundings even more.

Dane was somewhat amused as they started talking again, discussing other places they each had traveled, and the unique things they had seen and done.

Alexa made it clear that one of her favorite activities, when she wasn't on duty, was to visit the Gemini Ranch in Blue Larkspur—owned by two of her eleven siblings—and go horseback riding. She even had a favorite horse.

He was being driven by a cowgirl. Or so it appeared.

Although the scenery changed, he was glad when he started to see signs along the highway that they were approaching Moab. He knew Alexa wanted to stop there for a while.

A short while, he hoped. But it wouldn't hurt to get a break. Buy some more gas if they needed it. Get a drink. Find a restroom.

And maybe change drivers if it made sense, so

Alexa could observe what was around them even more carefully as he drove.

Only, as they got nearer, he felt the car slow a bit. He eyed Alexa.

She seemed to be looking a lot into the rearview mirror, and the side mirrors.

Her lovely face seemed…well, more than uneasy. Maybe apprehensive.

Maybe even disturbed.

"Is something wrong?" Dane asked, also looking into the side mirror nearest him.

A couple car lengths behind them was a large silver SUV. He'd seen the same vehicle, or one like it, just a short while ago when he'd been checking out the appealing terrain around them.

It was traveling at the same speed as they were, slower than the traffic had been.

"I think," Alexa said, "that we're being followed."

"Damn." Dane knew his voice came out as a rough whisper. What was his protector going to do?

What was *he* going to do?

He hoped Alexa would pull over, maybe, and let that SUV pass.

And if it didn't, they both could do their best to evade their pursuer. They would pull their weapons at the occupant as a last resort.

Alexa changed lanes, without pulling over. She sped up a little.

As far as Dane could tell, the SUV followed without getting closer.

"I'm calling Vince on my Bluetooth," Alexa told him. "Letting him know. Hopefully, this is one of the scheduled stops where he's got backup waiting."

"What's up, Alexa?" boomed the voice of Marshal Cudahy. "Everything okay?"

"I don't think so," she said. She related to Vince her—*their*—concern about the SUV following them. "But we haven't been able to see the license plate."

"And you're just outside Moab?" Vince's tone was brusque.

"Right, maybe ten minutes away."

"You're a little early, but the deputies I sent should be there by now. And I've also contacted local law enforcement. You still planning on heading for that shopping center to gas up and rest for a little while?"

"That's right." She looked over at Dane. "I'd already chosen our pit stop, in case we did need backup. That's where we'll still go."

"Sounds okay to me," Dane said, wondering if it really did.

Alexa continued her conversation with Cudahy for a short while longer. Dane kept checking the mirrors. That silver SUV was still there, even though Alexa sped up again, changed lanes, then slowed down a couple of times.

Soon they reached the Moab exit and Alexa drove off the highway. "We'll be there in a few minutes," she told Dane. The GPS on the dashboard designated where they were heading. Dane knew nothing about the shopping center but he figured it would be a good place to go, thanks to the backup Cudahy had promised.

They'd arrived. It was called The Moab Place, and a large gas station lined its west side.

Alexa pulled up to a pump and looked around, even as she started the process of pumping gas.

Dane got out of the car, too, to help, or at least to watch. "Get back inside," she hissed at him angrily.

Right. She was supposed to be protecting him, and they'd no idea if the person, or persons, following them were here, too.

"Okay," he said. "But I'm driving next."

"Fine." Her tone suggested it wasn't fine at all, but he nevertheless entered via the driver's door.

While she stood there, Alexa put the phone to her ear again. In just a few seconds, she was back in the car.

"Damn it all!" she said. "I called Vince again and he confirmed our backup was to be here by now, like he'd said. There's supposed to be at least one unmarked car containing deputies, but also a local police vehicle, or more. I don't see anyone who appears to be looking for us."

"I do," Dane said through clenched teeth. "Isn't that the SUV that was following us on the highway?" He nodded toward the next row of gas pumps.

That sure appeared to be the same SUV that had been behind them.

"Damn!" Alexa said again. "I shouldn't have gotten off the highway. Where's our backup?"

"Looks like we can't count on it." Dane wasn't the kind to panic, but he certainly didn't feel happy.

What were they going to do now?

Chapter 4

Alexa wasn't sure how she felt about Dane driving the car now, though she'd been okay with the idea initially.

Oh, he'd seemed from the first like a good presence behind the wheel, staying in lanes and going with the flow of traffic in the downtown Moab area between the tourist-attracting stores and occasional office buildings, none of which was particularly tall.

Dane didn't signal when he was going to turn, though. Normally, that would annoy her. Not now. Assuming they were still being followed despite not seeing anyone, why give whoever it was any more advance information about their route than necessary? And hopefully they wouldn't be pulled over for a ticket, since that could also put them in danger.

Alexa sat in the passenger's seat, her phone in her hand. She'd tried to call Vince again but only got his voicemail.

Had he neglected after all to send backup to help them on this path to Dane's trial testimony?

That wasn't like Vince. But maybe his equipment had been hacked somehow. That might mean all the Marshals Service equipment had been hacked. Or not. But she wished she knew. She especially hoped her phone hadn't been.

Or maybe there'd been no hacking. Maybe it was simpler, yet more complicated. Maybe Swanson had gotten to someone inside the marshals' office to elicit inside information about Dane's path.

In either case, or even if it had been something else, Alexa had ideas about what to do, but she also wished she had some expert advice within the service. Sure, the guy she was protecting was in law enforcement, too, but she didn't want to rely on him for answers. No, he was to rely on her.

Though she might ask him some questions, depending on how things went from now on...

A thought occurred to her. Several members of her family might have suggestions, and she quickly decided which one to call: her brother Dominic. He was one of the fraternal triplets who were now thirty-six years old.

More important, he was with the FBI's International Corruption Unit. She wasn't certain where he was located at the moment. Although he had an apartment in Denver near his FBI headquarters, he went undercover a lot and lived wherever his job took him.

Alexa had all her siblings' numbers programmed into her phone. Another good reason for Dane to be driving right now, since it took her a moment of looking away from the road to scan her contacts and find Dom.

She pressed his number, using neither Bluetooth

nor her speaker. Not while she was talking with her FBI brother about something requiring his expertise.

Although Dane would hear her end of the conversation, he didn't need to hear Dominic's.

"Hey, sis," her brother answered immediately. "What are you up to?" Dom was fully aware of Alexa's position with the marshals, just as she knew of his with the FBI.

"That's why I'm calling, bro." She could picture her good-looking brother with his shaggy blond hair and dark blue eyes standing...well, somewhere. And she also pictured him with his lovely fiancée, Sami, though this wasn't a good time to talk about her. Even so, Alexa's usual tinge of envy that they'd found true love that way slipped into her mind, and she immediately thrust it out. "I don't know whether you can help at all, but I'm on a witness protection assignment, and I've got a dilemma or two."

She quickly explained that she was in the process of getting one of the people she was guarding from one town to another, without explaining who, why or where. He'd understand her need for discretion.

"We saw a car along the way that appeared to be following us. That was dilemma number one."

"I'd say so," Dom agreed. "Were you able to shake him off?"

"Not sure. I'm going to take the position he's still around, since I don't know otherwise. And things are even worse than that."

"How?" her brother demanded.

"I was advised by the marshal I report to that I should stop in towns along the way, and he'd have backup at the places we discussed, so I'd have assistance there if anyone appeared to be following us or I otherwise felt we needed support. We just stopped in one of those places, though, and no one was there— no deputies, and no local law enforcement, either, although they were supposed to be informed and assist us as well. I'd even confirmed it with my boss, but now I can't reach him." She hesitated for only a second. No more needed to be described except... "So what would the FBI say? Any idea what I should do now?"

She assumed he would tell her to call the local police, even without knowing who her boss's contact was. But instead—

"Yeah," Dom said immediately. "Change your plans right away. Whatever you agreed to do with your marshal in charge, figure out a way to reach the same result, the same location, but use a different route or vehicle or whatever to make it harder for whoever's after your person under protection to find you. And don't contact anyone else yet, since you don't know who to trust."

"Great idea. Will do. Thanks, bro." Alexa didn't ask for any specifics. Her mind was already whirling in that direction, as it had been before. Dominic hadn't said anything she hadn't already considered, but she appreciated his confirmation. She had to ask before hanging up, "Is everything okay with you?"

"It's fine. Now, you take care of your charge, but be sure to take care of yourself, too. And if there's anything else you need from me, advice or even FBI support if your own remains lacking, be sure to let me know. It's not the best idea, though, to continue to call one person, so try not to do it often if you can avoid it."

"Got it. Thanks again. And you take care."

"You too, little sis."

They hung up, and Alexa found herself smiling grimly down at her lap, where she now held her phone again. Dominic understood her issues and her dilemma. He'd undoubtedly given her the best advice possible under the circumstances.

Now she had to run with it. And ignore the unease that swept through her.

"So, what did your brother say?" Dane asked. Alexa looked at him. He was driving just above the speed limit, watching the road, passing a car now and then— and keeping watch in the rearview and side mirrors. Just as he should be. Like a cop would be driving while not after a suspect. "I gathered he's with the FBI. Did he make any useful suggestions?"

She'd already started pondering what she could do to disappear from whatever radar their follower might have on them. She'd come up with some ideas and needed to focus on them even more closely to determine which way to go.

True, it would have been more convenient if Dom had suggested more specifics. But she purposely hadn't been specific with him, either. That was the way she was supposed to handle cases, even when she talked with law enforcement family members.

Secrecy was vital—not just to protect Dane, but also herself.

"Yes," she said. "I think he did. But now I have to figure out the best way to follow those suggestions— safely and in a way that will ensure our ability to get to Phoenix as planned."

"Let me know what I can do to help."

Good guy, Alexa thought. But of course he'd want to help, since it was his life that was in danger.

Hers, too, since she was protecting him…

"Just keep driving for now," she said. "I need to do a little research." Once more, she pulled her phone from her lap.

She looked at the map to Phoenix again, and began researching the metropolises, big and small, along the way.

She decided they would stop in the next town, though she hadn't planned it before, with Vince or otherwise.

That town was Monticello, Utah. It appeared to have the limited kinds of facilities she'd be looking for. And so, once more scanning the road behind them both through the side-view mirror and turning around to look, she said, "I don't see anyone following us at the moment. That doesn't mean we're not on someone's radar. But I want you to get off the highway at the next town. That's Monticello." Even though that could be obvious to whomever might be following them. But if it seemed appropriate, they could zigzag through various streets while they were there.

"Okay," he said. "What's in Monticello that'll help us? Any indication there'll be backup from the marshals, or local cops?"

"No. But if all goes as I'm beginning to plan, we'll still be okay."

"Fine. Care to tell me about it?"

"Sure, Dane. Er, Daniel. Er… Whoever you are. And whoever I am."

"What does that mean? Are we both changing identities there?"

"You'll see."

It didn't take much longer to reach the Monticello

exit. "We're here," Dane told her unnecessarily. "I assume I'm to get off now."

"Good assumption," Alexa agreed. Then she had to ask, "Do you see our buddies who seemed to be following us before? Or anyone else I should be aware of?"

"Not now. But that doesn't mean—"

"Got it." And she did. Could be those who'd been following had changed places with others, and even more cohorts of former police chief Swanson could be in on this game. Chasing them. Planning to stop them, in whatever way they chose.

Not if Alexa could help it.

Dane drove carefully. Alexa watched her phone and what she'd been researching on it, as well as the road around them.

In a short while, she had Dane drive into a two-story parking structure and stop on the first level amid a bunch more vehicles, backing in so the car's trunk was facing the wall but not close to it. She kept watching the entrance but saw no other car drive inside. Good.

She hadn't told Dane about what was in the backpacks and suitcase she had stashed in their vehicle's trunk along with the stuff he'd brought, but everything was geared for her job. She was the one to extract them, digging first for herself; she pulled out a man's wig and hid her head under the trunk lid while putting it on. She also extracted a black hoodie that she pulled on over her head. Plus, she removed a face wipe and quickly rubbed off all her eye makeup, then, using a small mirror she brought out, too, daubed on some darker stuff in lines that should hopefully make her appear more angular and masculine.

Still hiding behind the car, she looked herself over. With the jeans and athletic shoes she'd already been wearing, she now resembled a man. She hoped.

She'd insisted that Dane stay in the car, and, ignoring his amazed stare, now brought him a bag from the trunk that contained what she wanted him to wear, handing it to him as she settled in the passenger seat. No, he wouldn't look like a woman, but hopefully an overweight man. Too bad she couldn't inflate him, but she did tell him to slouch and keep the front of his new sweatshirt pulled out. His hairpiece? Well, it made him appear partially bald, with his hairline swept back.

It didn't make him look any less handsome, though. And who'd have thought she would consider that sexy?

She told him to move to the passenger seat to change, since he'd have a harder time with the steering wheel over him. Besides, they wouldn't be in this car much longer, so it didn't matter which seat he was in now.

She'd also brought his suitcase out of the trunk. She figured he wouldn't want to leave its contents here.

"Interesting that you have all this disguise stuff along," Dane told her as he pulled off his shirt, revealing his muscular body beneath his T-shirt.

Alexa tried unsuccessfully to make herself glance away.

"Some of it's what we're taught as part of witness protection," she said, "although I added to it. I liked the idea but wasn't sure it went far enough. My own change of wardrobe is essential, too, for example."

He fluffed out the large shirt that would make him look heavier when he stood. "Got it. And you definitely look like someone else. Me, too. In fact, if you tell me to lose some weight, be sure not to sugarcoat it or I'll eat that, too."

Really? A corny joke? She tried to ignore it.

When he was done changing, she said, "Okay, now. Here's what we'll do." First, she exited the car briefly, removed some of Dane's belongings from his suitcase and stowed them in the empty backpack she'd kept their new clothes in.

Getting in on the driver's side, she told him they would each exit the parking structure alone, via separate doors—and stay alert. Individuals, both males, were not as likely to attract whoever was stalking Dane, she said, since he had already been spotted that day with her. His appreciative expression when he said he agreed made Alexa blush—or at least she felt slightly warmer for a moment.

She then gave him detailed directions to where she intended to go and told him to walk there directly. She'd take a more circuitous route, and she would be in charge of the bags with his stuff, including his suitcase, while he took care of hers. If they were spotted, his stalkers would most likely assume she was him.

"That way," she told Dane, "we definitely won't look like we're together. Hopefully, Swanson's accomplices are aware you're in witness protection and will assume you'll have your protector with you at all times. And that means—"

"That means while we're separated, I'll need to be particularly careful." Dane nodded toward her. "Staying in shadows or behind buildings or whatever seems to work. So far, I like your plan. But what is the place you're directing me to?"

"A car rental agency. I've already texted them and they have vehicles available."

"Another thing to like about your plan," he said, nodding. His eyes captured hers, and she felt like blushing even more at his approving—and alluring—look.

"Thanks," she said almost brusquely. She needed to get any inappropriate thoughts about this man far away from her consciousness. Too distracting. She had to concentrate. And keep him safe.

That meant they had to join up at the car rental agency really quickly, and she told him so.

"You want me—Daniel Brennan—to rent the car?"

"No, I've got some alternate credentials to use," she said. "Are you ready to head that way? You'll go first and wait inside a store near the office. I'll take a nearby route where I should be able to keep an eye on you and your surroundings. But put your own figurative cop hat on and be damn careful. Got it?"

"Sure do," he said.

They both exited the car she'd been assigned. She locked it, wondering when she'd be able to let her superiors know where it was.

Alexa watched as Dane started in the direction she'd told him, first to the parking lot door. She couldn't help grinning. He did walk fast but hunched forward a bit as though following an enlarged stomach beneath his oversized sweatshirt. He must have been a good undercover cop, she thought, then set out.

The car rental place was a block away, and she headed that way, watching all the while for someone attempting to find him—or who had already been successful.

She saw no one except a few faraway pedestrians.

But she was relieved when she reached the rental place and saw Dane duck inside the bookstore beside it.

She soon got a car rented—under an assumed name and with assumed credentials she'd been given. For the moment, she was Bradley Brown.

The car was a light blue midsized sedan from a US manufacturer. Finding it in the filled rental shop parking lot, she quickly stuffed the backpacks, along with Dane's suitcase, into the trunk.

She didn't need to go get Dane. He'd apparently been keeping watch, and he was soon with her. She put her suitcase into the trunk, too.

Her turn to drive again, she'd decided. She motioned for him to enter via the passenger door and half expected him to object.

Fortunately, he didn't.

She soon pulled out of the rental car lot, telling Dane to crouch down in his seat, which he did, though he didn't look thrilled. She figured it was because anyone looking their way would see her. She'd be the potential target.

But that, too, was part of her job. She would just remain watchful. And careful.

Okay, here he was, Dane thought as Alexa pulled the car onto the small-town street. Being driven by this gorgeous woman who now resembled a not-so-good-looking guy. Following her orders in the hope he'd get to Phoenix, testify against Swanson, then return to his own life where he was in charge.

And Alexa, too, would regain her usual appearance—and her life. And they'd go their separate ways, probably never meeting again.

He knew that her precautions were in his best interests. Maybe the only way he could do what he needed, to get Alvin's killer into prison for the rest of his life.

But Dane wasn't used to following instructions this way. Sure, till recently he'd done what his superiors in the Tempe PD told him to. That was his job. Although those superiors weren't all that great, he admitted, given Swanson's crimes.

But he at least worked in concert with other law enforcement agents—he wasn't the one being protected. Usually, he was the protector. Now things were different. This was his life, for the moment. And he didn't like it.

Not even he could come up with a corny joke or two to ease his tensions. Not now, at least.

"So what's next?" he asked Alexa. Despite how early they'd started, a lot had occurred that day. In fact, it was late enough that he doubted she'd try to make it all the way to Phoenix.

He was right. "My research suggested we not try to get to Phoenix tonight," Alexa said. "Our followers might assume that's what we're doing, since they know our destination. But we can spend the night in an upcoming Utah town. It's small but has several motels and other amenities. It's not far from here, and we can keep an eye out for anyone following us on the road— or when we get off it."

"Fine with me," he said, though his mind glommed on to the fact they'd be spending the night together. In the same space, at least. They were both disguised for the moment, he reminded himself. But that wouldn't necessarily be for any longer than until they got into their room. Maybe two rooms would be better—except for the whole thing about keeping him safe. That meant they needed to be close to one another—and he didn't mind it one bit.

"Okay, then," Alexa said. "Bluff, Utah, here we come."

Chapter 5

Alexa had heard of Bluff and had researched it previously along with the rest of their route. It was a bit of a tourist haven, since it was near a variety of state and national parks and other sightseeing attractions such as Bears Ears National Monument and Natural Bridges National Monument.

Not that she'd get to see them on this trip, but maybe someday she could come back and check them out.

With Dane? He might appreciate them, too.

But by the time she could return he would most likely no longer be in her life.

That made her frown as she watched the road in front of her. Not that they had a romantic connection. Romantic connections? Not her. Not really, although she'd been involved with a few men, one almost seriously, but she'd never found a guy she really felt she could spend the rest of her life with.

She pulled onto the highway once more and headed south toward Bluff.

Maybe she'd been better off when all those she'd been guarding in witness protection had been women. There'd been no emotional overload then. She'd liked them. She'd taken care of them. She'd helped to get them through whatever crisis they'd each been in—which, most often, had been getting them to trials where they testified.

That was all this situation could be, too.

Never mind that she found Dane handsome, charming, sexy and more. Oh, and brave. And a bit silly at times, though in a surprisingly appealing way.

But he was her assignment. That was all.

To convince herself of that, she looked over at the passenger seat, where he appeared to be viewing something on his phone. He was still dressed like the portly guy she'd helped to manufacture while they were still in Monticello. But now that they were on their way, he had removed the head covering that had suggested he was going bald.

That made him look a lot better.

She glanced at him as often as felt safe, enjoying his appearance of concentration as he studied his phone.

Phone. Just in case, she figured it wouldn't hurt to send a text or two to her boss to protect them.

No one needed to know they intended to stop as soon as Bluff.

She pulled her phone from her lap and handed it to Dane, who seemed rather surprised but took it from her anyway. "I'd like you to use my phone to text Vince in a little while, after you do some research," she said, "and tell him we're stopping before Phoenix for the night. But since we don't know what's happened, why he didn't have the backup he'd promised when we got to Monticello, let's assume there's an issue and deal with it. We'll give him a town, but we won't tell him where we're really stopping."

Dane turned to look at her, a sly smile on his face. "You mean, you want me to lie to your boss."

"Exactly." She grinned back. "In a manner that he'll think it's me, but won't know it's a lie, at least not at first. So, please figure out a town along this route that's closer to Phoenix that we can mention."

"Okay," Dane said, then began concentrating on his phone again.

As he did his research, she watched the road. Listened to the car's tires on the asphalt below. They hummed, but she didn't find it as pleasant as her own car that she'd left at home.

Oh well. They were safer for now. Not as obvious as they'd apparently been before.

She hoped.

She snuck a peek at Dane, continuing to enjoy the look of concentration on his handsome face. She had an urge to stroke his cheek.

Good thing she was driving. Touching anything but the steering wheel and, occasionally, her phone, wasn't a good idea.

A short while later Dane looked up from his phone and suggested, "How about Kayenta, Arizona? It's farther toward Phoenix than Bluff, part of the Navajo Nation, and it has some facilities like hotels."

"Sounds fine with me, if you're happy suggesting it. Now, use my phone and text Vince as if you're me, telling him that's where we'll be overnight. Let him know

I'm still concerned about the lack of backup before but want to keep him informed about how we're doing."

"You think he'll respond now?" Dane asked. "He didn't before, right?"

"Yes, and I don't know if he received my correspondence then. He didn't answer his phone or any texts for a while. But time has passed, and we're in a different location, which might affect the phone's cell reception and all. Let's just give it a try."

"Whatever you say, Madam Protector."

When Alexa glanced at him this time, Dane's dark brows were raised and his smile was challenging, as if he figured her response would be irritated.

Instead, she said, "Glad you recognize I'm in charge, Mr. Protectee."

He laughed then looked down and got to work texting, while Alexa kept her eyes on the road around them, including, via the mirrors, behind them. A few semis rolled by, again heading in the opposite direction, and a car or two going in their direction passed them.

Nothing to make her worry about whether she and Dane were currently under observation. But she knew better than to assume they weren't.

"Okay," Dane said after a minute. "The text is on its way."

But there was no immediate response. And after five minutes, Alexa requested that Dane try again. "Maybe we were in another location with no service."

"You sure your office has service?"

She sent a quick glare at him. "What do you think?"

"Then—maybe it's your phone."

She shrugged, though she concentrated even more

when the car bumped a bit on the road. She wasn't sure what that meant, but she judged it wasn't serious. "Why don't you try your phone?" she asked then.

"Sure." But Vince didn't respond to him, either. And when Alexa suggested the cell number of one of her other colleagues in the office, there was no response to that as well.

The road turned gradually toward the left. Alexa started seeing signs to Bluff. Good. But she did want to let the world erroneously know that they were headed for—what was the place's name? Oh yeah. Kayenta.

"Tell you what. Please call my brother Dominic. His number's the last one called on my phone before your latest attempts to reach Vince."

"Got it."

"And put it on speaker so we both can hear him."

It only took an instant before Dom answered. "Everything okay, sis?" he demanded.

Alexa glanced at Dane, who'd raised his brows again as if he was ready to join in, so she hurriedly said, "I think so. My charge and I are on our way. But I'm glad to talk to you since no one in my office is apparently getting my texts, and my boss doesn't answer my calls."

A moment of silence. "For how long?" he finally said.

"Quite a while." She didn't get into what had happened before. "That might have been the cause of the lack of backup I mentioned previously. And they couldn't be reached on my charge's phone, either."

"Ditch your damn phone," Dom commanded loudly. "Your charge's, too. Replace them with burners when you can, but assume now that they've been compromised. Make sure you get rid of them in a way you can't be followed. Can't say for sure they're causing a problem, but you need to make sure they aren't."

"Thanks, bro," Alexa said. "You're probably right."

"And be sure to contact me and let me know how things are going once you get your burners, you hear?"

"I hear." Alexa hung up.

"I'd wondered about that," Dane said. "But I figured your marshals' people would have control of such things."

Alexa snorted. "I figured they would, too. But Dom is right. We shouldn't take any chances." She paused then shot a quick look at Dane. "Know what I'd like you to research now?"

"Hmm. How about whether there are places in Bluff to buy a burner phone?"

"You read my mind," she said with a slight smile. It wasn't a surprise that he knew what she wanted. He'd want it, too, if they wound up ditching their phones.

It didn't take Dane long to find the answers. "Bluff's got it," he said. "In fact, there are several stores where people can buy techy stuff."

"Good," Alexa said. "We'll pick a couple up tonight or tomorrow. Oh, and please figure out a good, dumpy motel we can stay in, one anyone following us would assume is too much of a hellhole for smart officers of the law to hole up in."

"Excellent idea, although we'll only need one new phone. I'm carrying an extra burner that I've never used yet. Oh, and one more thing we need to do, and I've got an idea how to do it."

"What's that?" Alexa asked.

"The best way to dump our current cells."

* * *

Alexa exited the highway, though not at the first sign for Bluff, which made Dane smile. She'd already warned him to keep his eyes open when they did get off to see if anyone else had gotten off at the same exit.

Fortunately, no one did.

He told Alexa to pull into a large service station just off the major road. It contained several rows of pumps, indicating lots of drivers must stop there on their way to wherever they were going. He indicated a parking spot behind the convenience store off to the side, and Alexa pulled into it.

"Okay," she said. "Now what?"

"Now you do what I tell you," he riposted. "If there are any phone numbers you care about or other info you'll need in the near future, I suggest you jot them down. I just happen to have a couple pens and pads of paper, in case my phone's not handy and I need to make sure I remember a joke I hear." That was somewhat true, he thought as he met Alexa's exasperated yet lovely expression with a smug one of his own. He mostly wanted to be prepared for anything.

Like having to ditch his usual phone…

She pulled a small, spiral-bound memo book out of her purse as well as a pen, and started making notes.

Him? He didn't have to. As part of his witness protection program—and his own practices as a detective—he carried that extra burner all the time, plus a charger. Although it was almost always turned off, it had all the info he'd need to call those he wanted to stay in contact with.

He'd have to change the number he'd added to it as Alexa's, though, once she obtained a new phone of her own.

When she was finished, she turned to him again. "Okay, what do we do next?"

"Next, go into your contacts again and delete them all."

She grimaced but appeared to do as he said, even as he did the same himself on his regular phone.

When they both were through, he said, "Just watch what I do next. First, say good-bye and hand it to me."

Her expression grew glum, as if she really did regret saying good-bye to her high-tech possession, but she did reach out with it. "Here," she said. "Oh, and good-bye, my phone."

He took it from her, amused by what she'd said. But surely she wasn't developing a sense of humor.

Fortunately, this service station was as busy as he'd anticipated. Lots of cars and a number of big rigs.

Dane quickly exited the car, both phones in his hand, and sidled along to the nearest semi. There, he looked around to make sure the driver wasn't watching, or anyone else. Then he wedged both phones between two prongs of the metal connector fastening the cab to the trailer.

Finally, he returned to the car. Good timing, since the driver of that truck approached and got inside. In moments, he left.

So did their phones.

"Now," he said, "if anyone happens to be monitoring our location via those phones, they'll assume we're going the opposite direction, for now at least." For, happily, and as he'd anticipated, judging by the way the big rig had been facing at the station, it embarked on the route from which they'd come.

"That was a good idea," Alexa said. "I've worked

out leaving phones and other electronics before, after deleting potentially damaging info, at various places for the people I'm protecting, or tossing them in the trash, but I've never actually sent them and us in different directions. I'll definitely do that again."

"Good. And here's the extra burner I mentioned." He pulled it from his pocket and turned it on. "There. Since I haven't used it, no one should be able to follow me because of it. Now, next step. We need to figure out where we'll stay tonight. I want to check out all possibilities, but I've pretty well narrowed them down to a couple places that look absolutely horrible online."

"Sounds perfect. Let's drive by them."

Alexa followed the directions Dane gave her, forcing herself not to shudder.

For the most part, she enjoyed seeing the small town of Bluff. Some of its areas appeared better than others, and some of the motels and inns also looked nicer than their rivals. Alexa was glad that Dane and she, in their discussion as they cruised the various districts and neighborhoods, soon narrowed their potential choices down to a couple—the rattiest-looking ones.

On their route, they stopped at a fast-food place to pick up their dinner plus some water, then got going again.

As they were on their way, Dane said, "Pull over here for a second." He gestured to the curb on a narrow street.

Alexa noted an option about a block away. She assumed Dane had, too, and was checking it out. A sign indicated it was the Stone Motel. No indication why that was its name. Alexa saw few stones around, mostly paving and enclosures of small gardens with grass and a few flowers.

"Is that place our goal?" Alexa asked.

"The first we'll look at," Dane replied, "and hopefully it'll work out. I checked out some of the local reviews on a couple popular online sites. That one has some of the worst."

"Perfect." Alexa grinned as if she really meant it. In some ways, she did. "I assume whoever is after you will figure that, if we don't make it all the way to Phoenix tonight, we would only stay in a nice, secure place. Which does make the most sense. Except—"

"Except that we're better off staying in a place they wouldn't be looking for us."

Alexa nodded. "Exactly. So…" She turned the key in the ignition, starting the car again. "Let's just hope this delightful place has a room available for us."

A room where they would stay together. A room in which she would be close to Dane, overnight…

Okay, she could admit to herself she was attracted to the guy, and the idea of that kind of closeness shot surges of heat inside her. But she would of course keep things cool and professional.

She had to.

"Do you really have any doubts that kind of place has rooms available?" Dane asked.

Alexa did, though just a few. The town hadn't seemed especially busy, so there might not be much overflow from the nicer motels to the dumps. But people sometimes chose accommodations based on cost instead of convenience and cleanliness.

They'd find out in a few minutes, she thought as she parked the rental car on the rutted paving of the parking lot just outside the two-story motel with the equally rutted walls. The windows, presumably one or more per room, were unbroken, but the caulking around the frames appeared uneven and damaged.

Oh yeah. If they stayed here this night, sleep wouldn't be highest on Alexa's agenda. Nor would it be anywhere else.

Staying aware and awake, and protective of Dane, would be her top priorities.

And the fact they'd be alone together? Irrelevant.

First, though, she had to book the room, if possible. She considered telling Dane to wait in the car. But although she was hopeful, she couldn't know whether they'd been followed here. And the only way she'd truly be able to protect him was to remain in his presence.

"Okay," she said. "Give me a minute, then we'll go to the reception area and see if they've got a place for us to stay."

"Fine. Are you—"

She assumed he was going to ask what she needed the minute for, but she figured it became clear pretty quickly since he shut up. She'd turned and knelt on the seat, then brought a backpack up from where she'd laid it on the back seat and put it on the center console.

She extracted her wig and some makeup.

"You're becoming a guy again?" Dane asked.

"Since we'll be seeing other people, yes. It makes more sense for us to remain in disguise so we can't be recognized. So, here." She reached into the bag again and pulled out Dane's bald wig from where she'd stowed it before, handing it to him. He wouldn't need makeup. He already looked like a man.

Quite a man.

She nevertheless also extracted the big, bulky sweat-shirt that would help him appear overweight that he'd taken off as they continued this direction.

No sense in either of them looking like who they really were.

Alexa next unzipped a pocket inside that bag and pulled out an envelope. She wasn't merely looking like a man. She was taking on the persona, too, at least for certain purposes.

Like paying for their room that night.

She had several different identities she could use, in-cluding other women. Too bad neither of her male IDs had the last name of Brennan. That way, she could turn herself miraculously into Daniel Brennan's brother.

But when she'd gotten set up with these additional identities, she hadn't known who she would be protect-ing. And so she'd had to decide between being Roger Jones or Bradley Brown, or a different woman tonight.

She extracted an appropriate driver's license and credit card from the envelope. "You ready to go in-side?" she asked.

"Sure," he said. He'd already turned to look at her. "Since I see you have cards there, I assume my protec-tor is going to attempt to pay, but—"

"But nothing. As you know, I'm in charge. And if you talk to me at all with anyone else around, I'm Roger Jones."

She wasn't surprised when his dark eyebrows rose and his head tilted slightly. "Roger?"

"You got it."

His laugh sent a ripple of pleasure up her spine, which she recognized was absurd. "Okay, Roger. You're in charge...sort of. And Daniel is ready to prepare for our night here in Bluff." He turned and reached for the door handle, then stopped and swiveled back to her. "Question, though. I know we're both men, guys who are buddies, right?"

She nodded. "That's right."

"Are we staying in the same room together? I mean, guys don't always take each other on as roommates while on the road. I still could pay for my own."

"Nope. We're staying together. Yes, we're good friends. We'll have lots to discuss about our road trip before we drop off to sleep, after all. Or that's what we'll allow whatever clerk who's there to believe."

"I got it. But—"

Alexa wasn't finished talking, so she interrupted Dane. "But dropping off to sleep is only on my schedule now and then. Even though staying in this hellhole, not as close to Phoenix as we should have been by now, isn't what I would have preferred, it should work best under the circumstances since we were followed before—and there's a good possibility our now-disappeared phones were hacked. I still really like what you did with them, by the way. And before we head off tomorrow, we'll stop in one of the local stores to get me a new one."

"Fine, but—"

"Let's get going," she said, interrupting him again. She'd heard the additional irritation in Dane's—no, Daniel's—voice. She'd better not forget that. As far as she knew, WITSEC had even given him official-looking ID with that name. Maybe he needed yet another name now, in case the people after him knew this one, but she couldn't be the one to work that out—not here, and not now.

And she couldn't allow herself to worry about his being annoyed.

She would do all she had to, to protect him. If that annoyed him, tough.

Alexa turned her back on him in the car and opened the driver's door, reaching back inside for the bag she'd been removing items from. Time to put it in the trunk and take out the small suitcases that would make them appear to be checking in to this motel.

She hadn't seen any other people around, so maybe the place's façade and reputation would mean they would be alone.

She would be damned careful in any case.

As Alexa walked around and opened the trunk, behaving in all manner the best she could as a guy around her age, she was glad to see that Daniel had exited the passenger's side and now approached her at the rear of the vehicle.

She liked that he was bent forward a bit, to help emphasize his appearance as a lot bigger than he was.

She didn't like his scowl, but she would live with that.

Although she always seemed to enjoy it when he smiled... Enough of that.

As he joined her, she made herself smile in as masculine a manner as she could, even as she looked around his shoulder at a few other cars parked in the lot.

Still no people, but the other vehicles' presence did indicate some rooms in the place might be occupied.

She let Daniel pull out the handle for the suitcase containing some of his belongings, and she did the same with her own.

"Under other circumstances," he grumbled as they

started forward, "I'd offer to handle both pieces of luggage."

Because, no matter what she looked like at the moment, she was a woman. "Glad you recognize the current circumstances," she said, deepening her voice, in case anyone was listening, although she didn't think so. "You need to remember that no matter what I look like, I'm in charge."

"Yeah. I get it."

"Good."

"Not many cars here, so I assume they'll have room for us." Daniel had modified his voice, too, making it gravellier.

"We'll soon see." They strolled at a leisurely pace toward the ground-level, glass-fronted door labeled "Office."

Inside, the place was as grungy as it appeared from the outside. The decorative tiled floor looked ancient, edges worn off. There were a couple of chairs where people could sit, but they both appeared sunken and likely to scratch anyone on them. Two vending machines looked like the best part of the place, where people could buy water and soft drinks from one, and candy from the other.

The girl behind the reception counter, with shaggy brown hair and thick glasses, looked to be in her late teens, and her sweatshirt and jeans were both torn, highly in fashion, Alexa thought. She seemed fairly young for this position, but Alexa assumed the place was family owned and run. Or maybe the owners had just hired anyone who'd applied for a job.

They did have a room. The girl hardly talked to them but got them to sign some paperwork—and Alexa signed everything as Roger Jones, paying for the room with cash. Never mind that she had a credit card in Roger's name and also a false driver's license. It would be preferable for whoever was after Daniel not to know the identity Alexa had taken on for this case, but if they did find out by tracking them to this motel, at least they'd only have a name.

Soon the receptionist handed them a couple of actual keys in a small envelope that had the number 16 on it.

"Thanks," Alexa said in her disguised voice, a much lower register than her normal tone. "Where is it?"

"Floor right above us." The girl then started doing something on the computer on top of the counter, ignoring them.

Time to go to their room. Together. Alone.

And Alexa again resolved to herself to remain professional, no matter how sexy the man with her appeared once undressed for the night.

Chapter 6

She'd paid for their room with cash. Dane had figured that the marshals providing witness protection must carry a lot, as well as alternate identifications. That made sense.

He carried quite a bit, too. He'd had to keep all the assets he could with him since he couldn't exactly show up at a bank or anywhere else using his real identity to get cash. He had a credit card with his current ID but didn't want to use it unless he had to since it would be paid by the Marshals Service.

Well, when this was over, he'd reimburse Alexa, or the Marshals Service, for all his expenses.

Now, as Alexa and he left the office and started up the uneven paved stairs to the second floor, Dane—no, Daniel again for now, he reminded himself—couldn't help wanting to grab the suitcase from Alexa, even though it was carryon size.

But that was simply a masculine urge to help a woman. And she was a he for now, he reminded himself unnecessarily, considering not only her neutral outfit but also her masculine hairpiece and makeup. She'd undoubtedly get damned mad at him if he attempted to act like a polite guy, let alone protective of her. But he had to admit he was drawn to her, despite their circumstances, and wanted to make sure she stayed safe, too.

At least for the moment, when neither of them appeared to be in danger.

He preceded her up the stairs. At least, along with his own suitcase, he carried the paper bag that contained the dinner they'd picked up. Alexa—Roger—lagged behind a little, apparently glancing around to make sure they remained alone. Protecting him.

Although if there was anyone after them here, that person could be on the motel's upper level, waiting for them. For *him*. He was the one under witness protection, and for good reason.

Dane was completely aware that Swanson was likely to do anything to keep him from testifying at the murder trial. Swanson knew full well that Dane had been a firsthand witness of the killing, as well as a victim of his shooting rage. And Dane felt certain Swanson was furious he had survived and had most likely hired assassins to go after him.

They reached the top level. It was also paved, with a railing along the steps and the perimeter of the balcony walkway. He stopped and looked around again.

He heard voices from inside one of the nearest rooms, maybe a parent and child. If so, it was unlikely it was anyone waiting for him, although he would still remain alert in case it was a ploy to fool him.

Alexa caught up to him. "Okay, Roger," he told her, "I'll go open our room." He didn't bother telling her why he'd stopped, what he'd heard or how he felt about not helping with her luggage.

Their footsteps shuffled along the balcony paving. The room nearest them at the top of the stairs was number 14. It didn't take long to pass that one and number 15, then reach 16.

Dane pulled the envelope from his pants pocket and used the key to open the door. No problems there.

He wasn't surprised when Alexa, leaving her suitcase just outside, edged her way past him and entered the room first. He watched her check out every inch of it, including opening up the doors to the bathroom and closet, her hand on that hip bulge beneath her shirt. That had to be where her weapon was, where she kept it a lot of the time.

Then she knelt on the floor and checked under the two twin-size beds across the room. She coughed a little, and he figured that was an indication of how unclean the place was. He'd noticed right away that it smelled rather musty.

But Alexa didn't do anything to suggest there was anyone or anything under there that shouldn't be.

He wondered, though, how he'd be anticipating their night together if they'd had only one bed to share, no matter what size…

"Okay," she said. "You can come in now."

He already had, though not very far. He'd wheeled both their suitcases in, too, and shut the door behind him.

He'd also been prepared to grab his gun, at his hip

beneath his bulky sweatshirt. He'd hoped it wouldn't be necessary. He doubted anyone could have anticipated they'd be here. They hadn't anticipated before where they'd stay the night, either, other than to hopefully find the kind of place no one would figure they'd hang out in.

Like this motel.

Even though Alexa had checked out the entire room, Dane scrutinized it again, from the beds he'd been studying to the TV hung on the wall across from them and the dresser with a scratched mirror on the wall across from the bathroom. He walked to the closet and looked inside, too. It was small, and the hangers on the rod at the top were of many kinds, from bent wire to plastics of several colors. There was a luggage rack at the bottom that he pulled out, intending to put his suitcase on it, unless Alexa preferred that to placing hers on the dresser.

"Guess we're staying the night," she said unnecessarily, but he figured she was in her way asking him if he was all right with it.

He was. "Guess we are," he said.

He asked her preference for the suitcase. The dresser worked for her, so he put her bag up there. They both entered the bathroom and washed their hands. They each then sat on one of the beds, facing each other, as they ate their dinners. He'd gotten a burger and fries, and Alexa had a chicken sandwich. His tasted okay, but he wasn't very hungry. He had too much on his mind.

Including how things would go in a short while when they got ready for bed, then lay down in their respective places.

Heck, this woman shouldn't be getting into his

thoughts the way she was. He didn't want to seduce her, no matter how she was dressed now or would be later. He wanted to get his time in her presence over quickly. Safely. For both of them.

And yet... When they were finished eating, it was only about six o'clock, and even at that they had taken a bit of extra time to drive there. Alexa said nevertheless, "I know it's early, but I suggest we get to bed soon, since tomorrow will be a big day."

Yeah! Dane's hormones cheered, but he of course tamped them down.

Getting to bed individually, to sleep, was what she'd meant. He knew that, even as every fiber of him wanted to hold her.

"Good idea," he said. "We'll want to get on our way early tomorrow."

"Right."

"I usually like to take my shower at night," Alexa said, "but I figure the sheets aren't likely to be that clean, so I'll wait till morning to remove any added dirt. How about you?"

"Yeah, that sounds like a better idea to me, too."

"I'll go change now, then you can." She meant she'd run through the bathroom first, which was fine with him.

While she was in there, he put the TV on, which was likely how they'd spend their time that night till they fell asleep. There was apparently a cable connection, and he found a news station right away.

It provided national updates as he watched, not local. And certainly not Tempe's news. Or Phoenix's.

He wondered what was going on in Phoenix, in preparation for the trial. They'd arrive there tomorrow, so he'd find out…and he'd say goodbye to being on the road with Alexa.

She soon exited the bathroom. She no longer had her hairpiece on, but her pajamas appeared unisex: nothing feminine about them.

Even so, there she was, in his motel room with him, in pj's. With her lovely blond hair framing her face that was again highly feminine now that she no longer wore her wig or any masculine makeup.

He hurriedly grabbed his own pajamas and toiletries kit and went into the bathroom.

When he came out again, Alexa was under the covers of the bed she'd chosen, sitting up. She appeared wide awake, but he wasn't sure.

The news was still on, and they watched it for a while longer. And Alexa rose, pulled the draperies back a bit and looked out the window several times before returning to her bed.

"You ready to turn off the TV?" Dane eventually asked.

"Sure. I'll set the clock radio here for seven o'clock since we don't have our phones now. We can go out and grab breakfast at one of the fast-food places. I assume the shops here open around nine, but if they don't open earlier, we can continue on and stop somewhere else for my new burner."

"I figure I'll wake up early on my own, but setting the alarm is fine," Dane said.

In a few minutes, she was done fussing with the alarm. "Good night, Daniel," Alexa said.

"Good night, Roger," he said, and swallowed his laugh.

It was a good thing to think of her as Roger right

now, he realized. He'd found his protector much too sexy a woman.

He'd remain aware of her presence not far from him that night. He wasn't sure he'd sleep, but at least he wouldn't make any attempt to seduce her.

Darn it.

Only… Well, it wouldn't hurt to thank her. The light on the nightstand remained on, very dim. Was that okay? Apparently, Alexa thought so. But if someone was looking for them, and tried peeking into the room despite the closed curtains…

At least it gave him an excuse. He got out of his bed on the side nearest Alexa's and reached for the light switch.

"Are you uncomfortable leaving it on?" she asked. "I've got a flashlight, so we don't need to keep it lit."

"I think that would be better," he said. But before he turned it off, he bent down and gave Alexa a deep kiss, tasting her mouth, her tongue… And was delighted that she responded passionately. Wow.

Too bad they couldn't do anything more. That would be unprofessional on both their parts. Plus, it would be too distracting if anyone was around here pursuing them.

Still… Well, when that kiss was over, he started another. And Alexa put her arms around his neck to tug him down even more. The kiss continued, and he felt Alexa stroke his back, then downward, which caused his penis to become erect.

He debated stroking her as well and did let his hand touch her buttocks.

But before he could do more, she was the one to pull away. "Okay, we've gotten that out of the way," she said.

"And I, for one, enjoyed it. But that's all. Go to bed, Daniel." She reached around him and turned out the light. "And I hope I don't bother you too much when I get up and check our surroundings a lot tonight."

Sleep? After *that*, and knowing sexy Dane was just across the room from her?

Alexa knew she shouldn't have participated in those kisses, let alone encouraged them—and more. She'd anticipated…something. And was glad they had done what they had done.

But she'd been serious when she said it was a good thing they'd gotten them out of the way.

Never mind that she'd become so sexually aroused that it was damn difficult to move away.

Well, it was over now. One less thing to worry about this night.

Except that she'd have to force herself to focus on her real reason to be there.

Fortunately, Alexa hadn't intended to get a good night's sleep.

Her intent was to doze, off and on, and listen while awake for anything going on outside their room. Walk around inside it, too, a few times and check out the window some more. Maybe even throw on a shirt and her hairpiece, go outside onto the upper area of this motel and look around a bit, but she'd only do that if she felt they'd been compromised at all, and so far she didn't.

She lay awake a lot, listening for sounds indicating trouble, but that wasn't all.

She listened to the sounds from the other bed. Dane sleeping deeply, shifting around sometimes, maybe even snoring.

She heard that briefly a couple of times though not particularly loudly. She otherwise became aware of his deep breathing that might indicate he was asleep—or just resting.

Maybe even keeping track of her late-night noises as well. She considered getting into his bed with him and snuggling—but forced herself not to.

Did she snore? She wouldn't be surprised if she did on other nights. But that night she didn't ever sleep deeply.

She might not have slept at all.

And not just because she was doing her job.

She kept thinking of the two of them together for the night, in the same motel room. Especially after those kisses.

Sure, during the day right now she was just another guy accompanying him, appearing to the world, she hoped, like a buddy, and that was all.

But even in disguise Dane was one good-looking guy. She couldn't help thinking of him sexually, at least a bit...well, maybe more than a bit. Especially since she knew he'd taken his clothes off to change into pj's, as she had. Only a few feet from one another, though separated by the bathroom door.

And then those good-night kisses...

Cut it out! her mind kept yelling at her. But for now, she hadn't been able to get those thoughts about Dane out of her mind.

She wondered what it would have been like if they'd actually made love. She'd had sex with other men, of course, but nothing that had made her want to keep any of those guys in her life for long.

Would it be different with Dane? No matter. Wasn't going to happen.

But he was one attractive, brave, sexy guy…

Good thing he mostly stayed in his bed, even when she got up to check that the room was secure, which probably woke him at least sometimes. As she'd mentioned, she had a flashlight in her overnight bag, just as she carried extra weapons, to go along with her job.

She'd wanted to keep the room lamp on a little longer, but Dane had been right. It had been time to shut it off.

She'd have been glad to use the light on her cell phone, but that object was probably in Grand Junction or Blue Larkspur, or that far away at least, right now.

Okay. She was thinking too much. Again. She glanced toward the clock radio on the nightstand between the two beds. The night was passing more quickly than she'd figured, considering the fact she hadn't slept through it. The time was nearly five o'clock. They hadn't planned to get up for another couple hours, which was fine.

But Alexa once more itched to get out of bed. She pulled the flashlight from the nightstand and turned it on, planning to check the perimeter yet again.

"You're awake again." The voice from the other bed startled her.

Even when she'd wondered previously if Dane was awake, he hadn't said anything.

"So, apparently, are you," she responded.

"Yeah. Everything okay?"

"Seems that way."

"Good." Dane sat up a bit, putting his back against

the wall at the head of the bed. "Need any help making sure this time?"

"No. You can go back to sleep for a little while," Alexa told him. She intended to get back in bed, even though she doubted she would sleep any more.

"Oh, but I'm a little chilly. Care to join me to help me warm up? A kiss might help."

She hadn't really heard that, had she? He wanted her to join him in his bed? Kiss passionately again?

He was right, it was a little cool in the room. This was a desert area, but it was October. They hadn't put on the air conditioning, but neither had they turned on any heat.

She figured that wasn't the reason for his unexpected invitation.

An invitation that made her shiver a little, and not because of any coolness.

But this time she had to stay professional. Aware of their surroundings. Aware of how to protect this man under her observation and care.

"I think you can warm up on your own," she said. "Just burrow down under your sheet and blanket. And think about the day we're going to embark on soon. I think that'll take any chilliness away."

Alexa no longer had any desire to nestle back down in her bed. Not the way her thoughts were going. She thrust her sheet and blanket aside and stood up.

"You sure you won't come over here?" Dane's voice suggested he was smiling.

"Is this another one of your corny jokes?" Alexa retorted, even though on some level she hoped he was serious.

"Who, me? Joke?" Dane got out of bed, too. He stood

across the room from her now, and she aimed her flashlight in his direction. "Gee," he said then. "Guess you're getting better at figuring out when I'm teasing."

That made Alexa deflate inside.

What? Had she hoped, on some level, that he *was* serious?

Hell yes.

But she'd never admit that to him. Instead, she decided to respond with a dry word or two of her own. "Damn. I was hoping you were going to say no, that it wasn't a joke, that you really wanted me to jump into bed with you and have some hot sex. After all, I'm not the guy I look like during the day right now. And you've already tested that with those kisses."

"Those kisses. Hey, I wouldn't mind some more. After all, we're both dressed. We're wearing pj's, both of us. We're protected and—"

"You know, Daniel," Alexa made herself say drolly, "this is getting out of hand. A little more sleep—sleep, and nothing else in our beds—will probably be a good thing for both of us. And—"

"And you're right." This time Dane started walking around the room, pulling back the curtains on the windows just a bit before passing them, then walking close to the other walls. "Maybe this isn't the best of hours to kid around. No more kisses. Just a little more sleep."

"Right." Alexa also made sure no one was lingering outside their room, then snuggled back down in her bed. Alone. Of course.

Even realizing this guy was too clownish at off times like now, she couldn't help wondering what it would be like if they were sharing a motel room for other reasons and weren't both alert for trouble.

You'll never know, she told herself, forcing her eyes to close despite knowing she wouldn't sleep. *Stay professional. Don't even think about it.*

Dane got out of bed a while after that conversation of sorts with Alexa. He knew he wouldn't be able to sleep any more that night. Time to take his shower. Without saying a word, he went to the stand holding his suitcase and, using his own flashlight that he'd brought along, he pulled out underwear and the clothing he intended to wear that day as Daniel.

Sure, he was well aware that the danger to him was likely about to multiply, especially when he reached Phoenix, and even, potentially, on the way, in spite of his being in witness protection. His insomnia was largely based on concern.

And remembering those kisses.

Damn. He never should have started that. But he had. And he had to put it behind him.

It was critical that he get to court in time—and in one piece. He had to testify.

He had to do all he could to get justice, for Alvin's sake—and to bring down that murderous Swanson.

He'd shut the bathroom door. Time to strip and shower. But the idea of being naked now and for the next few minutes, with Alexa—not her alternate persona Roger—in the next room, made him think all the more about what he'd been kidding about before when he'd spoken with her. Teased her about their spending some time together in the same bed.

Kissed her last night…

Only, on some level, he hadn't been kidding or teasing. The idea of being that close to her in bed… Okay, he needed to direct his thoughts another way.

He hurriedly took a few steps on the dirty, cold vinyl bathroom floor and turned on the water. He let it run cold for a minute as he stepped inside. Ah. That helped him cool down in many ways.

He turned up the heat a bit then and completed his shower.

After drying himself, using a towel that actually appeared clean, he shaved then dressed.

Only then was he ready to face Alexa again.

She, too, had awakened and left her bed. She had turned on the TV. "My turn for the bathroom?" she asked.

"Sure."

While she was in there, Dane watched television again, trying damn hard not to imagine what she looked like in the shower and after…

She emerged from the room fairly quickly, smashing his imagination since she had definitely morphed into Roger again. "Okay, are we ready to go grab breakfast?" Damn, but her wig, covering her lovely hair, appeared to be real.

That was okay under the circumstances.

"Fast food, yes?" he asked. "I figure it should be fast, since we're hurrying today."

"Right. But our next stop after eating will be—"

"A store where we can grab you a burner."

"Exactly. And we'll get you another one, too, to make sure your extra one isn't compromised. You should keep it turned off. Let's check to see when the stores open around here, then decide whether to shop or continue on."

He obediently allowed Alexa, carrying her own bag, to go check them out of the ratty place.

She returned to their room after apparently leaving her suitcase in the car. "I think we're okay to leave, but let's be careful."

"When am I not careful?" he asked, raising his brows as he talked to the guy in front of him who was his supposed buddy.

"Don't get me started." She tried to grab his suitcase but he didn't let her, though she did take the backpack.

They were soon in the rental car, and she was letting him drive. They were learning to compromise, he observed. "I'll want you to drive a lot today," she said, "so I can be as observant on our route as possible."

"Got it," he said.

He drove them into a better part of town so they could more likely assume their breakfast would be sanitary. He was glad to see they passed a couple of stores that might sell cell phones.

They reached a family restaurant and agreed to eat there since they had time before the stores opened. Fortunately, that early, it wasn't very busy. They sat at a booth near the back. He ordered pancakes and coffee from their middle-aged server, and Alexa got a breakfast sandwich, also with coffee.

And as they ate, he appreciated how alert Alexa/Roger appeared to be.

"Which store do you think we should head for when we're done?" she asked him.

"Not sure, but I have an idea." He asked their server where the nearest shopping center was that had a name-brand discount chain store. He figured they'd carry phones. He'd seen some possibilities as they had driven here, but someplace close would be better.

She told them. Fortunately, it wasn't far away. And that kind of retailer should open early.

It did, they learned a short while later after driving there. And also fortunately, it had an electronics section that included prepaid smartphones.

"I'll buy them," Alexa told him. "I'll register both in my assumed name of Roger, too." She'd kept her voice low, and he understood what she meant.

This was another way to keep even his new identity secret.

It was her job, sure. But Dane really appreciated all this beautiful woman—no, this frumpy, short-haired guy—was doing for him. Even if he knew that whatever was developing between them couldn't last.

Chapter 7

She hadn't needed to set one up before, but Alexa was aware of the procedure her department used to get numbers for burner phones obtained for those under their protection. Soon, she was back in the car with the man she now always thought of as Dane but referred to as Daniel when they were out with others around, as they'd just been. Only then did she download the app that she recalled from her training days.

Fortunately, she remembered how to do it well enough, and she followed the procedure to obtain temporary numbers for each of them. And, surprisingly, these were free for a week or so.

They were both using their new identities, of course, not just him, and Dane was driving once more. She checked the phone again and set up the GPS so she could direct him how to get back on their way toward their destination. That would be Route 191 till they reached the Arizona border, then Route 160 for around two and a half hours, and they'd still have a distance to go.

Alexa was glad to see there weren't many other vehicles on the road around them. Since the landscape was mostly flat or rolling desert, places where anyone could hide were rare.

For now, at least, they could travel their route in peace, as long as no other cars seemed to hang around them.

"Okay, we have phones again," she soon told him, letting him know what his new number was. It had the Bluff, Utah, area code of 435, as did hers. "I'll write it down for you later."

"Good." He glanced at her then back at the road. "I'll probably need to let the prosecutor know as we get near Phoenix."

"Good," Alexa said, although she would handle communications as much as possible. His former ties were with Tempe, and that was where the crime had been committed, but, as they'd discussed, the court in Phoenix would be in charge of the prosecution. "Have you been in touch with the prosecutor before?"

"Not directly. Since I'm in WITSEC, I was told by your predecessors to let them handle any contacts, to try to ensure no one learns my identity or whereabouts by sneaking around using that angle."

"Glad you're aware of that." She would give him more info later, maybe even this evening, assuming they reached their destination tonight. And that looked quite feasible now.

That would be good, since the trial started tomorrow.

But for now? She didn't want to just sit observing the scenery, which wasn't changing much. She considered discussing last night, the fact they'd seemed safe in that motel.

Even more, she had an urge to mention those kisses— No. They'd been impulsive, a mistake. She didn't want to think about them again.

As if she'd really be able to get them completely out of her mind...

So what should they talk about now?

An idea came to her: their respective backgrounds.

"Have you always lived in Tempe?" she asked him.

"Pretty much," he replied, glancing toward her again. "I got my degree at Arizona State University in Criminology and Criminal Justice and attended classes for that in Phoenix. But I came back home to take on my job as a vice detective with the Tempe PD."

"Got it. So is your family in Tempe?"

"That's right." At her urging, he went on to talk about them. His mom was a transactional attorney for a downtown Tempe law firm, and his dad worked in finance at the local headquarters of a national bank.

"Any siblings?" Alexa asked. She was looking forward to telling him about hers, assuming he wanted to hear about them.

"A brother, Max. He went into finance like our dad and got a job in Los Angeles at a different bank. He's married and has a couple of kids, so I'm Uncle Dane."

His tone suggested he was happy to be an uncle. Did that mean he liked kids? She thought about asking him if he wanted a family someday, but stopped herself. That didn't seem appropriate, even though she was interested.

"Why did you wind up in law enforcement?" Alexa couldn't help asking. She didn't gather that anyone else in his family was the stimulus. As she waited for his response, she turned to check behind them. There were a couple of cars in the distance, but nothing looked threatening. She set her eyes ahead again and scanned the horizon. She only saw one car coming toward them and had no reason to worry about it so far.

"Got interested in it while still in high school. The Tempe PD had some programs for familiarizing locals with the department and various programs, including for kids, and I was hooked."

"Sounds good." Alexa watched as that car coming toward them passed and kept going. She took a deep, calming breath. Nothing to worry about now. But that didn't keep her from staying alert. She wanted to know more about him and his personal life, but he started talking again first.

"How about you?" Dane asked. "How did you get into law enforcement?"

Ah, here it came. "It's pretty complicated," she said. "Family related."

"I figured, since you're a Colton and your family's reputation precedes you."

She knew he'd heard of the Coltons before—who hadn't? How much did he know?

"But we've got time. Tell me about it so I can make fun of you." Dane shot a glance filled with a smile toward her before looking back at the road.

Alexa couldn't help shaking her head. This was a serious discussion, and yet Dane made it clear he wanted to joke about it.

Why did she find that appealing? She knew she didn't have much of a sense of humor.

But this guy seemed to stimulate what little she had.

"Okay, what would you think if I told you I wanted to get into law enforcement because my father was a crook?" A bit much, but it was definitely true. And considering her family's reputation, he probably was aware of some of it.

Even so, he said, "Tell me about it."

That, she did. She explained that she had eleven siblings, and that she and Naomi were the youngest. "Most of us are trying to help others with our careers. We go about it in different ways, but we hate what our dad did and we hope to make things better for those he harmed and others in need of justice."

She kept it short and sweet. Their father had been a judge in Lark's County, Colorado. He'd apparently worried about supporting his large family. At least, that had been his excuse for his heinous criminal activities.

"His corruption was brought to light eventually by the family of one of those he convicted. But before he could be sent to jail himself—" Alexa felt her throat close up. No matter what he'd done, no matter how much she'd wanted to help those other people, she'd cared for her father though she had been too young to remember him well, except for the hugs he had given her and her siblings. And it had been so hard to grow up without a dad. "Anyway, there was a car accident on ice, and he died."

Dane glanced at her again. "I'm so sorry." He sounded serious this time. No joking in his tone.

"But the good thing was how his evil stuff spurred so many of us to do good things. Like me, in law enforcement. And among my eleven siblings, two are attorneys who started their own law firm and also created The Truth Foundation, which helps to get innocent people, like those our dad convicted, exonerated. One's a former sergeant in the army. Another, Dominic, the one I've been in touch with, is with the FBI's International Corruption Unit. And one's a district attorney in Lark's County, where Blue Larkspur is located."

"That all sounds really good," Dane said. "A bunch of you are doing all you can to atone for anything bad your father did."

"That's right."

She didn't mention, though, that her law enforcement family members were all after drug smuggler Ronald Spence. He had been thrown in prison thanks to their father, and The Truth Foundation had gotten him released after evidence had seemed to prove his innocence. Only it had since become apparent that Spence was actually guilty.

He needed to be thrown back into prison, and Alexa knew she would do all she could to help accomplish that—at least, once this latest case was complete.

She continued. "But would you like to know one of the careers a couple of my siblings have that's my favorite?"

"Sure," he said.

"They own the Gemini Ranch. I get there as often as I can. Maybe I'm a cowgirl at heart."

That caused Dane to laugh aloud. Alexa, too. Maybe she had a sense of humor after all.

Or at least she enjoyed talking about her family, and the strong—and fun—parts of it.

"Got it. I'd wondered about that. But that's not all of your siblings. What else do they do?"

"Well, my twin is in show business." She explained how Naomi's career differed from her own, and how Naomi had fallen in love with an undercover cop recently while shooting a reality show at the Gemini. Her very lucky sister.

Naomi, Alexa couldn't help recalling, who seemed to know strange things sometimes, and who had expressed concern about what might happen on this journey.

Nothing bad had happened, though...so far at least.

But they still had several hours to drive.

"And the rest include a venture capitalist, a social worker and a journalist who's also a podcast host."

"That's quite a family," Dane said. "I'd like to meet them sometime."

Really? Alexa assumed that, after he testified against his former boss and hopefully helped to get him convicted of murder, he'd be out of witness protection—and out of her life.

But what if he wasn't?

She couldn't help recalling those kisses...

Fortunately, he started asking more questions about her family, including her widowed mother.

"Her name is Isadora. Isa. She's a freelance graphic designer, a really nice person."

And Alexa and her siblings had recently realized the depth of their mom's feelings for a new man—family friend and local police chief Theo Lawson. Alexa was happy for her.

Right now, Alexa was glad that they'd started seeing signs indicating they were getting close to the Arizona border. They were making progress. It would still be a few hours before they reached the Phoenix area, but not too long. She'd have to figure out where they'd stay that night.

Tempe, and anywhere near Dane's usual territory, would be a bad idea.

But now that she had her burner phone, she could try again to contact Vince for his take on what should come next.

She couldn't relax, of course. But at least for the moment she didn't have to feel stressed.

And she could enjoy Dane's presence for as long as they were together. Even as she made sure to protect him if any action to accomplish that became necessary.

They were approaching Arizona, he realized by looking at the terrain. Signs along the roadway confirmed it. Soon, they'd cross the state line.

Dane resisted the urge to push down on the gas pedal. He'd seen no highway patrol, but that didn't mean they weren't around. He drove slightly faster than the speed limit, and that was good enough.

They remained a distance from Tempe. But Phoenix was a bit nearer on the route they were driving. And every minute they continued this way brought them closer to his testifying in Swanson's trial.

How did he feel about that?

Glad. Very glad. He would bring that dirty police chief down, help get him sent to prison for the rest of his life.

For Alvin's sake. But how would it feel to go his separate way from the marshal he'd come to like?

"Hey, we're making progress," he said to Alexa now.

He figured she was well aware of it. She'd stopped talking about her family and seemed to be concentrating even more on their surroundings, glancing often around them.

Dane had found himself fascinated by what she'd said as they'd discussed their backgrounds. What a family she had! The Colton name was well known in law enforcement, so he had heard of them before, but it was interesting to learn how versatile they were, in so many areas of the law and peacekeeping. And bringing down bad guys, he figured.

As well as protecting witnesses in danger.

He'd been serious about wanting to meet some of her family. But he realized that once he was no longer the subject of Alexa's safeguarding, he would probably never see her again.

He was determined to move back home as soon as it was safe for him.

Like, hopefully, in another week or two.

Although, if there was any possibility of his getting together again, in some manner, with Alexa—

"You're awfully quiet." Alexa's soft voice brought Dane out of his reverie. "What are you thinking?"

Like, *Are you scared*? Dane figured that was what she meant.

And *heck*. He *was* somewhat scared. He'd have to be stupid to assume all was well, even with his own private protector with him.

But nerves wouldn't stop him.

Only another bullet…

Forget that. If nothing else, he would be prepared this time, or at least aware his life was in danger, which would keep him vigilant.

"I'm thinking about all I want to say tomorrow," he said in response to Alexa's question. "I've no doubt the prosecutor will ask the right questions to get me to testify about what I saw, what I know."

"I've no doubt, either." Alexa's voice was soft and encouraging, and Dane had an urge to pull her quickly into his arms and kiss her again in thanks...and more.

That was wrong, especially now. He was concentrating on his driving, as he had to be.

And drawing them even closer to their destination—and where he would ultimately help bring Swanson to justice.

"Hopefully, you will have time to discuss the trial and your testimony in advance with the prosecutor," Alexa continued. "That's what they usually do. I've seen it a lot before, with the witnesses under my protection. But this situation... Well, it's a bit different."

"Like, the perpetrator being tried was my former boss, a police chief, and he has a lot of cohorts who just might be happy bringing down a bigmouth like me. He might even pay them for it." As he said that, he recalled what Alexa had said about her father.

He appreciated that Alexa, and apparently a bunch of her siblings, had been horrified by what he'd done, enough so that they'd chosen careers that could help the innocent and those in danger.

Like him.

He couldn't help it. He scanned the horizon in front of them and, via the rearview mirror, the area behind him. Again. As he did often. And as he was fully aware the amazing woman who accompanied him to protect him also did.

The woman he thought about often as the subject

of his protection as well, if it ever came down to that.
Or at least he would be prepared to attack anyone who
targeted her.

"Say," he said, "tell me a little more about your
brother Dominic, the FBI guy you talked to. How did
he decide to go that direction?"

"Well, he's in their International Corruption Unit.
Oh, and he's a triplet, older than little twin me."

Dane laughed. He'd also thought that, of all the siblings she'd described, Dominic might be the one he'd
like to meet most. But the two oldest were lawyers
who had started that organization—The Truth Foundation, right?—to help the people their dad had hurt
by sentencing innocents or recommending harsher
sentences than crimes warranted. They also sounded
pretty darned interesting.

Well, someday the trial would be behind him, and
he could continue with his detective career, being even
more observant of what was going on around him.

And by whom.

Plus, he would be able to follow up on anything
he learned as a result of this situation, not only about
how cops should or shouldn't act, but also about their
families.

Having a chance to talk to some of Alexa's siblings
might be damned interesting for that.

There. They were just about to reach the turnoff
from Utah into part of Arizona.

They were getting closer.

The route they were on continued south, but the
next veered west a short distance before heading south-
west—mostly south, from what he recalled of the GPS.
He relied on Alexa to confirm the route as they contin-

ued, but for the moment he prepared to make the turn onto the interstate.

Several signs prepared him for the intersection. He slowed, flipped on the car's turn signal, and turned left onto Route 160. Soon, he accelerated to reach the speed limit.

That was when he saw an SUV come from the direction he hadn't taken.

It looked like a police car. Lights on top were flashing, but he heard no siren.

A police car. He was back in Arizona now. At least some of his former colleagues were now his enemies, if they believed whatever cockamamie story Swanson had undoubtedly made up to protect himself and throw blame for the situation that had resulted in Dane's injury, and Alvin's death, on Dane.

Well, what could he do but pull over? Although—

He glanced at Alexa. She was looking in the side-view mirror on the passenger side. She had already seen their pursuer.

"Under other circumstances, I'd be glad to pull over," he told her. "And we've no reason to think that Swanson's got any state troopers in his pocket. But they'd be in charge here on the highway, and—"

"Understood," she said curtly. "But for now, let's act like obedient regular citizens. I'll make sure my weapon is handy, though."

"Mine, too." Dane put on his turn signal as he started to slow down, preparing to pull off the road.

"Okay, but be careful. I don't want to kill or injure a law enforcement officer because we're nervous. Got it?"

"Yeah, I got it." Dane knew he sounded more than

irritated—that was just his anxiety talking. But he genuinely agreed with her.

Nerves were one thing, though. Danger might be related, but that was what he needed to watch for. What *they* needed to watch for. For better or worse, he'd realized, they were partners in this adventure.

He stopped and put the car in Park, though he remained ready to accelerate again. He didn't turn off the engine.

An African American guy in a beige uniform, with a badge on his chest and loaded belt around his waist, exited the driver's-side door.

Dane rolled down his window as he waited. He also checked to see how easily accessible his gun was.

"I'll take care of that, if necessary," Roger, beside him, said in a gruff, masculine voice, and Daniel, back in his own undercover identity, chose not to smile.

Nothing funny about this. And he understood why Alexa—no, Roger—would want every precaution to be taken.

As the trooper reached the open window, Daniel turned his head to look at him. "Something wrong, Officer?"

Like, were you hired to look for me by that SOB I intend to bring down, maybe even kill me?

The guy appeared to be in his thirties, with short, black hair and a scowling expression. "You didn't signal as you turned onto this highway from 191," the trooper said. He pulled out a pad from one of his many pockets. "Time for a ticket."

"Oh, but this is a rental car," Roger/Alexa called in his throaty, masculine voice from the other side of the car. "We just picked it up yesterday." He'd pulled the paperwork from the glove compartment and waved it. "See? And I saw Daniel flip the switch for the signal. It must be broken."

"Oh yeah?" the trooper said without asking to take a closer look at the rental lease or registration card. "Give it a try, and I'll take a look."

He did. Daniel flipped the blinker a couple of times, and the trooper checked it out from the rear. His partner exited the SUV, too, and the two of them talked for a minute.

The first officer came forward again. "We'll let you go this time since it appears to be defective, but you'd better report that to the rental company, maybe even pick up another car if they've got an office wherever you're heading."

Daniel felt relieved the trooper didn't even ask where that was. "I'll certainly do that, Officer. I'm really sorry. And thanks so much for being so understanding."

The trooper stomped off. Daniel gave a big sigh of relief as he glanced at Roger beside him.

"Maybe this is our lucky day after all," Roger/Alexa rasped.

"You, with your law enforcement background, know better than that. If we were really lucky, he wouldn't even have noticed." But despite his words, Dane—now feeling like himself again, rather than Daniel—felt at least a bit optimistic as he started off once more toward Phoenix.

The trooper's SUV passed them as Dane maintained the speed limit. Soon, the state vehicle was out of sight ahead of them as the road turned a bit.

There were other cars around, though not many.

More seemed to be going the other way, but a couple caught up with them from behind and then passed.

Dane had an urge to speed forward, and although he did increase his velocity a bit, he decided to behave for now.

He was well aware there were likely to be more troopers around.

He kept checking to make sure none of them, or anyone else, was following him, glancing often into the rearview mirror.

No one that he saw at first, but—

He was about to say something to Roger/Alexa but she spoke first in her usual voice, as she stared into the side-view mirror. "I appreciate how you've been staying near the speed limit and letting cars pass, but there's one back there—"

"That seems to be following at our speed."

"Right," Alexa said. "I'd like to get it to pass so I won't be worried about it, so please slow down a little more."

That, he did.

The vehicle appeared to decrease its speed, too.

And so Dane went even slower. A few other cars passed, but not that one. Snail's pace time.

Ah, the black sedan appeared to accelerate, maybe no longer wanting to stay behind a crawler. Only—

As it reached them and began to pass, it sped up. Someone on the passenger side glared at Dane; a young guy whose brown hair blew in the breeze of the open window. He had no facial hair, but there was a look of determination on his long, thin face.

He wore a dark shirt. It looked like it could be official, although Dane saw no badges from this angle.

Even so, could he be a cop? If so, what jurisdiction? Tempe?

Dane stared farther inside and noted that the driver, too, appeared to be in uniform.

And that was when that passenger pulled a gun and aimed it at Dane.

Chapter 8

"Speed up! Faster!" Alexa yelled, not even attempting to sound like Roger anymore. But she didn't really have to tell Daniel/Dane. They were already accelerating rapidly past the vehicle beside them, at least for the moment. Alexa had pulled her gun from her pocket but didn't have anywhere to aim it, for now.

She wasn't surprised that Dane had done the same thing, still holding the steering wheel with the other hand and moving his gaze from the road ahead to beside them.

But she did hear a sudden blast—clearly from a gun. Their pursuers must have caught up to them. Fortunately, with the way Dane was also swerving across the road, the bullet hadn't seemed to have hit anything. Not them at least, thank heavens. Alexa had no idea where it had gone.

There fortunately weren't any other vehicles close to them right now, so hopefully it hadn't hurt anyone.

But the shot had made a loud noise. Loud enough for the troopers who'd pulled way ahead to hear and come back and help them?

Apparently not.

Their car continued to race in that direction, though, thanks to Dane, who also kept zigzagging across the road to keep the other vehicle behind them. She knew his defensive driving was also designed to make the people in this front seat—namely, both him and Alexa—harder to hit.

She just hoped it worked.

For her own safety, Alexa figured she should have crouched down, or at least bent over to stay out of any line of fire. But that wasn't why she was there. Why she was with Dane. And so she remained sitting up, wishing she could throw herself between Dane and any weapon aimed at him, but in this car that wasn't possible.

She did keep an eye on the other vehicle, though. His safety was her responsibility.

And she would do everything she could to keep him safe—and not just because it was her job. She realized she really had begun to care for the man in her charge.

She kept her gun ready in case using it became practical.

And she additionally pulled her new phone from her pocket and pressed in the number for her boss, hoping it would work this time.

It did. Marshal Vince Cudahy answered his phone immediately. "Hello?" He didn't demand, in that one word, to know who was calling, but Alexa was sure that was what he meant. He didn't have her new number, so no identity would have showed up on his screen.

"Vince, it's..." She was about to identify herself as Alexa but didn't have to.

"Alexa? Where the hell have you been? What's going on? Is everything all right?"

"No," she said, and really meant it now. She used her shoulder to keep her phone at her ear. Their assailants had pulled up close behind them, the hood of the vehicle now very close to their bumper. "Turn!" she shouted to Dane, who obeyed by turning the wheel abruptly to prevent the other car from hitting them. He then braked suddenly, throwing them both forward into the dashboard.

The other car was now ahead of them again. A good thing? Probably not. Not when the occupants had taken a shot at them, and probably would again.

But Alexa resolved to take control of that angle, at least somewhat. She loosened her seat belt, kept her phone wedged where it was, crawled somewhat into the back seat, rolled down the left window and shot at the other car several times, aiming for the left rear tire, though missing it as they moved. She also memorized the Arizona license plate.

The car didn't brake immediately, but it did pull over to the right side of the road, then slowed a bit.

"Good! Now keep going. Fast."

"Yes, sir. Or ma'am."

"Tell me what's going on," came the order in Alexa's ear.

"I don't know why we haven't been able to communicate, Vince," Alexa responded. She put it on speaker so Dane could hear, too. "Maybe it was because the burners Daniel and I both had were hacked. We've sent them off in a different direction now. But we're still on the way from Blue Larkspur to Phoenix, and the occupants of a car just started shooting at us. And they could be cops. Here's the license plate information." She related it to him, figuring he'd have a way to jot it down. But she figured it was likely to be false or stolen.

"Damn!" Vince exploded. "Tell me where you are."

"Somewhere between—"

But before Alexa could say, Dane said, "Don't do it! Even if you're sure it's your boss, who knows if our burner phones are totally safe? Hope so, but just in case, don't give him any details."

"If I don't tell him, he won't be able to send help." Alexa knew she sounded desperate. But she was, in a way. Still, this was the kind of situation she'd known she might face while doing her job. She could handle it. She *would* handle it.

But having some assistance sounded damned good right about now.

Yet Dane and she were far enough from civilization out here that it would undoubtedly take forever before Vince could be of much help, unless he sent a helicopter. Or even drones.

And that apparently was his idea, too.

"Look. He's right." Apparently Vince had heard what Dane had said. "But you know it's me. And I understand that you don't want to give a lot of information under these circumstances. But I'm assuming you're at least in Arizona by now, right?"

Alexa looked to Dane, who shot an angry glance toward her as she said, "Yes. And we dumped my assigned car before and are in a rental car. It's a light blue sedan. The car we were shot at from is behind us."

"Okay, then. I'll get in touch with some of my contacts in the area you're probably driving in. You'll see helicopters overhead soon. Be careful in the meantime, stay as far as possible from the shooter, of course. And after help arrives— Well, I figure you'll determine the best course of action then. Got it?"

"Right," Alexa said. "Thanks, Vince. And I'll be in touch again as soon as it's feasible."

"At least I have your current number, for now. But do what you have to, to stay safe, even sending this phone...wherever."

"Got it." Alexa hung up.

But where were those guys now?

Behind them somewhere, since they'd pulled over and slowed. But Alexa didn't see them.

That, hopefully, was a good thing. She checked her phone's GPS.

Not far from a turnoff road. That might be good.

They had passed the town of Tsegi. Route 160 continued on, but Alexa had an urge to tell Dane to drive off the main road toward where the Peabody Kayenta Mine used to be.

Not too far, though. They needed to be near the primary roads when—or *if*—Vince was able to get helicopters headed in their direction.

"Drive south onto Route 41 here," she told Dane. "There's an old coal mine a little way off, but there are some local streets first that even have a few restaurants on them. Let's wait there for a short while."

"Sounds good," Dane said. "It might be easier for us to hide among crowds of people."

"My thoughts exactly."

They agreed not to spend much time here by getting food or anything else in this small town, but he parked and they continued to observe the roads around them.

Nothing.

Good, Alexa thought. But where were their attackers? Were they lying in wait, preparing to spring another deadly trap?

"Time to go back?" Dane made it a question after a few minutes, but he must have already decided the answer since he'd turned the engine on and headed the car back to Route 160.

Coincidentally—or not—Alexa saw a car a distance in front of them. It looked a lot like their pursuers' black sedan.

Damn. How had they gotten ahead?

She told Dane.

"Yeah, I saw it," he said through gritted teeth. "I don't want to turn back the way we were going to avoid them. We're losing too much time, and I need to be in court tomorrow."

"I understand. I think I'll call Vince again soon and find out if any copters are on the way. Oh, and he could call the prosecutor and let him or her know that you'll do your best to be there, but maybe not first thing in the morning, considering the situation."

"Good idea. I don't have to be the first witness to testify."

"And if they have any way of helping us, they should let us know." But Alexa doubted the prosecutors could do much.

They cruised along the road, letting others pass

since Dane wisely didn't floor it to get closer to the car they'd pegged as possibly containing their enemies.

That was when Alexa first heard the sound of a helicopter's whirring blades. Or was it two? She looked up through the windshield and saw a couple approaching overhead from the south. That would still make sense, even if they'd been sent from Vince in Colorado, since he would undoubtedly have contacted law enforcement closer to where he knew Alexa and the subject of her witness protection were currently located.

"Could those have been sent by your Marshals Service?" Dane asked, also looking in that direction as he drove slowly toward them.

"I'm fairly sure they were." Alexa allowed herself to feel a slight sense of relief. But not much. Just because they now had help didn't mean their jeopardy was over.

"Good. We'll just stay nice and slow for now till we see how things go."

Quite a few other cars passed them as they kept their speed just below the limit. The car they'd been checking out did not appear to slow down. In fact, as the helicopters kept circling the area, Alexa lost sight of it; she figured it had sped up to get out of the way.

She didn't see anyone, or any vehicle, that particularly troubled her—but that fact itself wound up troubling her. She wanted to know where they'd gone.

But she figured she could rely on the choppers that still showed up overhead with frequency to, if nothing else, scare off their potential attackers, at least for now.

They continued driving for quite a while, veering off the main road and back on again to keep an eye out for anyone following—and no one was. Alexa made her call to Vince, thanked him for the help and requested that he contact the prosecutor in Phoenix, which he agreed to do.

Dane and she didn't talk a lot, at least not like before. Dane did ask Alexa if she had ever experienced anything similar, like helicopters swooping in to help keep her, and the witness she was then protecting, safe.

"No, but I'd heard of similar circumstances. Now I have another experience I can add to my list of things I've had happen while on the job."

"Ah, so that's why the other car came after us. You planned it to add to your experiences."

Alexa had been scanning the sky yet again, but now she looked over at her driver—and the subject of her current assignment.

And the man who thought he was funny sometimes when she didn't see the humor.

Like now.

"Oh exactly," she said dryly. "I called on some suspects in other cases who wanted some current fun and told them to come after us in our rented car. And then I contacted Vince to get him to protect us."

Dane laughed. "Hey, of us two, I thought I was the joker."

"So did I," Alexa grumbled. She was looking at her phone. It was getting late enough in this day that she thought it would be better to stop for the night, then get up early enough tomorrow to drive straight through to the courthouse.

Hopefully, with more protection from Vince's allies. But this way, Dane's enemies, with a bit of luck, wouldn't know where they were or be able to figure out their timing.

"Hey, you know what?" she said. "I think we're get-

ting close to Flagstaff. And I think your pursuers are
going to assume, with those helicopter escorts, that
we'll roll into Phoenix tonight. I want us to find another dinky hotel, this time in or around Flagstaff, and
stay there till very early tomorrow morning. And I'll
let Vince know, too, in case we need any more help."

She thought about asking Dane's opinion. But she
was in charge.

"Okay by me," he said anyway. "How soon do we
reach a Flagstaff turnoff?"

"Not long. But here are my thoughts about that."
Alexa suggested that they exit where it was clear that
food and gasoline were available and stop for those
services. That way, if anyone had been able to evade
the copters and still follow them, Alexa and her charge
would have an obvious and necessary reason to get off
the route they were taking.

Only, then they would find a nearby hole-in-the-
wall motel to stay the night, maybe even leaving the
car parked near the gas station. They could use a ride
share to get to the motel, as long as they remained
careful and in disguise. And asked their driver to get
them there by a circuitous route while they observed
their surroundings.

"Sounds fine to me," Dane said. "Tell me the best
place to get off this road."

Dane was pleased when Alexa told him where to
exit the route they were on, then get back on the main
road, then off again.

So she could watch even more for anyone following, he assumed. She really was thorough, he observed.

At the second exit there were billboards for a nearby

service station and convenience store. That was where they headed, at Alexa's suggestion.

So did the couple of helicopters that had continued to show up periodically and circle their area.

"I think this might be a good time for you to talk to Vince and see where we are if we stay somewhere near here overnight—and whether he has spoken with the prosecutor," Dane said as they reached the shop.

Smart and helpful witness protector that Alexa was, she not only did what he requested, but she also put her phone on speaker as they parked in one of the few vacant spaces just outside the convenience store. Dane felt he could participate if it seemed appropriate, although he didn't wind up saying anything.

"Oh, hi, Roger," Vince began as he answered. "Thanks for calling."

Dane—no, maybe Daniel at this moment—looked toward Roger/Alexa's slitted eyes. She appeared concerned. Did her boss's use of her pseudonym mean they were in trouble?

"No problem, Marshal Cudahy." Alexa used her deep, disguised voice, and Dane continued to be concerned. "But I had some questions."

"Let me guess. And in case you're wondering, I'm assuming you aren't reaching your destination this evening, so those copters will only circle for a couple more rounds today."

Alexa nodded. "Correct assumption," she agreed, still using her male voice. "But your pilots know in general where we are. I don't want them to know where we're staying, so maybe you should call them off now."

So they could find someplace to stay and no one would know where, Dane figured.

"Will do, but, so that you know, I've made sure there are copters circling in a few other places so it won't be obvious where you are."

"Excellent idea," Alexa said.

Dane continued to sit there as he listened, staring at people who entered and left the store, and others behind where they were parked who were pumping gas into their cars.

"And in case you're wondering," Vince said, "I did speak with the prosecutor, District Attorney Moe Francini, to let him know that his key witness was getting close but, for security reasons, would not reach Phoenix till sometime tomorrow. I'll give you his phone number. You should call first thing in the morning, early, to give him a status report. Otherwise, he'll be hammering at me, I figure, and I won't have all the answers."

"Fair enough. Did he give any parameters about what might be too late for us to arrive?"

"Only that the trial will begin around nine and he'd like to have Dane there no later than eleven so they can discuss his testimony before Moe begins questioning him that afternoon."

"I think we can do that."

"Good. Sounds like you're doing well with your alternate identity, by the way. And I'd like you to call me again after you talk with Moe tomorrow to keep me informed, too. That'll possibly inspire me to get more copters over your heads if it makes sense in the morning."

"Thanks, Vince," Roger/Alexa said, and they soon hung up.

She looked at Dane. "I assume you're okay with all

we said, or even a jokester like you would jump in and tell us what was wrong."

"Who, me?" Dane spoke in the grittier voice he sometimes took on with his Daniel identity. "A jokester? Or a complainer?"

"Both sound just like the wonderful you I've come to know over the last couple days." Alexa/Roger sent him an irritated grin, then said, "Now, let's hurry into this place and grab some stuff for dinner tonight. Then, I have an idea where we can stay."

"Sounds good to me. Another hellhole like last night?"

"Maybe, but there's a place I saw online that might actually not only be in a somewhat safe location, but even possibly clean."

Dane gestured into the air with his fist. "Yay! Bring it on."

"Food first."

That was fine with him. He got himself back into the mode of being Daniel Brennan, big and bulky, with a lot less hair. He also appreciated that Alexa, already somewhat in disguise, went into thorough Roger mode.

Soon, they were both in the store. Each chose a sandwich from a refrigerator case. Daniel's? Ham and cheese. And Roger decided on tuna salad. They each additionally selected chips on the side, and they also bought a six-pack of bottled water.

There weren't a lot of other customers, but Dane wasn't surprised to see Roger shuffle along one side to stare down the couple of aisles at the other people there. He didn't appear concerned, and neither did Dane see anyone who particularly worried him. But he remained on high alert.

Soon, they were ready. He wasn't surprised when Roger pulled his wallet from his pocket—opposite side from the fortunately not especially noticeable bulge on the other side where the weapon was stuck in his pants—and paid cash for what they'd bought.

Another thing for which Dane would ultimately repay Alexa, or the Marshals Service, once everything was resolved.

Dane let Roger lope slowly in front of him as they left the store, acting as if he was the older man he looked to be, yet staying close enough to Dane to be the target if anyone tried to harm him. Yes, this was Alexa's job. Dane definitely knew that before and now found it even more obvious, even if the intent was that the limping senior appeared to find it too difficult to move away.

But now the other "man" accompanied Dane to the passenger side and watched as he got into the car, after Dane suggested leaving the car there and using a ride share service to head somewhere else. "That would just provide another possibility of someone unknown sneaking into our lives—one of those who's trying to find you," Alexa said. "I know I considered that before, but the idea began to worry me."

"Got it," Dane told her. And he did. He was getting used to having to second-guess every move he made.

But were they really out of the vision of whoever was after him?

In any case, it was Alexa's turn to drive. Dane didn't even ask.

Once they were both locked inside, Alexa started backing out of the parking space.

As she drove away, he asked, "So are we off to the place you found where we can stay tonight?"

"Exactly. But not directly."

Sure enough, she drove around the store and parked first at one of the gas pumps, where she insisted on getting the fuel into the car's tank.

Dane pretended to be looking at his phone but mostly kept an eye on Alexa. He couldn't help himself.

When she got back into the car, he had to ask. "Did you see anything worrisome?"

"Only the price of the gas."

Really? This woman who seemed to have little, if any, sense of humor was making a joke?

He, of all people, loved the idea but wasn't sure if she was actually being serious.

On the other hand, this gas station's prices were on the high side, maybe because of the location near the road and not too far of a distance into Flagstaff.

Maybe she wasn't joking.

He didn't ask. But he did say, "So how long will it take to reach our destination?"

"Not long."

And in fact, she was correct. She drove around the block again. Then she got onto a wider street that appeared to lead to downtown.

Except that she quickly edged into an alleyway between a couple of office buildings.

Nearby was a small but relatively nice-looking motel.

The motel faced another road and wasn't too close to any of the offices or any other structures.

But Alexa didn't park in the spaces surrounding the

motel. Instead, she pulled into a three-story lot at the end of one of the office buildings.

"Let's assume we'll be staying here and get our stuff," she said. "And let's be careful."

They soon had their belongings out of the trunk. And yes, they were careful as they at first stayed near the offices, then crossed the parking lot to the motel— but only after Alexa insisted on walking that way first.

Alexa had also insisted on being the one to check them in.

Dane hoped this place would be much better than last night's. But even if it looked better, Dane couldn't help wondering, *Would they stay safe?*

And could he get away with kissing his protector good-night again?

Chapter 9

Though she acted even older than she had before, Alexa felt she did just fine hobbling as Roger into the small but attractive lobby on the ground floor of the Welcome to AZ Flagstaff Motel, and rallying her huskiest, senior, masculine voice to ask the receptionist—a middle-aged lady in a fancy pantsuit—if they had a room available.

She certainly hoped so. She'd done some quick digging on her burner phone to find a motel in an area where there was nothing to particularly attract tourists or anyone else. This one had not only come to her attention quickly, in a business-oriented neighborhood with a few but not many similar accommodations, it had also stood out as a potentially okay location, despite its remoteness.

Pictures had showed it was a couple of stories high

but not particularly large, with limited windows and a visible outdoor path to reach the rooms. Their website had indicated the rates were reasonable, and the photos had depicted rooms that were more than decent compared with the place they'd stayed the night before. Those rooms appeared clean, with a couple of beds in each, and other amenities, including free bottled water in the small refrigerators.

And it hadn't been far off their existing path. Although that might have been more of a problem than a plus if anyone following them had managed to elude the helicopter pilots and continued to surreptitiously shadow them.

"Do you have any rooms available for just tonight?" she asked.

Daniel was standing at the door, looking out as if he was fascinated by the neighborhood. They'd planned that. He stood back far enough that he wasn't particularly visible, nor was he at an angle where he was likely to be shot if any of his enemies turned up, assuming they'd recognize him in his disguise.

Smart guy. He was doing a good job of keeping an eye on things for his protection, and even hers. And despite his ugly disguise, he still appeared somewhat good-looking to her.

"Yes, we do," the receptionist said in a calm voice, nodding so her brown hair caressed her shoulders as she regarded Alexa through her large, black-rimmed glasses. Her ID pin said she was Bobbie. She turned to the computer beside her on the wooden counter and typed something in. Alexa wondered how many rooms were available. Maybe all of them, judging by the lack of parked cars or other activity in this location surrounded by businesses that apparently didn't otherwise include places to stay. Bobbie looked back at them. "One room for the two of you?"

"That's right," Alexa groused as Roger, wondering if they'd get any kind of argument. Could be the place was so empty that management hoped a pair of guests might rent out two rooms.

But Bobbie nodded, typed some more and said, "I have a room on the second floor for you. We don't have an elevator, though. Would you like me to send someone to carry your bags up there?"

"No thanks," Alexa said, still grumping. "We'll manage."

Of course. She was strong enough to manage her stuff, and with the help of Dane/Daniel there'd be no problem at all.

They hadn't requested it, but she was glad they were getting a room upstairs. Maybe the place wasn't as empty as it appeared. But it'd be easier to keep an eye on their surroundings from up there.

Alexa showed her special Roger ID and paid by cash again. She felt Daniel's glare—did he really manage to exude irritation at not being in control while hiding from potential killers?—but had already told him she had sufficient cash, and it was certainly less traceable than credit cards, even obtained with fake, protective names.

More likely, he wanted to pay, as he'd said before. Well, who ultimately got stuck with the bill wasn't up to her. She was simply following orders. And *she* was the one in charge—she'd thought he'd come to terms with that, but apparently not the way she'd hoped.

She got the receipt and two keycards from the receptionist. It all felt a bit like last night, although Alexa definitely hoped their room tonight wouldn't be as ratty.

But even if it was, this was where they would stay. It was only for one night, after all. And if she'd done a good job selecting the place, they'd hopefully remain safe. *But is he going to kiss me again?* she wondered.

"Thanks," Roger said deeply and politely.

Alexa led Daniel out of the reception area, both of them rolling their carryon bags behind them. Daniel held the plastic container with their dinner food and his backpack.

At the base of the concrete steps, Daniel said, "I'll carry both suitcases. One at a time, though."

Even though Alexa considered herself totally able to take care of her own things, the Roger she was acting like around here might not be able to, and it wouldn't be a great idea to indicate to the world that he could. As a result, she agreed with her companion. "Thanks," she said in a deep mutter. "Let me carry the backpack and food, at least."

She followed large Daniel as he carried her bag upstairs first. She walked slowly, balancing the backpack and holding on to the thin rail at the side of the steps, as if she needed to do so to maintain her steadiness. Since she still had both keycards, she opened the door to their room, which was the closest to the stairs.

She hurried in and, hand on her covered weapon, she checked the place out. Looked okay. No one was there. She went back outside to watch apparently overweight Daniel strain his way up the stairs with his own bag...and, even more important, to keep her eyes on their environment to make sure no one else was watching her charge.

Fortunately, the area, despite having taller buildings around it, appeared quiet. She saw no one looking at them either from below, or from any windows in those buildings.

At the top, Daniel grunted and moved around Roger into their room, where she joined him and closed and locked the door behind them, then checked to make sure it seemed secure.

"Not bad," Daniel said in his normal Dane voice, standing taller, ignoring his distended stomach.

"I agree," Alexa said.

As with the other place they'd stayed, this room had a window looking out onto the upper walkway, and Alexa was pleased that it had slatted blinds that were closed. It would most likely be easier to move a slat or two to look out than it had been to deal with drapes.

And when Alexa walked around to study the place, she was even more pleased. The room not only looked clean, but the furnishings gave it a higher-quality feel. Both beds had fluffy, attractively lacy beige coverlets, decorative area rugs sat on the wooden floor and there was an ornate wooden dresser along one wall. There were photos of buildings hung on the plain white walls, and a very large flat-screen TV on the wall facing the bed.

Very nice, she thought. At least as far as the décor. But was it safe?

Well, she wouldn't sleep much. She'd pace the room often instead of sleeping, and peek out those slats through the window. Maybe even go outside and look around, although if she did that, she would have to be Roger—an armed Roger, with his weapon still not visible if anyone happened to see the codger out and about in the middle of the night.

Didn't sound like fun. But there were always parts of her witness protection job that weren't enjoyable. It was about justice, not fun.

And those parts were overrun by the good stuff, like getting her subjects to their trials safely and allowing them to testify against whomever was threatening them.

That was what she would do tomorrow with Daniel/Dane. And she'd resist the temptation to kiss him while they were in this room together, she vowed.

Dane. He'd slipped into the bathroom, although the door was open. Even so, Alexa figured it wouldn't be appropriate for her to peer in while he was there.

She pulled off her hairpiece for now, which made her a lot more comfortable, and quickly changed her clothes.

He soon emerged. And it definitely was Dane who emerged. He'd removed the clothes that made Daniel seem large and ungainly. He still had a T-shirt on, and his somewhat baggy jeans, but he appeared a lot better than when she'd seen him last.

A whole lot better.

And now they were again about to spend the night in the same room.

"So what are our plans for tonight besides eating dinner?" he asked as he sat on top of the bed nearest the bathroom door. His voice was back to normal. So was he, she assumed, although that question didn't hold a bit of humor in it.

And she had no intention of doing anything funny.

She was going to do all she could to keep this man, her subject, safe. *And nothing else*, she added silently.

"Early to bed," she said.

"Early to rise," he added. "Makes a man healthy, wealthy and—"

"On his way to testify in court, as he is expected to do," Alexa broke in. Okay, maybe a little humor was called for after all. Although there was nothing particularly funny in her modified last line. Wise? Maybe. But they definitely would need to rise early tomorrow and get on their way.

"Sounds good to me," Dane said. The way he smiled at her, his rugged face back to its usual handsomeness now that he again looked like the Dane she was protecting, made her insides quiver.

Cut that out, she told herself.

But she couldn't completely ignore his sexiness.

Not that she would do anything about it.

"So," she said, "let's eat."

Each sat on a bed as they ate. Different beds, hers the one nearest the door.

She put the TV on and they watched some local news, although she kept the sound low. No items about the sudden appearance of helicopters over their route earlier in the day.

Alexa's tuna sandwich was fair, but she wasn't hungry.

Or maybe she simply didn't have an appetite because of her assignment.

Or because of her discomfort that evening being in a hotel room again with the man she was protecting.

The man she was much too attracted to.

They both were side by side somewhat, each sitting

at the foot of their respective beds. Alexa glanced over at Dane—and saw he looked at her, too, as he ate.

Neither looked away, not immediately. And Alexa felt her insides flutter, as if they were there for a reason other than having someplace hopefully safe to stay the night.

But she forced herself to ignore that.

"The news here isn't too exciting," she said when she turned away, as if giving him an excuse for having stared at her instead of the TV. But the idea of him watching her that way... Surely he was wiser than she, had no particular interest in her except as his protector.

That was as it should be. She couldn't allow any kind of distraction from what she had to accomplish.

And tomorrow would be a day where her skills would undoubtedly be put to their highest test so far in this assignment.

She would take care of Dane. It was her job.

And, she admitted to herself, it was also something she had to do, for her own peace of mind, as someone who really liked a lot about her subject. He seemed smarter, more reliable, even sexier than any guy she had ever dated—never mind how inappropriate it was for her to even think about that.

"Yeah," Dane said. He was regarding the TV then, and obviously responding to what they'd already been talking about. "Doesn't sound as if they're excited about a certain trial that'll start tomorrow south of here. A murder trial. They haven't mentioned it, at least not since we started watching."

"Assuming the news people even know about it," said Alexa.

"Oh, they do," Dane said. "Or at least I saw, around

the time of the murder, that the media anywhere near Tempe ran stories about that situation, and Phoenix and the national media surely picked up on it, too. It isn't every day that a police chief is accused of murdering anyone, let alone one of his own subordinates, and shooting another. I kept looking for all the information I could at the time, even as I was taken into custody myself by the FBI, and then your marshals, for my protection."

"Still, that doesn't mean they necessarily kept up with what was happening." But Alexa realized that the media always glommed on to any exciting news they could.

And the upcoming trial was definitely, at least potentially, exciting for a local audience.

"Do you believe that?" Dane responded in a highly skeptical voice, even as he grinned at her.

If only she wasn't so enticed by that grin.

Or everything else about this man...

"No," she admitted, smiling back. "Not really. I assume you were a media star back then."

"Pretty much. And I'm prepared to get in the spotlight again now, although I hope it's because my testimony is a major factor in putting that miserable SOB who used to be my boss away for life."

"Great idea, as far as I'm concerned."

And Alexa found herself beaming under that still growing, intimate smile of her subject.

He was off-limits. How many times had she reminded herself of that? Did she really need to again?

She'd finished eating. So had he. She pulled out her phone and checked the time.

With all the care they'd taken and veering back and

forth to avoid being seen as much as possible, they'd eaten up a lot of the day before.

Now it was nearing nine o'clock. Good enough for bedtime tonight.

First, though... "I think this old man needs to take a quick walk outside to act nosy again. But the other man in this room should stay here. I'll be back soon. You could even start getting ready for bed."

"Not till my old man companion is back safely." Dane was standing now, almost glaring at Alexa as if he expected her to object.

She didn't, but his protectiveness made her glow inside. Not that she'd mention that, either. "Well, if anything goes wrong, you have Vince's number," she reminded him as she had before. "And if it goes really wrong, you can always call 9-1-1 first."

His glare deepened. How could that be so alluring at a time like this?

"Things had better not go wrong at all," he growled. "And if anything—"

"I know. You were in law enforcement, too. You'll want to come intervene." She glared at him, hoping he would be obedient, but figuring he would do what he wanted. "Well, don't do it. We checked this area out as well as we could, and I think we're okay. I just need to make sure."

"I get it. But—"

"I'll be back soon. I promise." And Alexa hoped it was a promise she could keep.

She grabbed her Roger clothes, and more. After going into the bathroom and dressing again as Roger, she stuck her weapon into her belt beneath her loose shirt. Back in the room, she glanced briefly at Dane.

He was watching her.

She picked up a keycard from where she had put them, on top of the dresser, and prepared to leave the room.

"I'm listening, in case anything's out there," Dane said. Alexa realized he had turned down the sound on the TV.

"So am I. And looking." She unbolted the door and limped outside, pulling the door shut behind her.

The sky was dark. The motel area was lit, though, by a series of streetlights along the parking lot. Alexa stayed close to the wall.

There were a couple more cars in the lot now.

Did either belong to someone after Dane?

Alexa saw no people outside, nor did she see any movement of the slats in windows of the upstairs rooms as she limped by, pretending to be fascinated by the sky above and the parking area below.

Well, she actually *was* interested in the parking area, though she spied no activity.

Still walking like Roger, she returned inside, then locked the dead bolt on the door behind her, glad there was one.

Dane was sitting on the same bed he'd sat on while they'd eaten dinner, his back against the headboard. The TV on the wall still had the news on, not a surprise. "Everything okay out there?" he asked.

"Far as I could tell."

He grinned. "That wasn't especially positive. Do you ever say anything definitive?"

"Only if I'm sure what I'm saying is correct. If you want me to tell you you're safe for the night, the best

I can say, as I have before, is that I'll do everything in my power to make sure you are."

Dane laughed. "I got it. So, what are my protector's plans for the rest of this evening?"

"Evening? It's night. My plans are to shower now so I won't need to take the time to do so in the morning, and I suggest you do the same. Then it's bedtime." Alexa felt herself swallow as she said that. It was bedtime, but the idea of them going to sleep together, even in separate beds in this very nice room, crept into her mind.

Well, she shoved it out as she walked across the room and placed her carryon bag on one of the foldable stands after taking it from the closet. She removed her pj's and the case holding her travel paraphernalia and headed toward the bathroom. "I'll go first, since you seem wide awake. Your turn now to listen for anything out of line. If so, let me know. Knock on the door or whatever."

"Will do."

Alexa was soon in the bathroom, with its door closed. As she stripped to prepare for the shower, she felt her body react as if she was removing her clothes in front of Dane, to seduce him.

She quickly started running cold water in the shower, hoping that would cool her off and make her stupid body regain its senses instead of continuing that warm reaction in her most sensitive areas, though she doubted anything had changed.

She made it a quick shower, wanting only a short time from her protective detail. Soon, she dried herself, put on her pajamas and brushed her teeth.

Ready for bed? Yes. But also ready to go back into

the room and take up where she'd left off in protecting her very handsome subject.

She opened the door and strode toward the far bed, the one where Dane wasn't. "Your turn," she said. "And as I said, I'd prefer if you shower tonight, too, so there'll be no delay for it in the morning."

"Yes, master. Or mistress."

"Ha, ha." Alexa forced herself to stop thinking of the alternate meanings to *mistress*. Or at least she tried to.

Dane had already placed his suitcase on another foldable luggage stand and had put a small pile of clothing on top of his coverlet, as well as his masculine-looking travel case that most likely held a razor as well as toothbrush. Alexa hadn't noticed much of that last night as they'd attempted to deal with the filthy room they'd stayed in.

But this space was comparatively nice and welcoming. And clean.

Alexa just hoped she'd be able to get a little sleep while ensuring that Dane remained safe.

And also knowing he was across this special room from her...

She might wind up sleeping in a room with him for more nights once they arrived in Phoenix, although additional marshals could be sent by Vince to help out. Maybe one of the guys would instead stay with Dane then.

Alexa had mixed emotions about that possibility. It would be better. More practical. Maybe even safer.

But she'd miss being with him...

For now she grabbed the TV remote and turned up the sound of the news. That way she wouldn't be as aware of what Dane was doing in the bathroom, when he showered and all.

Or at least she'd hoped she wouldn't be. But the idea led her to listen despite the droning of the TV newscasters talking about a robbery at a grocery store in downtown Flagstaff.

In a short while, Alexa no longer heard the shower running. Dane didn't emerge immediately, but he soon returned to the room.

Alexa glanced in that direction, ready to tell him good-night.

Only—where were his pj's? He had emerged from the bathroom with a large white bath towel around his private parts.

His muscular chest, with hair as dark as that on his head, was showing. So were his long, hard legs.

Last night in their room together, Dane had put on deep blue pajamas, nice enough looking but they covered everything, as they should.

But now— She had an urge to call out to him to go back into the bathroom and put his clothes on.

She doubted he'd do it, though. Not considering the way he had started looking at her with those suggestive green eyes of his. Smiling sensually.

Communicating with her without saying a word.

Well, she didn't have to do anything about it. She could ignore him. Turn off the TV and settle down under her covers, turning her back in his direction.

She could… Yes. But instead she first listened for any inappropriate sounds outside and, hearing none, found herself smiling back, as sexily as she could.

"You ready to go to sleep?" she asked, but she knew her tone suggested anything but sleep.

"Soon," was his reply. "First, though—well, I can't help thinking we should kiss good-night again, like we did last night."

Just kiss? She doubted it.

But— "Sure," she said. "Why not?"

She knew exactly why not.

Yet that didn't stop her from standing as he approached. He held on to his towel with one hand as his other arm went around her. She threw both her arms around him.

Their kiss made their prior embraces seem almost juvenile. This was hot, sensual, enticing—as intimate a kiss as Alexa had ever shared with a man. Maybe more. A lot more.

Dane growled as his lips pressed hard against hers. His tongue slid inside her mouth, drawing in and out in a way that suggested what might happen if they actually engaged in sex.

Would they? Oh yes, Alexa hoped so. No matter that it was inappropriate. This man's hot, hard body tempted hers in a way she had never felt before. His chest against hers was strong and muscular and hot and—naked.

She still had her pajamas on. He was still draped in his towel.

Alexa could do something about both. And did.

After checking the door again to ensure it was locked, she rejoined him, reached down and gently tugged the towel out of Dane's hand, then let it fall to the floor.

And felt, and heard herself, gasp as she glanced down to his rock-hard, large erection that pointed at her.

She didn't let herself touch him—yet. Instead, she

started unbuttoning her pajama top but felt her hands pushed gently away as Dane took over.

In moments, her top was off, then her bottoms.

"Dane," she breathed. How did they get onto the bed—her bed, the closest? No matter. They were there. She now lay beneath Dane's naked body, feeling his hands caress her breasts as his legs wrapped around hers. Her shoulders rose as she moved upward to savor his touch, how he caressed her, smoothly rubbed her nipples, then moved to suck them gently.

She didn't just lie there, though. She reached up and grasped his erection, moving her hand to allow her to feel the hardness, stroke it in the way she'd like to have it move if it entered her.

No, *when* it entered her. Not immediately, though. His right hand slid downward to her most sensitive area, caressing it, moving a finger, then two, inside her. She nearly cried out—and did moan when he suddenly pulled away, got off the bed. Where was he going?

To his bed, where he'd left his pajamas. Also his night case. He extracted something from it, and Alexa realized it was a condom. Smart man, to come prepared for this—as well as bringing a weapon.

That thought brought her up short. She was supposed to be protecting him, not having sex with him. This was a terrible distraction.

But she heard nothing to make her stop.

"You ready?" his deep voice, rough and seductive, asked. Good guy. He was giving her the opportunity to opt out.

She didn't. "Oh yes."

He stroked her again, and she reached around to hold his taut buttocks. In moments, he entered her.

She felt her hips rise and then settle into the irregular but wonderful rhythm of his plunging in and out. She breathed fast, irregularly, and heard him do the same.

And then... She inhaled deeply as she reached her climax and heard Dane's deep groan at the same time.

All movement stopped. They held each other as Dane gently lay on top of her.

Wow. It was over. It was wonderful.

And no matter how wrong it had been, Alexa knew she wouldn't regret it.

As long as it hadn't prevented her from keeping him safe.

Chapter 10

Concentrating on the heat of the soft and gorgeous skin beneath him, as well as the irregular, deep breathing beneath him, Dane continued to lie gently on top of an amazing woman.

She was clearly there for him in more ways than one.

Not that they'd planned what had just occurred. Well, not exactly. He'd thought about it a lot since she had first insinuated herself into his life, but he hadn't anticipated it could really happen.

It had. And he was pleased. No, more than pleased. He was delighted. And satiated.

For now.

"Wow," he said as he rolled off her. But that caused reality to reappear in his mind. "Do we need to check outside to make sure all's well now? Or—"

"Or not. I'll look through the blinds after we turn

our lights out just to make sure I don't see or hear anything I need to deal with. And if all's well, we'll simply go to bed."

Dane couldn't help feeling somewhat sad and disappointed as he watched that sexy woman move her slender but curvaceous body off the bed and grab her pajamas, pulling them on again.

Highly appropriate, yes. But it made his immediate thoughts of having yet another enjoyable session, or several, that night rush out of his mind.

Well, no, the thoughts were there. But the likelihood of doing anything more about them? That was what disappeared. Fast.

"See or hear anything?" He kept his voice low in case someone was out there, or at least to make it evident to Alexa that he would do what he could to assist her.

"No. But I'll continue to check tonight. Let's get to bed."

Dane sighed. Good idea, but he figured he'd not get much sleep thinking about what they'd just done, and wishing the woman across the room from him was at least closer.

Hey, maybe he could convince her to share a bed. "You know…" he began, but she interrupted him.

"It might be a bad idea," she said, "but it wouldn't hurt to stay closer together tonight. I might be able to protect you better that way."

"You mean, sleep in the same bed?" He felt his grin grow wide at their matching thoughts.

"Why not?" Her lovely blue eyes were narrowed now, and she, too, smiled—although that expression evaporated as she looked at him. "As long as the operative word is *sleep*. With our pj's on. As much as I enjoyed what we did, we need to rest, not do it again. You should let me know, though, if my getting up periodically to check on things will prevent you from sleeping. If so, we shouldn't stay in the same bed."

"I'll be fine with it."

At least he thought so.

They soon settled under the coverlet on the bed that had sort of been designated as his, him on one side and Alexa on the other.

The room wasn't entirely dark, since Alexa had left the bathroom light on. She'd closed the door except for a slit that let a little light in, presumably to help her when she got up.

That allowed him to see her lovely face as, head propped on her pillow, she closed her eyes. He watched her, observing all he could of her beauty.

Memorizing it, since he probably would never have this opportunity again. And keeping his thoughts deep inside.

Difficult thoughts. Yes, he'd had women in his life, quite a few now and then. Enjoyed sex when he could. Nothing recently, though.

But his former lack of sex wasn't why this had felt so wonderful. This woman was amazing in so many ways, professionally, sure. But also…well, now this. Sure, he had been spending a lot of time with her during the last couple days, but this was something more than proximity. It was attraction and admiration and— well, he couldn't hope for a future with her. Not even any more sex.

But still…

When Dane couldn't fall asleep, yet heard Alexa's

breathing grow deep enough that he assumed she was, in fact, asleep, he slowly moved his way over until he first felt her warmth.

She didn't move, so he edged a little closer so their arms touched.

Yes, they both wore their pajamas, but somehow Dane felt they were attached in a sensual way, nonetheless. Not that he would do anything about it...

Except fall asleep, too.

He figured he'd done so a while later when Alexa's slowly getting out of bed woke him. He considered joining her but figured she wouldn't like it.

And since she soon got back in bed, he figured all was well.

Except his own state of mind. He had an urge to at least put his arms around her and pull her close.

And maybe remove those pajamas of hers, as well as his own...

He didn't laugh aloud at himself, but he laughed inside. He knew better. Way better.

It took him a while to fall back to sleep. Or at least he assumed he did, since he felt his eyes pop open sometime later when Alexa once more arose and did her checking.

He considered telling her he'd do it next time but figured she'd say no, so he stayed where he was. And fell asleep again after her return. Or at least he believed so the next time, too.

When he next awoke, it was because Alexa had snuggled up against him. Really? He reached out and put his arms around her.

"Good. You're awake. It's time to get up and get going—nearly six o'clock."

"Got it," he said. Although she started moving away, he couldn't help it. He pulled her close again. And, right or wrong, he gave her a big good-morning kiss.

Yes, a sexy one. Well, so what? She wanted them, rightly, to get going, so nothing else could result from it.

Not then. And probably not ever again.

He'd stay alive, at least, with her help. But he realized how much she was putting herself in danger to help him. He'd known, from the moment he got into witness protection, that those guarding him could be the ones to die while they took care of him.

He hated the idea. He'd considered it a lot with his former protectors but even more now with Alexa—the woman he'd just made love to, a woman he wanted to spend even more intimate time with.

He also wanted Alexa to stay alive and…well, and not get injured, or worse, as a result of protecting him.

He pulled away first. "Okay if I use the bathroom now?"

"Sure."

He found himself saying, "About last night…" He stood there looking down at her lovely face. Her eyelids remained low, as if she hadn't completely awakened. Or maybe the ensuing look was the result of his mentioning what they'd done… He finished by saying, "Do you want to talk about it?" Like, blame him for getting her involved in something so improper.

"No," she said, her tone abrupt. But she didn't look away. Maybe she was trying to figure out where he was going with this.

Well, so was he. "Do you want to do it again?"

Okay. It was inappropriate to ask that, too.

But he was glad he had.

She hesitated. Then laughed. "We'll see."

Yay! It wasn't an absolute no.

Wanting to end this conversation, wanting to do what he needed to now, he grabbed his travel kit, underwear and clothes, and hurried inside the bathroom. There, he washed his face—and observed it in the mirror. He still looked like himself, although there was an aura of sorts that suggested both satisfaction and frustration. Maybe he just imagined it, but it seemed to remain as he shaved. Even got worse.

He had to do something.

Last night had changed a lot inside him. And his mind had started focusing even more on today and the future, on the danger that remained out there.

He soon changed from his pajamas into his disguise, including the hairpiece. He felt a hint of amusement that that gorgeous woman had made love with him, while his usual appearance during the day was as such a big frump of a guy, and she'd been dressed similarly.

But she knew what he really looked like. Not that he thought himself to be a great-looking hunk…but apparently he was appealing enough to her. Maybe irresistible?

Even if they wanted to again—and he certainly did—the circumstances likely to transpire over the next few days could make that impossible.

But what would happen now? Yes, his mind had mostly focused on Alexa and their time together, yet not entirely so. Now he allowed the other vital thoughts he'd been repressing somewhat to take over while he prepared for the rest of this day.

Okay, where were they—the deadly killers who had come after him?

Did they know where he was? Were there more of them?

Had they really been turned away by those helicopters flitting around and around in the sky?

Right now, it all seemed easy. Too easy. When would they, or someone else, show up again?

For he was certain their attempts to stop him from testifying, Swanson's determination to shut him up, weren't over.

Would those who'd attacked before now stay away and hide wherever they'd gone yesterday, let him get to Phoenix and testify against Swanson?

He doubted it. They were most likely waiting for him, maybe somewhere near the courthouse.

Even so, he had to get there. And at the moment, it felt even more important to accomplish it without Alexa getting hurt.

Never mind that she was his designated protector. An idea had come to him, one in which she wouldn't accompany him there, no matter what her Marshals Service's plans were. He cared too much now to allow her to be harmed while protecting him.

He would get to the courthouse alone, so Alexa wouldn't be endangered if his foes caught up with him again. He had an idea how.

And it was time. He fortunately hadn't been in there long. He knew Alexa was eager to get going. Well, so was he—but not the way she intended.

He exited the bathroom and noted immediately that Alexa had taken advantage of her alone time to get dressed, too. Roger/Alexa stood near his suitcase, organizing things within it. As soon as he saw Daniel, he grumbled, "About time," grabbed a toiletry bag and rushed past him into the bathroom. He stopped at the door, though, and looked back. "I'll be ready in a couple minutes. Meanwhile, just stay there. I'll check things out, then we can get on our way."

He used the opportunity to finish packing and unhook his phone from its charger, which he also packed. He then grabbed his backpack and suitcase, and exited the motel room.

He didn't intend to be foolish, though. He waited right outside the door, which he'd closed gently, ready to duck back inside if he saw anything of concern.

Fortunately, he didn't. He saw a couple people getting into a car at the level below, a senior man and woman. A disguise like his or Alexa's? Maybe, but it didn't appear that way.

Even so, he remained cautious as he carried the backpack and suitcase down the steps, one hand over the weapon thrust into his jeans beneath his long denim shirt. He limped a bit as if he was the big guy he appeared to be, but still managed to hurry. And look around. A lot.

When he reached the bottom, he couldn't help glancing up to the room where he'd stayed the night. The amazingly wonderful night, thanks to Alexa.

The woman, the witness protector, whom *he* now intended to protect.

He didn't see her. She must still be in the bathroom.

It was therefore time for him to hurry.

Alexa had washed her face, put on makeup to ensure she resembled the man she was supposed to look like and was about to leave the bathroom when her phone, in her pocket, sounded to indicate an incoming text message.

She was a little surprised to see the message had come at this hour from her boss. Sending an unscheduled text around 7:00 a.m. seemed a bit strange, unless there was a problem.

In a way, there was. His message told her to call District Attorney Moe Francini immediately. It included a phone number with an area code that was probably Phoenix.

It seemed rather early to call a DA, especially one she didn't know, but Alexa was now under orders from her boss, and so she did it, holding her breath in case the guy hadn't been primed and got upset.

She also headed for the bathroom door. Depending on how the call went, she could put it on speaker and let Dane hear, too.

"Hello?" the male voice nearly shouted over the phone. "I'm assuming this is Marshal Alexa Colton, right? I was told you'd be calling now."

"That's right," Alexa said. "Marshal Vince Cudahy asked me to call you. My job is witness protection, and one of the witnesses in your trial of Samuel Swanson is my charge at the moment."

"Yeah, yeah, Vince told me that. He also told me my key witness, Detective Dane Beaulieu, isn't going to be there when the trial begins in a couple hours. What's going on? When will he appear? Is there something wrong?"

"Yes, there is something wrong," Alexa said, "so we're running later than planned." Since she'd been given his info by her boss, she assumed she could be at least somewhat specific in her description. "We started driving in plenty of time from the location where Detective Beaulieu had been living under an assumed name and in witness protection since the time of the homicide, but on the way we were attacked by unknown assailants." Maybe cops, but she didn't mention that. "We took some evasive maneuvers and got away. Local authorities directed helicopters to protect us and perhaps to capture the assailants, but as far as I know, they got away. As a result, we are still being highly cautious as we continue toward Phoenix."

A silence for a moment, while Alexa opened the bathroom door and stepped into the motel room.

The empty room.

Where was Dane?

Her heart pounded. Was he okay? She hadn't heard anything, so hopefully no one had grabbed him. But had he left on his own? Why? Suddenly terrified while also holding back any pending anger, she had to end this conversation as soon as possible and find him.

"So when do you anticipate getting to the courthouse?" Francini demanded.

"This afternoon," Alexa said, repeatedly scanning the room to make sure she hadn't missed anything. "Assuming we don't have to do any further time-consuming evasive maneuvers. If you can delay Detective Beaulieu's testimony until tomorrow, that might be best." She didn't attempt to explain her concern about time. Yes, they were close.

But she didn't know where her charge was.

Better to plan on his testimony tomorrow, after she found him.

And yes, she would find him.

"You'll be here for sure tomorrow, then?"

"Yes, although if anything else comes up I'll call to let you know." Like the disappearance of the witness, Alexa thought grimly. Had Dane simply started packing the rental car?

If only it was as simple as that. She could hope...

Well, damn it, he knew he had to stay with her so she could continue to protect him, even if he was wearing his disguise. He shouldn't even go out to load the car without her.

Oh, Daniel, she thought. *I'm about to ream you out for leaving my presence.*

Assuming that all was well, and she could find him now, and they could get on their way again.

"You do that," Francini said, apparently almost spitting into the phone. "Damn it, I was considering changing my original plans and opening with the star witness's testimony. But— Well, I get it. You be damned careful and get him here just as soon as you can. Got it?"

"Yes, sir," Alexa said, hating lying but resolving to fix the problem before Francini even knew something had gone wrong. She'd accomplish her goal, preferably today, but no later than tomorrow because of the weekend. "And now you have my number as well, so please keep me informed of anything we need to know."

"I'll do that." Francini hung up.

Good. Alexa dashed to the motel room's door and opened it, almost leaping out—till she reminded herself she was in disguise, too. And disabled seniors like Roger couldn't exactly jump around like that.

Instead, she hobbled onto the balcony area and

looked around, down toward the parking lot first. Not seeing Dane or Daniel, she began to scan the area, and—

There. Was that him in the distance, also in his disguise? If that was him, Daniel had reached the far end of the walkway in front of the motel, pulling his suitcase behind him and crossing the street, heading in the direction of the closest shopping area.

What, he was that eager for breakfast? He could have waited. They'd have stopped on their way.

Okay. Time to get out of here. Time to catch up with him. She was already pretty well packed, so she ducked inside only long enough to grab her bag, then hurried to get the rental car.

In moments, she was driving in the direction she had last seen Dane head. She would catch up with him.

She *had* to.

Dane hadn't focused on it as much yesterday as he wished he had now, but when they'd been driving around deciding what motel to choose, he'd checked out what kinds of businesses were in the area, mostly out of curiosity. And concern over his safety, and Alexa's.

There appeared to be more offices than retail around here. Several motels besides theirs, though not many. Convenience stores and liquor stores and fast-food restaurants on nearby blocks.

And a rental car place.

Fortunately, he had noticed that. And that was what he needed now. That location was where he headed, albeit carefully. Keeping watch around him to attempt to be sure no one was paying attention to him.

And keeping watch around the motel he was leaving to make sure he didn't see Roger/Alexa. Or, more important, that she wasn't outside anywhere watching him.

Was that their rental car driving in that area? Could be, darn it. He'd have to be even more careful.

Was it foolish to ditch her at this point? Probably. But it had gotten personal. He appreciated her watching over him, sure. But even though they hadn't become close friends—exactly—as he'd done with Alvin, he really cared about her, especially now. He couldn't bear the idea that Alexa might get hurt, or worse, because of him. Even if he had been hurt in the line of duty, he was determined that she would not be.

So now he stayed as much in the shade as possible. Moved off the sidewalk to use parking lots of some of the stores nearby. Ducked around the block to get there a different way. Checked his GPS often to make sure he was ultimately heading in the right direction.

Fortunately, he was. It took about ten minutes, but he was soon outside the location.

Also fortunately, it was open, despite the hour. He saw someone coming out with a car key in his hand and heading into the parking lot in front.

And so, Daniel, patting his pocket to make sure he felt his wallet there, headed inside, dragging his carryon bag behind him, the backpack over his shoulder, and making it appear that every step was an ordeal. After all, not only was he Daniel at the moment, but he was the form of Daniel that Alexa had created, big and senior and bulky.

But he did want to hurry, or at least not be visible from the street much longer. Alexa was hunting for him, and he didn't want to be found by her.

He entered the room that mostly contained a reception stand. Two desks were located behind it, each occupied by a woman. The one closest to the door stood as he entered. "Can I help you, sir?" she called.

"Yes, please," he responded in Daniel's cracked voice, although he had removed his hairpiece since he'd need to resemble the photo on his fake driver's license. "I need to rent a car for a couple days. Do you have any available?" He didn't mention he would return it to one of their facilities in Phoenix. The fewer people who knew his destination, the better.

"Of course. Please join me over here. I'm Marcia."

"And I'm Daniel," he said.

Marcia shot him a big smile. She appeared to be just a kid, barely out of her teens. This could be her first job. Her brown hair was curly, and she wore a very short peach-colored dress with long sleeves.

She waited till he reached the counter, then walked a few steps away to pick up some paperwork from the desk she'd just left. "Are you okay with a small domestic sedan, or do you want something larger?"

"That sounds fine," he said. "I just need it to get around."

"Very good."

In a minute, he found himself entering information onto a contract form Marcia had put on top of the tall counter. No problem with Daniel Brennan filling the thing out. Yes, that was his name. His address was in Blue Larkspur, Colorado.

"Everything look okay?" Marcia asked.

"Sure." And, fortunately, it actually did, or so Dane believed. At her request, he signed the form.

"What credit card will you be using?" she asked next.

Dane told her. Though it was also mostly to be used for confirming who he supposedly was, he'd been told he would be able to charge things on it, although he might be required to repay at least some of those charges when he got his real identity back.

At her request, he also showed her his alternate driver's license.

"Okay, looks good, Daniel," she finally said. "The car's in our lot right out front, in the space designated as A-26. It's a red Chevy. And you'll be returning it here in two days, right?"

Unlikely that he would but he nodded.

He took the keys that Marcia handed him and made his way unevenly, as large Daniel, to the rental office's door. He looked out the glass for a moment. Except for the cars he saw there, the parking lot appeared empty. A good thing.

He headed toward the back of the row of cars parked near the office, where he could see the space numbers painted onto the cement. Number A-26 was several cars to the right.

In a few seconds, he pushed the button on the key fob to unlock the doors and was close enough to hear the low thump. Good. He reached out and opened the trunk, pretending to take a lot of effort to lift his small suitcase and place it inside, along with the backpack.

After he stuck his hairpiece back on and closed the trunk again, he walked to the driver's side.

He tried not to hurry too much, or at least not to get out of his character as large Daniel. In moments, he reached for the handle and started opening the door.

"Let's not be too hasty," growled a voice from behind him. A gruff, male voice that didn't sound like Alexa's, even in character as Roger.

Dane turned slowly and found himself facing a tall man whose black shirt and black pants could have been a cop uniform, although it had no patches or badges. The guy had short brown hair, wide ears and clenched teeth, visible as he scowled at Dane. He looked familiar, like the guy in the other car who'd shot at them. He held his weapon low so that anyone around would be unlikely to see it.

But Dane could definitely see it.

He considered his own weapon that remained at his hip beneath his large shirt. But he felt certain he wouldn't have time to draw it at the moment without getting shot.

"Hey," he said, keeping his voice husky to remain in character but trying to maintain a friendly—false—note in it. "Are you one of those cops who shot at me on the drive here?" He considered yelling at the guy instead but figured that acting friendly might buy him more time. What he wanted to do, though, was beat the crap out of his assailant. Better yet, shoot him first.

"What makes you think that?" The guy grinned slightly, clearly not denying it.

"Just a guess." Dane hesitated. Was there some way he could call this guy off? "Look, I'm assuming you're working with Samuel Swanson, or at least believe he's in the right and shouldn't be standing trial today. I get it. But I was one of those he shot. Now, if he's paying you to go after me, I'd be glad to—"

"Gee, are you about to try to bribe me?" his assailant drawled. "Don't bother. I know what happened, and I'm fine with it. But I need to make sure Swanson— Never mind. You don't need my opinion or anything else. I think we've talked enough, in fact. I don't think it'd help for me to try to get you to accompany me someplace else. In fact, that might let you think you may find a way to get the best of me. So—"

The guy glanced down at the gun he held and started manipulating it, apparently flipping the safety off.

Dane figured he didn't have time to draw his weapon out and ready it to fire. But if he ran—

Damn it. He grabbed for his own gun anyway but before he could get it out of his belt he heard a voice he'd hardly anticipated hearing so soon.

Alexa's. And she, still dressed as Roger and sounding like a man, stood behind the armed cop.

"Hey, you know I'm ready to shoot you in the back if you don't put that safety back on and place your gun on the ground. You can ignore me if you want, but I wouldn't suggest you do that. Or, you can turn to see whether I'm really armed, and how much time you might have to get me first—which is none."

"You son of a bitch," the guy blurted. "You were in that car, too, right?"

He did slowly turn around, although he didn't move his gun.

But when he saw Alexa aim her weapon, the guy swore again and knelt down, placing his gun on the ground.

"Atta boy," Alexa said in her Roger voice. "Now, you're coming with me." She directed a glare at Dane. "You, too."

She—Roger—winked at Dane as she stepped forward, pushed the guy onto his knees on the ground and began cuffing his arms behind his back.

Dane felt relieved. Definitely. And yet he felt embarrassed Alexa had figured out what he had done and caught up with him.

Well, he was safe now. And he would deal with her anger—and possibly gloating.

Chapter 11

Alexa had already determined what to do with this hit-man cop. She felt certain she would have recognized him, even if he hadn't been aiming a gun at Dane. He'd been the shooter from the car that had come after them near the Arizona border but had been chased off by the helicopters.

Where was his partner?

"Okay," she said to Dane as she pulled her prisoner back onto his feet and behind the car. She'd already grabbed his weapon, checked to make sure it wasn't ready to fire and stuck it inside the waist of her jeans. Plus, she'd taken a few pictures on her phone of his accosting Dane before jumping in so she would have evidence of his attack. "This guy's coming with me. I've already called Vince, and he's got some local authorities on the way. While I take our buddy the short

FREE BOOKS GIVEAWAY

HARLEQUIN INTRIGUE

THE BODY IN THE WALL

RITA HERRON

USA TODAY BESTSELLING AUTHOR

LARGER PRINT

HARLEQUIN ROMANTIC SUSPENSE

COLD CASE COWBOY

JENNIFER MOREY

2 FREE SUSPENSE BOOKS!

2 FREE SUSPENSEFUL ROMANCE BOOKS!

GET UP TO FOUR FREE BOOKS & TWO FREE GIFTS WORTH OVER $20!

We pay for everything!

See Details Inside

Complete the survey below and return it today to receive up to 4 FREE BOOKS and FREE GIFTS guaranteed!

FREE BOOKS GIVEAWAY
Reader Survey

1

Do you prefer stories with suspenseful storylines?

◯ YES   ◯ NO

2

Do you share your favorite books with friends?

◯ YES   ◯ NO

3

Do you often choose to read instead of watching TV?

◯ YES   ◯ NO

YES! Please send me my Free Rewards, consisting of **2 Free Books from each series I select** and **Free Mystery Gifts**. I understand that I am under no obligation to buy anything, no purchase necessary see terms and conditions for details.

☐ **Harlequin® Romantic Suspense** (240/340 HDL GRPH)
☐ **Harlequin Intrigue® Larger-Print** (199/399 HDL GRPH)
☐ **Try Both** (240/340 & 199/399 HDL GRPV)

FIRST NAME   LAST NAME

ADDRESS

APT.#   CITY

STATE/PROV.   ZIP/POSTAL CODE

EMAIL ☐ Please check this box if you would like to receive newsletters and promotional emails from Harlequin Enterprises ULC and its affiliates. You can unsubscribe anytime.

HI/HRS-122-FBG22_HI/HRS-122-FBGVR

HARLEQUIN® Reader Service — Terms and Conditions:

distance to where he'll be picked up, you're staying right here. Got it, Mr. Brennan? I'm in charge. I was, and I still am."

Despite her appearance, she made no attempt to pretend that she was Roger just then. She needed her captive to follow her orders, too, and even though he might not like listening to a woman dressed like a guy and looking old, that was the way things were. She was the one with the gun now. She was in charge—just like she should have always been with Dane, who had tried and failed to sneak off on his own, terrifying and frustrating her. She'd have a stern talk with him later.

She was protecting the witness who'd soon be testifying against the man this cop—whether real or pseudo, whether paid specially by Swanson or just following orders given at his station—wanted to capture. Or worse, kill.

Alexa definitely was not going to allow that to happen.

"At least let me come along as your backup," Dane said. "I can—"

"What you can do, if you come along, is to follow my instructions. If you promise to do that, you can join me. Us."

She hadn't taken her eyes off her captive, so she saw the guy's expression change slightly at her words. He didn't look at all happy. Nor should he. But she recognized he was attempting to figure out what he could do to escape.

The answer? Nothing. As she'd told Dane, she was in charge. Of both of them. Of this situation.

And she expected that Vince would follow through

and do what she'd discussed with him over the phone—sending local authorities.

Never mind that the subject was also her lover, or had been. Fun, yes. But irrelevant. And in the past now.

Dane used the key he held to lock the nearby car he'd apparently rented. Good. At least he wasn't attempting to slip inside now and drive away while she took care of this evil goon who wanted to kill him. Alexa would have figured out a way to deal with both at the same time, but fortunately didn't have to.

"So," Dane said in his Daniel voice, bending over. "What's next, boss?"

She knew he was trying to be funny, as Dane so often did. Under other circumstances, she'd make a point of responding in an official but perhaps humorous way.

Not now.

"We're going to walk to the end of this row of cars and cross the street to the parking lot of the office building there," she said softly in her normal voice. "There's a shed at one end of that parking lot, and we're going inside. I've already checked, and it's not locked."

"Got it," Dane said, although Alexa knew he couldn't be aware of the reason she intended for them to go there. But it sounded as if he was doing as he should for once: obeying her.

In any case, Alexa stood on one side of their captive, her left arm through the guy's right as his hands remained cuffed behind him. He was quite a bit taller than she, but she was the one who was armed and untethered. She maneuvered him somewhat in front of her so she could hide his wrists at least partially from any observers.

"Like this," she said, and Dane clearly understood.

"Got it." In seconds, he was standing at the man's other side, not far from Alexa, and also shielding the bound hands from view.

"Before we walk away, I'd like you to put the keys to your new rental car under its driver's seat," Alexa instructed him. "You're going to notify the company that you changed your mind and just left the car there for them to lock up again. And don't bother attempting to have them give you credit on your card for non-rental. That'll only complicate things further. Got it?"

"Of course." He shot her a sad grin from the other side of their captive. Yes, he looked ashamed, as he should be. But that didn't quell her anger with him—or her relief that he was okay.

He quickly removed his backpack from the back seat of the car and arranged it over his shoulder, then grabbed his suitcase. In a minute, after leaving the keys inside, he was back in the position he'd been in before.

"Now," Alexa said, "let's go."

They did, walking slowly behind the row of rental cars. One man stood near a driver's-side door, but fortunately he only glanced at them briefly then slipped inside. There was no one else around.

As they walked, Alexa looked up into the face of their captive. He glanced at her once then continued to stare straight ahead.

"So where is your partner?" Alexa asked, watching him carefully. But not only didn't he answer, he also didn't glance around as if searching in a direction that partner might now be hiding.

Alexa wasn't convinced another man wasn't around,

but neither was she certain he'd stayed with this criminal to get at Dane.

It took several minutes to reach the end of the rental car parking lot, then dutifully await the green traffic light before crossing the street. No sense making themselves look like scofflaws, Alexa figured.

The lot on the corner there held two five-story buildings, and both appeared to contain offices. There could be people looking out the windows that they didn't see, but at least no one anywhere close seemed to be paying any attention to them.

As they reached the shed, she opened the door, and she and Dane ushered their detainee inside. "Sit down," Alexa commanded, pointing to a spot in the corner, on the floor. Since she waved her gun, the guy obeyed—notwithstanding his furious scowl.

"Now stay here with him while I check." She didn't say what she was checking, but Alexa ducked outside again, still looking like the old guy she'd pretended to be and once more limping in character.

There. A black SUV pulled up alongside the shed. An undercover cop car, Alexa hoped as it drew closer. A real one.

She approached the driver's door cautiously, though. And, as she'd hoped, a cop in uniform got out of the driver's side, and another from the passenger side.

"Marshal Colton?" the nearest man, who'd been driving, asked, his voice low. "Flagstaff police. We were sent here to help you as the result of a call from Marshal Cudahy." A badge on his shirt indicated his name was Williams.

"Yes," she said, allowing herself to feel a little relieved. He certainly sounded legit. "That's me." She didn't bother to explain she was a woman marshal in disguise as a man that day, but waited for him to continue talking. She still had to remain cautious. She couldn't be certain where they'd gotten Vince's name— or if they'd just been sent to attempt to grab, or kill, Dane.

"I understand you have someone in custody who needs to be taken to our nearby station and booked. Is that true?" Officer Williams said. He was short but seemed muscular beneath his cop shirt. His taller partner, Officer Shaler according to his badge, joined him.

"Yes, that's true. He's in the shed." So someone, hopefully Vince's local contact, had given them at least that much information. Unless that was just a guess.

Williams drew closer and leaned over, talking even more softly. "I was told you also have someone in witness protection. Correct?"

Someone who was setting Dane and her up would know that, too, though. She pulled her phone from her pocket and motioned for Officer Williams to join her as she walked a few feet away. Officer Shaler stayed where he was.

"Who told you that and directed you to come here?" she asked Williams.

His grin moved his dark facial hair. "I get it. Here, you can call our chief and check us out." He pulled his phone from his chest pocket and typed in Flagstaff PD. The online search came up with a site that appeared genuine, and Williams had her press in the number for Chief Sanchez.

"What's up, Williams?" was the immediate answer.

"This is Marshal Alexa Colton," Alexa began. "I'm—"

"You've got my team there grabbing your subject's attacker, right—Williams and Shaler? And you're on Williams's phone."

Alexa smiled. "Exactly. And you've made me feel more comfortable that your team here is actually your team. Thank you, Chief Sanchez."

"You can thank your boss, Marshal Cudahy, for contacting me about it."

Alexa did, silently and fervently. She would call Vince later.

For now, she answered a few questions, but she kept her responses brief, without giving details about what her subject and she were up to, where they were going or why. It was safer that way, if Sanchez didn't already know.

She led them into the shed where Dane was keeping an eye on their captive, who sat on the floor in one corner.

"That's our suspect, I assume," said Williams, and Alexa confirmed he was.

It was time to go. "Thank you, officers," Alexa said.

But she wanted to leave first, with Dane, in case someone was out there and saw what was happening, particularly the partner of the man who'd just been taken into custody.

"We'll get on our way now," she said, to notify both the cops and Dane, who stood leaning against one wall of the shed, arms crossed, watching all that was going on.

"Sounds good." He tossed his backpack over his shoulder, grabbed the handle of his suitcase and bent forward a little to resume his character. That made Alexa appreciate his efforts, despite the fact he had nearly fled her custody.

"Be careful," Shaler said. "And be sure to call us if you need any more help in our area." He pulled a stack of business cards out of his hip pocket and handed one to Alexa.

"Will do. And thanks again."

Alexa saw Dane drawing closer to where she stood by the door. She nodded to him, and both soon dragged and limped their way in character, with her pulling Dane's suitcase.

Alexa told Dane, "My rental car's in the lot on the other side."

"Got it."

They both headed that direction. Alexa stepped up her pace a little, despite resembling a geezer. Even seniors could sometimes go faster if they had a reason. And she noted happily that Dane followed her lead.

Nothing, and not one of the few people they saw, appeared out of the ordinary.

In a short while, they'd reached her blue rental car, in the middle of a row of other parked vehicles. She drew the key from her pocket.

"I'd like you to drive," she told Dane. "I want to make a couple of phone calls."

"Sure." Dane placed his bag on the back seat of the car, then got into the driver's seat. Alexa maneuvered the suitcase inside. Hers was in the trunk.

Soon, they were ready to go. Good.

It was definitely time to get to Phoenix so Dane could begin testifying at the trial.

* * *

First thing, as Dane started to drive, Alexa started to lambaste him, then apparently stopped herself. "Why on earth would you run away like that? To protect me? Never mind."

Before he could respond, she pressed a number into her phone and brought it to her ear. Dane felt a bit relieved that they weren't going to talk about what he had done.

"It all seemed to go fine, Vince," Alexa said in a moment. Her boss must have responded immediately. "Thanks for calling your Flagstaff contacts."

She put her phone on speaker apparently so Dane could participate, too, but for now he just listened as he watched the road, driving just over the speed limit. There weren't many other cars going either direction that day.

"But you said they only got one of your attackers," Vince continued.

Dane didn't know Vince, but the marshal definitely sounded miffed. "We don't know where the other one went," Alexa responded. "And the guy we got wasn't talking at all. But we're being as careful as we can be about watching around us. And if things look bad on the main road to Phoenix, we'll figure out another way to go."

That had been on Dane's mind, too. He had even attempted to find an alternate route, but nothing direct had popped up on his GPS. Any other way would take much longer to get there.

And if he wasn't likely to get there this afternoon, he'd need to let the district attorney know.

"Just be careful, damn it," Vince said. "I'm glad you

got the one guy before he could hurt Dane—and you, too, for that matter. And I'm glad my contacts were able to help. But it isn't over till it's over. Stay in touch as much as you can, and if you need any further help, let me know right away. Got it?"

"Got it," Alexa confirmed.

Dane glanced over to see she was nodding her head—in its costume that included odd makeup and a wig with short hair.

That was a shame. He enjoyed the look of her lovely face, including her special blond hair. The feel of it when they'd made love...

Okay. Of course he would think about that now and then. It had been an amazing, memorable experience.

A one-time experience. He knew that. Even though his mind, his body, reacted to the very thought and kept reminding him of how wonderful it had been. And urged him to find a time and place to do it again.

No matter how impossible that was, if for no other reason than Alexa would most likely never want to be intimate again with him after his essentially fleeing her custody. His betrayal of her—even though he had done it in an attempt to protect her.

Dane listened as Vince and Alexa said good-bye to one another, and he added his own good-bye. Alexa ended the call and put her phone on the console between them.

So what were they going to talk about now? He wanted to start a conversation with her but figured things would be awkward between them.

Should he mention the time, to start something? Fortunately, since all had started early, it was only midmorning. If all went well now, it should take less than three hours to reach Phoenix.

If all went well. That punched at his brain.

When, on this trip, had anything gone well? Or since the situation that had thrust him into witness protection, for that matter.

Although he'd had some good caretakers.

None better than Alexa…

At least it should be a scenic trip to Phoenix. Some of the terrain was mountainous. Some was forested.

He figured it might be useful to get Alexa's opinion on how his testimony should go, so he pondered what he should ask first to get the conversation going.

Only she began talking first.

"Okay," she said, staring at his face. He knew that because he glanced at her. And she wasn't smiling. "Maybe it's irrelevant now, but I want to talk about it anyway. I'm still really peeved that you tried to run off without me this morning. We already knew someone was after you. At least we caught him, or at least one of the two we're aware of. And if I hadn't been with you before—"

Not exactly what he wanted to discuss even now, but he could understand why she wanted to.

"I appreciate that you were there and helped out the way you did," he said, interrupting her.

"You're welcome. Sort of. But if you hadn't run off that way, we might be farther along toward Phoenix, and your treacherous buddy might not have caught up with you."

She was right. He knew that. But he'd had a good reason for doing what he had.

Only—she had put herself in danger before this situation. After all, she was trained to do so, and he'd tried to subvert that; he hadn't doubted her abilities, he'd just worried for her. She'd known she could be hurt or killed while protecting one of the people whose problems she took on.

And she'd done so again today when he'd put himself closer into harm's way, sort of. She was right. He might not have been attacked again if he hadn't tried to protect his protector by running off.

Maybe he should keep quiet about his rationale. It wasn't particularly rational, after all. Or she was bound to think it wasn't.

Still—

Okay, he had to say something. "Look, you know of my law enforcement background," he said. Out of the corner of his eye he saw her move, so he quickly continued. "I know about witness protection, of course, and what it's about. And why it occurs. Plus, as you know, you're not the first marshal to help me that way over the past weeks. But—"

"I've just been doing my job," she broke in.

That was true to a point, he realized.

But their time together went far and away above her call to duty.

And he couldn't be happier that they'd engaged in it.

"I know," he responded. "And you know I've just been doing my job, as well, preparing to help convict a murderer. But that doesn't have to include someone else getting hurt, as you might if you step in while I'm under attack. And—"

"And you're the one who'd have been hurt if I hadn't gotten there when I did." As if she had to remind him again. "You know that."

He prepared to interject a protest. But he realized, ultimately, she was right. She was plenty capable, and he knew it.

Before he said anything, Alexa continued, in a much softer, more controlled voice. "I appreciate your concern for me, Dane. I really do. But I think it's at least partially the result of our inappropriate behavior by having sex."

Dane opened his mouth again. But Alexa didn't stop talking.

"Oh, I found it wonderful. I really did. And the idea of more…well, it's not going to happen, but I truly relish the thought. But if that's even part of the reason you ran off to try to protect me, knowing full well that my responsibility is to defend you no matter what the peril you face right now— Well, thanks but no thanks. Can you even imagine what I'd feel like if something happened to you on my watch like that? I'd be devastated. The fact I'd be out of a job is only part of it. I care about you, Dane. A lot. I think you know that. And right now…well, I need for you to promise you won't do that again. That you'll let me stay in charge and take care of your safety. Okay?"

He didn't want to admit that he wasn't *really* okay with it, no matter how much he appreciated it. And understood it. But he needed to come to terms with that.

And found himself glowing inside at her admission that she cared about him.

They had to stay together now, and he did have to allow Alexa to do her job. To protect him, even as he intended to protect her, too, no matter what she said.

For the moment, though, he had to concede, or at least appear to. And so he said, "I understand, Alexa.

And appreciate it. So, yes, I promise I'll allow you to remain in charge. I'll listen to you despite whatever danger we come across." He shifted slightly to look into her eyes before turning quickly back to the road. "Thank you," he said, wishing he could hug her and kiss her in appreciation…and more.

"You're welcome," she replied.

Chapter 12

Despite his thanks, his verbal acknowledgment of her duties and his appreciation of how she was attempting to meet them, Alexa wanted to slug Dane.

No, she really wanted to hug him. Hold him tight now that he was safe again, at least for the moment. Or both?

But neither was going to happen.

She had every right to scold him for putting himself more directly into trouble that way, when he knew full well she had a duty to protect him. Because he thought he was protecting her instead, he'd indicated.

A swear word came to mind, but she thrust it out immediately. That kind of thought would do no good.

Reprimanding him the way she had, had been a good idea. He seemed to understand, agree with her. Maybe.

Or he at least knew better than to criticize her any

more—for now. And he'd been sweet enough to even thank her.

Was his gratitude real, or had he just professed it to try to get her cooled down?

Drat. She was riding in a car with him and would be for a while—and she was thinking too much about this bad situation that, fortunately, had had an okay ending, mostly thanks to her calling Vince.

Vince. She looked around them again, as she'd been doing a lot, as always. But fortunately she still saw nothing that indicated she should have asked him to send copters again.

There was someone else she needed to call, though. Or at least text. Only, she figured that District Attorney Francini was most likely in the middle of the first morning of the trial now. Even if he wasn't conducting a witness examination at the moment, he probably wouldn't want to answer the phone, or even respond to a text message.

But he was the one most likely to know what was going on. Where she should take Dane when they arrived near the courthouse. How to keep him safe from anyone who might be watching for him. And if there were any local resources there who would help.

Plus, keeping Francini informed about Dane's progress in reaching the place would be appropriate. In fact, they might hear from him even if they didn't contact him first. But who knew when?

If all went well, they could arrive in a couple of hours. So, she had a little time, but she definitely needed instructions about the best way to handle things when they got there.

Should they park in the regular lot and just walk inside?

Had any efforts been made to ensure Dane would be protected as he entered the court, and not just by her?

Where were Swanson's peons now? Were any in custody, or at least under observation?

Okay, maybe calling Francini wasn't a great idea at the moment, and she'd no idea when he might try to contact her, if ever. But she knew who she could call again who would be able to tell her what to do: Vince.

"You're awfully quiet," Dane said, breaking into her thoughts. "What's on your mind? Is everything okay?" He took his eyes from the road for a moment to look into hers, and he appeared highly concerned.

"I hope so, but that's exactly what's on my mind," she responded, not even attempting to appease him. He knew what was going on. Trying to protect him mentally as well as physically wasn't exactly her job. In fact, he'd been wary before, even if he hadn't completely acted rationally, and she needed to remain careful now.

"So everything's not okay? What's wrong?" He sounded uneasy, as well he should.

"Nothing I know of now," she said. "And I want it to stay that way. I'm going to call Vince again and ask him a few questions. I'll put him on speaker as usual so you can join in if you want."

"Sounds good."

Before calling, Alexa scanned their surroundings yet again. Nothing seemed concerning. They were still headed in the right direction on a road with minimal traffic and no obvious threats.

Obvious being the key word in Alexa's thoughts. She could never assume there were no threats around.

The same somewhat mountainous landscape surrounded the route here. Attractive to look at, but also concerning since the bumps and curves could hide danger.

Right now, she grabbed her burner phone from where she'd stuck it on the car's console and searched it again for Vince's name—not hard to do not only because of their prior conversation—but also because she hadn't added many contacts to this phone since she'd gotten it. Dane, of course, and Vince. And her sister Naomi and brother Dominic. She'd added Francini's number but didn't want to call it now.

She pushed the phone receiver symbol to start the call, then put it on speaker.

"Everything okay now, Alexa?" was Vince's greeting.

"Everything's fine right now, thanks," she replied. "But I need your advice. We're moving right along and hope to get to the courthouse in a couple hours. But I want to talk to Mr. Francini about what to do as we get near there, how best to park near the courthouse and get Dane inside, and—"

"Got it," Vince responded.

Dane, meanwhile, had aimed a quick grin toward Alexa. He didn't say anything just then but he blinked and tilted his head as he mouthed, *I didn't know you cared.*

That, of course, was absurd. Of course she cared. It was her job to care. *But not as much as I do...*

And the fact she cared beyond only wanting to ensure his safety? Well, that she would keep to herself.

"Okay, I just texted Moe's assistant DA. Her name is Cora Canfield, and I'll text you her phone number so you can confirm it's her. I've told her to give you a call in five minutes to discuss status. Moe gave me her contact info for just this kind of reason, in case we needed to get in touch with him at a time he was likely to be in court. She's probably there, too, but she can step out."

"Got it. That should be really helpful. Thanks, Vince."

"No problem. Oh, and by the way. I've talked to both Moe and Cora about how you've been handling Dane's protection so they'll know what to expect, although I assume Dane will want to look like a detective and not a witness in disguise when he's inside the court."

"I agree," Alexa said. She'd already been considering how they'd change back to themselves but figured they could determine that closer to the appropriate time.

"Anyway, glad you called," Vince said. "And keep me informed, like I said before."

"Will do."

"And, Dane?" Vince added, apparently recognizing he was on speaker. "Are you ready to testify?"

Silly question, Alexa thought. He'd better be. But his answer was definitely important.

"The sooner, the better," her driver replied. "I hope I get a chance to talk to Moe or the ADA beforehand, though, so we can go over what he'll ask and my best way of responding. Telling the truth, of course. But making sure I phrase it in the best way possible to convict Swanson."

"Amen," Vince said. "Talk to you both later."

And meanwhile, they'd get to talk to Assistant DA Cora Canfield, Alexa hoped.

For now she said, "We should get to the courthouse as fast as possible, and hopefully we'll soon have our questions answered."

My questions, she thought, but figured Dane desired those answers, too—like how he could get into court most safely. But he was human. They both were. And so she felt compelled to ask, "Would you like to make a brief stop for coffee, or anything else? We'll be passing a few small towns before we get there." She'd checked the map on her phone and looked at the Arizona Veterans Highway, which was another designation for Interstate 17. They'd be going by some places such as Lake Montezuma, Flower Pot and Black Canyon City. They'd pass Sedona first, but it was farther from them than the others.

"Not unless we want to check out anyone around us to see if they're following," Dane said. "Still don't see anyone. But this seems too easy, especially after being attacked earlier. Something's got to happen before we arrive. Someone's got to try to stop me."

"Unfortunately, I'm sure you're right. But—"

Her phone made its noise indicating she'd gotten a text, and she checked. Vince had sent her a phone number, which he'd said was Cora's. Her phone rang then. She glanced at the number. It was Cora.

"It's her," she said to Dane, then swiped her phone to answer. "Hello?" she said in a serious, professional voice.

"Hello, Marshal Colton?" asked a female voice.

"That's right." She waited for the other person to identify herself, just in case something was off.

"This is Maricopa County Assistant District Attorney Cora Canfield. Marshal Vince Cudahy—your boss, I believe—gave me your phone number. I understand you're on your way here to court with our key witness in the *State vs. Samuel Swanson* murder trial, Dane Beaulieu, correct?"

"Definitely correct," Alexa replied.

"I understand you have some questions, which I'll be glad to answer if I can. But first—where are you? How close? I need to get an idea about when you'll arrive."

"Of course," Alexa said. She felt a little uncomfortable giving the information, but other than being professionally paranoid to keep her witnesses safe, she had no reason to disbelieve this woman was who she said she was. "I see some signs along the road." She'd been watching the roadside as well as the cars around them as she spoke. The area was somewhat hilly and dry around the road, with some green bushes and trees along the desert-like ground. "I believe we'll be at Camp Verde soon, and I assume it'll be an hour and a half or so after that when we arrive in Phoenix. We'll have to get to the court then."

"Which won't take too long. Good. And more questions from me. Vince indicated that you and your subject are both in disguise as senior men, correct?"

"That's right." Alexa was starting to feel a bit more uncomfortable again. Why did she need to know that?

But her next statement clarified why she'd wanted to know, and also made Alexa feel more at ease, at least a little.

"Good. The situation is potentially dangerous enough that we're going to assume that the people who are apparently attempting to save Mr. Swanson are aware of your disguises. I understand that you and Mr. Beaulieu have already been confronted on your way here, correct?"

"Yes," Alexa confirmed. "And I have an idea that should help protect us as we get there." She'd been considering it for a while, and now requested that they have a couple of Phoenix's law enforcement officers dress as Dane and she were disguised now and walk into the courthouse as a diversion. "That way, if anyone's out to stop us, they'll hopefully be caught first."

"Good idea," Cora said.

Alexa watched Dane's face, too, and he appeared pleased as he looked out the windshield, even smiling a little. "But what should we do when we arrive?"

"Are you driving?" Cora asked.

"Not at the moment," Alexa replied. "Dane is."

"Good. I assume you have something to write with. Here's the location we'll want you to park at. And we'll need the description of your car and its license. Other plainclothes officers will accompany you into the courthouse by using back doors and seldom-used stairways."

"Sounds good to me." The driver was talking. Well, that was fine. He was entitled to participate, Alexa thought. "This is Dane Beaulieu, Ms. Canfield," he said. "And I might be less obvious if I go in alone rather than with Marshal Colton. She's been great, taking care of me in witness protection, but—"

Alexa glared at him. Participate, yes. Modify the situation to comply with his own thoughts, no. She was the protector, not him. "Detective Beaulieu has been overstepping his limits in witness protection, Ms. Canfield—" she said.

"Just call me Cora already," she interrupted, sounding annoyed.

"Cora. It's my job to ensure he remains safe before, during and after his testimony. And though I very much appreciate the help you're describing, I'm going to tag along, and more if necessary." She kept her voice strong, and her gaze on her charge, who only shot a glare back at her as he kept driving.

"I understand," Cora said. Did she sound amused? Alexa couldn't be sure.

"Glad to hear that," she said anyway.

"So your car info?" Cora pressed.

Alexa turned and pulled the tote bag with her rental car info in it. Was she comfortable giving the information to a stranger, even one who'd been vouched for by her boss?

Not really. But she had little choice.

And she'd be there to protect Dane anyway, no matter how hard he tried to get her out of that situation.

She provided the details to Cora.

She then jotted down the information Cora provided to her, including the location of a parking lot in the vicinity of the courthouse, though not its main one.

"Definitely call me when you park," Cora said. "I'll send those plainclothes cops to join you and ensure you get to the right place safely."

"Thank you," Alexa said.

"Let's get this thing done right," Cora replied. "We have potentially enough evidence to convict Swanson without Dane's testimony, but with Dane's story about watching his partner die and getting shot himself...

Well, that should take care of the situation and ensure the conviction."

Alexa certainly hoped so. Otherwise, this entire journey might have been in vain.

They might actually reach their goal of Phoenix, Dane observed to himself. And have backup so he could safely get into the courthouse. And testify.

Although considering how late they'd get there, he probably would not be able to finish his testimony today. Not with all he had to say about Swanson and what he had done.

"Look," Alexa said now into the phone. How could she still appear so attractive while she was disguised as a grungy old guy?

Maybe it was just because Dane knew who she was underneath all that.

Too bad he wouldn't get to see it again.

Or would he? Would she stay with him that night?

Maybe only if the local authorities turned out to be scum like Swanson, and Alexa and he had to disappear till the trial's next day.

"I appreciate all your efforts and ideas," Alexa continued. "And I'm sure you know how concerned I am about keeping my subject safe, both in court and otherwise. And—"

"And you don't know if you really can trust me. I get it. Well, though my preference would be for our cops to take over Mr. Beaulieu's protection as soon as you reach the courthouse, I figure you'll want to remain with us to ensure he really is safe. Right?"

"Yeah, you got it," Alexa said. Her cold, efficient voice somehow made him smile inside. Sure, she was just doing her job. But he didn't want to permanently part ways with her just yet.

"Fine with me, and with my boss, Moe, too. He and I talked this over before. And though he's in court examining a few introductory witnesses for now, he's dealt with people in WITSEC before and knows how paranoid they can be. Their protectors, too. For good reason."

Dane couldn't help glancing toward Alexa at that. Her grin was wry; she was also looking at him, nodding slowly.

"So how do you intend to make us feel better?" she asked.

"Well, for one thing, we did come up with that scenario about getting Mr. Beaulieu into the courthouse, with the support of plainclothes backup. But if there's something else you want us to add to it, just let me know."

"I will, of course."

Why wasn't Dane surprised about that?

Well, could be because this smart, determined woman was full of good ideas to protect him...

When he looked in the rearview mirror this time, he saw a large gray SUV passing everything behind him, barreling in their direction. Was this it?

Were the occupants after him?

He gestured to Alexa, using his thumb to point toward the rear of the car.

"Hold on a sec," she said to Cora.

She pulled her gun from her pocket and turned around—just as that SUV pulled up beside them.

Dane prepared to slam on the brakes and pull his own gun out as he bent sideways—but the SUV kept going. Fast. He didn't see whoever was inside, but that also indicated no one was particularly staring at them.

And in moments that potentially scary situation was over.

"Guess that was simply a speeder," Alexa said. She quickly explained the situation to Cora, who laughed a little.

"Glad that's all it was," she said.

"Me, too." Alexa took a deep breath as Dane again looked at her. Then she said, "Okay. Here's what I was going to say...

"I'm going to ask that Vince get the local authorities to have most of the plainclothes officers dress similarly, appearing like possibly disabled senior citizens, to throw off anyone who might know how we appear now, and potentially capture anyone who's out to harm Dane."

Dane liked what she'd said. It was another small but important step on the ladder of protection she was building around him.

"Interesting idea." Cora's tone suggested she was musing on it.

"Do I recognize that the villains could figure out what's going on, even potentially dress like older people, too?" Alexa said. "Of course. But we'll have to take that into consideration with everything else. And if it works out, it may help Dane get into the courtroom more smoothly and be able to testify and participate in the conviction of that particular murderer."

Chapter 13

Alexa's heart rate was finally settling down as she continued to sit in the passenger seat, still anxious despite the more relaxed tone she was using with Cora.

Oh sure, she'd been fully aware that a fast SUV passing them didn't necessarily constitute, or contain, any danger. But she'd nevertheless tensed up as she'd prepared to take on any attackers, if necessary.

Thank heavens, it hadn't been. Right now, even with Cora still on the phone, she carefully eyed their surroundings,

"Okay," Alexa said. "I think it's time for me to call Vince and let him know my idea. He's a smart guy, and well connected, and I'm sure he'll know which authorities in your area to contact to ensure that lots of plainclothes cops dressed like us show up around the courthouse. He'll probably try to contact Mr. Francini, too, to confirm what's happening. I assume you'll also let him know."

"Of course," Cora said. "And if I didn't have to appear in the courtroom to help, maybe I'd dress up to look twice my age, too."

"Sounds good," Alexa said, smiling. "As it is, I hope we see you in or around the courtroom so we can meet in person."

"I'll look forward to it," Cora said. "And I'll head back in to let Moe know what's happening whenever there's a break."

"Fine," Alexa said, and hoped that, and all other contacts Cora had, went well. She had no reason to mistrust the ADA, but she didn't completely trust anyone just then.

Except Dane.

She wished suddenly that she could hug him. Hold him tightly even as he drove.

Protect him with her body. And do even more than that with her body...

But that had to remain only in her thoughts. "I'm sure we'll speak again," Alexa said to Cora. "Hopefully soon. And please let us know if you, or anyone you speak with, has any other ideas about how best to get Dane inside the courtroom safely."

"Will do. I look forward to seeing you. Oh, and by the way, I have a good idea how Moe wants to approach questioning you, Dane, but I'd rather you and he have that conversation before you're put on the stand. Okay?"

"Fine with me," Alexa's driver said, nodding. He now looked serious again.

"You okay with all this?" she asked Dane after hanging up. In his senior's getup, he certainly wasn't as handsome as he really was, yet she still liked his looks. Liked him.

Too much...

"I'm more okay than I was before." He glanced toward her before returning his gaze to the road. "And I'm looking forward to seeing all those geezers around the courthouse."

"Me, too." Alexa couldn't help grinning as she looked back down at her phone. She soon pressed in Vince's number again.

"Everything okay?" was Vince's immediate response as he answered.

"For now," Alexa said. "We're getting closer and being careful about other cars around us. But things are too quiet, I'm afraid." She told him about their conversation with Cora. "And of course I'm hoping no one's bugging you now to find us, burner phones or not."

"I've got our techs checking it constantly. Far as I know, all's well."

"Glad to hear that," Alexa said. "And to also help keep it that way, I have an idea I want to run by you." She told him about her plan.

"Hmm," Vince said. "I like the idea. But I've only talked to the local Phoenix authorities about having two enter the courthouse around the time you get there. Not sure they can grab enough other people and get them dressed like oldsters on time."

"I understand," Alexa said. "But Cora's on board with it, though she may need help getting oldsters in disguise there fast."

"Well, I'll get in touch with the DA and see if he can delay Dane's testimony so it can start first thing tomorrow, not later today. Meanwhile, we can try to get lots of young apparent senior citizens, with protective weapons, prepared to take care of any bad situations that might arise."

Alexa felt like cheering. "Sounds good to me," she said.

"It may take me a while to talk to Moe, since he's already in court. But I'll let Cora know I need to talk to him, which it sounds like she may already know."

"Right," Alexa said.

"Anyway, keep me informed how things go as you get closer to Phoenix, and I'll also keep you informed about how my upcoming conversation progresses."

"Great," Alexa responded. "Cora gave us a detailed description of what we should do when we get near the courthouse today, but I can let her know we'll conform to what she said tomorrow instead."

"I'll do that," Vince said. "She can get back in touch with you if there are any questions." He paused. "You listening to all this, Dane? Are you okay with it?"

"I'm listening, and I like what I'm hearing," he said, leaning slightly from the driver's seat toward where Alexa held the phone.

"Excellent. I'll be in touch again soon." Vince hung up.

"Interesting," Alexa said. And maybe a little worrisome. She'd considered what they'd do that night anyway, after the court closed. But she'd also considered that the local authorities might take over protecting Dane.

Not that she'd drop out of the picture, but she might have less ability to make decisions. And she wasn't sure she wanted to give him up...

"So we might wind up avoiding the courthouse till tomorrow." Dane expressed some of what Alexa was thinking.

They'd have another night together. But where?

And would it be even more dangerous, since they were going to be so close to where Dane would be testifying against the murderer? Swanson had apparently been able to get a lot of support from those who had formerly reported to him or whomever the people were who had come after Dane.

She saw Dane aim a brief glance in her direction. Oh yeah. She needed to respond to what he'd said.

"That's right. We'll be together another night, but one where your safety might be even more in jeopardy."

"So how are you going to take care of me, O Protector of Mine?"

He sounded sarcastic.

And yet Alexa did hear reality, and true questioning, in what he'd said.

"Unless I hear otherwise from Vince or someone else in charge here," she responded, "I'm going to find us a place to stay that's off the beaten path, close enough to downtown Phoenix to get to court early in the morning, but somewhere your enemies are highly unlikely to find us."

Sounded good, she thought. But how was she going to accomplish it?

"So where's that?" Dane's tone was serious now, and so was his expression beneath his elderly disguise.

Good question. And then a thought occurred to her.

"Not sure yet, but I've got some ideas. First, I've been thinking about another phone call I need to make, to my brother Dom. Maybe the FBI would have some suggestions."

"I'm all for getting as much backup as possible," Dane said. "And getting advice from your FBI brother? Why not?"

Why not indeed? Alexa thought. She'd keep her phone off the speaker, at least at first, though, to help keep Dom's privacy, but also to allow him to say whatever he wanted about protecting Alexa's subject without that subject chiming in.

What was going to happen?

Would it wait till they got to the courthouse either later today or early tomorrow?

Or had the confrontations they'd already had been all they'd face?

She wished. But for now, she would make that call.

She pressed Dom's number into her burner phone but kept it off the speaker.

Her brother answered right away. "You okay, Alexa?" Of course he recognized the burner phone's number since she'd used it before.

"Pretty much so, Dom." She wanted to act as cool as possible, even though she was going to request his assistance to help keep her subject, as well as herself, safe. And this also wasn't a good time to ask about his fiancée, Sami, though she hoped all was going well with them.

"What's not okay?" He leaped immediately on the negative part of what she'd said. Unsurprising. He was her big bro.

She chose not to tell him about Dane's inappropriate attempt to rent a car on his own and show up at the court without protection. But she did describe her conversation with Assistant DA Cora Canfield.

And also how far along they'd gotten, and not gotten, on their way there.

"If we arrive at the courthouse today, there won't be much time, if any, for District Attorney Francini to talk to Dane and prep him for his questioning on the stand, let alone starting that testimony," Alexa told Dominic. "I'm thinking we should stay somewhere in town overnight, then show up first thing in the morning at the court. I can let our contact, ADA Canfield, know that. My boss, Vince, might already be doing that. And I did come up with a way to hopefully keep us a bit safer."

She next described her plan.

Dominic laughed. "Sounds like something you'd come up with, Marshal Colton," he said. But then he added more seriously, "And I'll be glad to request that a few of our Phoenix special agents show up there, too, though I can't promise they'll be in disguise as oldsters. But they can arrive armed and observe what's going on and step in if further protection is needed. I'm pretty sure the office there will be glad to send people, but I'll let you know if there's any problem."

"Great. Thanks." She could let Dane know about that. In fact, it wouldn't have hurt for him to be in on the conversation. But Alexa had more to ask Dom. "So how are things with you and the rest of the family?" Even though she'd seen Jasper and Aubrey at the Gemini Ranch recently and talked to Dom and Naomi over the past few days, there were always things going on.

"Far as I know, we're all doing fine. Only—well, if what you're asking about is if there's been any fur-

ther progress that I'm aware of in releasing the innocents our dad got convicted, I haven't been working
on that at the moment or staying in close touch with
our Truth Foundation siblings. And that drug smuggler Spence, who should be back in prison? Oh yeah,
my eyes and ears are open, but he's still on the loose,
as far as I know."

"I figured. Anyway... One other question. I don't
know if you know the Phoenix area well, but since it
looks like we're not going to the courthouse tonight,
we'll need a place to stay till tomorrow morning. Any
ideas?"

"Let me check with one of my fellow agents there
who's my buddy and text you some suggestions. Okay?"

"Sounds good," Alexa said.

Before they hung up, Dom said, "Now, I know
you're on an assignment and you've been doing witness protection for a while, but now that you're getting
down to the wire and about to deliver your subject—"

"I know where this is going, bro," Alexa said. "I'll
appreciate any help you and the FBI can provide, as
well as the local police and my marshals. And you can
be sure I'll be damn careful."

"Yeah, be careful. That's exactly where I was going."

Alexa could almost see her dark blond, blue-eyed
brother staring at her with his head tilted and his gaze
insistent. She smiled.

"Talk soon, Dom," she said.

"Yes, talk soon."

Alexa pressed her phone to end the call. But her mind
was racing a bit regarding her conversation with Dom.

The family was still concerned about Ronald Spence,
also as always.

Dominic gave a damn about his US Marshal sister who was performing witness protection.

Good thing Alexa had such a wonderful, caring family, even as large as it was. She loved her siblings.

And wanted to stay alive and healthy and see them all again soon. Including the significant others some of her brothers and sisters had found, the people they intended to spend the rest of their lives with.

Now, if only she too could find true love—and she kept her mind far from the man with whom she shared this car. Or tried to. That certainly wouldn't work—even though she now was about to spend another night with him.

It would help if Dom found a place around Phoenix for them to stay, and she directed her mind that way.

But as much as she relied on her brother, she couldn't assume he'd find all the answers. He was still in Colorado, after all, at least as far as she knew. He'd be relying on his Arizona colleagues for their help.

That might be perfect, and keep Dane, and her, safe.

But perfection was hard to achieve.

"So how's your brother?" Dane interrupted her thoughts. "Is he going to get a bunch of FBI agents to the court tomorrow along with the local cops? I heard you tell him about what you planned and how you're getting your own boss to get some contacts together in Phoenix."

"Doing fine. And I'm not sure how many FBI agents might show up, but I gathered he'd make sure some are there, armed and ready, in case any additional federal protection is needed along with the local."

"Good guy, I gather."

"Yes, he is," Alexa said. A thought about the other

part of their conversation shot through her mind. Her brother, and other siblings, were all good people. And though she still missed the idea of a loving father, it was really hard to realize that, despite what had been good about their dad, it was outweighed by the bad stuff that hurt quite a few people.

Too bad that actual crook Spence hadn't remained in jail, though.

Signs along the road indicated they were getting closer to Phoenix, a good thing since it was nearly three o'clock in the afternoon.

Dane said, "I think we're still doing fine, but I want to get off at one of these exits and just make sure no one follows us." He paused then added, "Things have seemed too safe and calm, under the circumstances. I'm waiting for the next shoe, or tire, to drop."

"You're reading my mind," Alexa told him. "So, yeah, go ahead and exit. And I'd be glad to take over driving, if you'd like."

"Maybe for a while," he said. "But I want to be the one at the wheel when we enter Phoenix. That'll give you more ability to concentrate on who and what's around us, O Wonderful Protector."

His tone was intended to be humorous, she was sure. But what he'd said made sense. Dane Beaulieu, aka Daniel Brennan, had apparently come around to relying on the US Marshals, most especially her, to keep him safe at last.

Or he wanted her to think so. Alexa had no doubt he'd jump into any fray to try to protect himself. And her. But she appreciated his attitude, feigned or not.

They sat in silence for a few minutes, Alexa's mind

spinning on the topics she expected involving keeping Dane safe.

Getting to Phoenix.

Getting to the courthouse. Presumably, it closed around five, so even if they arrived before that, there wouldn't be much the DA or his assistant or Dane or Alexa could do to help convict the killer tonight. So forget that.

Tomorrow? Oh yeah, they'd potentially have a whole day for Dane to testify about what he'd seen and experienced.

So—what about tonight?

What about something near Phoenix Sky Harbor International Airport? There'd likely be so many visitors in those hotels that the people out to find them might get confused.

But then, so might they. And Alexa certainly wouldn't want to do anything that could get them lost, or stuck in traffic, in the morning.

Something downtown near the courthouse? She started looking for possibilities, even though her mind told her that wasn't a great idea, either. They might wind up being too obvious to anyone attempting to find them.

How about contacting Cora again and asking if Dane and she could sleep at her home that night, wherever it was? Was she married? Did she have kids? In case she did, that was another bad idea.

Alexa didn't want to endanger anyone else.

Still, contacting Cora again seemed like a wise choice. Alexa could ask her for her suggestions for a hotel, plus confirm the time they should arrive at the court tomorrow.

At least they already had Cora's plans for where Dane should head.

Just then she got a text from Dom with some suggestions, too, that his Phoenix FBI contacts must have provided.

"Hey," Dane said from beside her. "What was that text? And enough of the silence. What are you thinking?"

"I'm still attempting to figure out how to figure out where to stay tonight. The text was from my brother, with suggestions, but I'm not sure whether to follow what he says or figure something else out."

"Hey, a joke of sorts. I like it. And thanks to the joke, I'm getting off the highway at the next exit. We could use some gas, and I could use a rest for... Oh, say five minutes. I'm still driving into town, and I know we're getting close, but maybe I can help you figure out how to figure out—"

"Got it," Alexa said. Yes, she'd attempted to be a bit humorous, which was interesting. But despite believing she had hardly any sense of humor, being in this sexy jokester's presence somehow got her thinking about how to make him smile.

And how to get him into bed— *Stop that*, she shouted internally to herself. Yes, it appeared they were going to spend another night together, probably the last. Alexa was likely to be out of the picture once the local authorities took over Dane's protection.

That made it all the more tempting to consider what they could do together this night.

To consider what they'd done in last night's hotel...

"And maybe while we're stopped," Dane said, shooting a sideways glance toward her and a wink, "I can be the one to figure out a hotel or two in the area we're heading to. We need to get lots of rest tonight to prepare for tomorrow."

Alexa felt her heart sink. He was absolutely right. They needed to sleep tonight, in advance of his testimony tomorrow.

Although she would still have to be on guard to ensure Dane's safety tonight, more than ever.

But anything else…?

"Of course, we have to get some exercise before we attempt to drop off to sleep to ensure we sleep well," he added as he slowed to approach the off-ramp. "Now, I know you'll try to stay awake anyway. But I intend to do my best to wear you out so you actually do get some sleep, while I'm the main one of us who watches for anyone after us. My turn. Maybe my last turn. But I do intend for us to have fun first."

Really? She should brief him on reality. Tell him that wasn't going to happen.

But she stayed silent.

Chapter 14

Dane needed a break. Oh, he was fine with his driving, but his state of mind needed some time out.

Reaching a ramp, he turned at the last moment after making certain no one else had a turn signal indicating they were going that way, too. He didn't use his signal, either.

No sense giving a hint of what he was up to if any of the cars that appeared in the moderate traffic contained someone following him.

Fortunately, no one appeared to follow, turn signal or not. He couldn't be certain all was well, but no danger was currently apparent.

"We're heading to Cordes Lakes?" Alexa asked.

"I saw some signs for travel stops off the interstate." He noted that she hadn't expressed delight at his suggestion of how to spend part of the night. But she hadn't told him to bug off, either. "We'll check out one of them and spend a few minutes there, maybe get some coffee and visit the facilities."

"Sounds good to me."

He glanced over and saw Alexa nodding, her phone still clutched in her lap, but she wasn't talking to anyone at the moment but him.

They were only about an hour away from Phoenix now, as far as he could tell. Maybe they should head for the courthouse right now after all. But if they did, it was likely to be after four o'clock when they arrived. Sure, he could stop in and say hi—and potentially get attacked today rather than tomorrow—but it would certainly not be the grand entrance he hoped for.

Not that he intended to stride in as Dane Beaulieu in his Tempe police uniform or even a suit. No, he'd go along with the protection lovely, and smart, Alexa had been providing him, and stumble in as senior Daniel Brennan, hiding among whatever authorities or undercover geezers showed up.

And talk to the DA. And eventually have the fun of entering the courtroom—probably wearing the suit he'd brought—smiling at his enemy, and give his testimony to bring Swanson down forever for killing Alvin.

And, oh yeah. For shooting Dane himself, too.

"Looks like you're doing a good job of staying alert," said the geezer beside him. She, too, was scanning the area around them, as she always did. Apparently nothing concerned her, or she'd have said so.

Oh yes, Dane trusted the lovely, disguised woman. Knew she was smart.

Knew she was goal-driven. And her goal, at least for now, continued to be to protect him.

And not to head to bed with him again, most likely.

Not tonight, but sometime in the future? Could they have a life together after all this? Maybe. He could contemplate—well, something. But reality...

"Trying to," he responded to her. "And by the way, I'm feeling fine. I want to do some more driving, including into town. We'd discussed changing drivers before but I'm fine with the fact we didn't. And I do want you to be our official observer as we get to Phoenix and decide where to stop."

"Fine with me, if you're not too tired."

"Here we are," he said, still cleaning up the idea of another night with Alexa in his mind. Or trying to. He already felt pretty tense about what was going to be happening over the next few days.

That was a kind of tension he could control. At least, theoretically.

Although... Well, once he was done, once Swanson was done, the reality he was contemplating was that Dane would return to Tempe and hopefully get his job back. Alexa would be back in Colorado. Would they ever see each other again, let alone have another night together?

Oh, yes, he could hope so. He realized he *did* hope so. But he knew better. And the idea of no longer having Alexa in his life was more than depressing.

"Are you okay?" Alexa, beside him, was regarding him with concern. "Did you see—?"

"I see a gas station and a nice large convenience store. And cars, some SUVs and a couple of semis parked there. But did I see something alarming? Nope. Although I have to admit that worries me. We haven't seen much of anything or anyone coming after me, and

I know Swanson wouldn't have made it easy for me to get to court to have him convicted, if he could help it."

"Maybe he couldn't help it," Alexa said. "I hope not. We've already been confronted by at least one of his paid peons. And we'll be prepared, with help, when it's time for you to get to the court."

Dane nodded as he pulled up beside one of the self-serve gas pumps. "Ah, time for this old geezer to limp his way over and fill up this car. Unless the other senior citizen in this car, who's in charge of me, chooses to do it."

He watched Alexa's face as amusement eased her expression. "Oh, I think you're perfectly capable of pumping gas, Daniel. But this oldster will get out of the car, too, to stretch his legs…"

In less than a minute, Dane had inserted the credit card with his new identity into the dispenser and started pumping gas.

He had an urge to touch her, to rip off her disguise and see the real Alexa beneath. He didn't do it, of course. Certainly not here, in public, even though there weren't many people around.

But he still couldn't help hoping he'd at least have one more chance to do that while they were alone tonight.

He heard her phone ring. Roger pretended to have a hard time finding it in his pocket, but soon had it up to his ear. "Hello?"

Dane couldn't hear the rest of the conversation, but he watched as Alexa took a few steps away to concentrate on the call. It was short but appeared rather intense.

Who was it? Was everything all right? Worry surged

through him. But if there was a problem, he—they—would deal with it.

When he finished pumping the gas, he approached her, just as she swiped her phone to hang up.

He made himself smile. "Hey, should I have been in on that conversation?" She'd mostly let him participate while they were together, although she hadn't when she'd spoken with her brother.

"Maybe, but I'll tell you all about it once we're back in the car. I want to go inside the store first, and you need to go with me."

He bought them some water as well as pretzels, to tide them over till dinner, once they decided where they'd stay and what takeout they'd bring to whatever room they had for the night.

At least now he felt his mind had recharged a bit despite his concern over what Alexa might reveal. He was ready to get back on the road.

And to ponder again about what would happen beyond tonight.

First, though, he carefully waited on the walkway near the store to get back into the driver's seat, partly because someone was getting out of the car beside theirs—a tall, muscular, young guy with an angry expression as he looked at the person getting out of his driver's seat, an older guy. His dad?

His boss?

His cohort in attempting to take down Dane?

Okay, he could allow his imagination to run wild—and suspect everyone of somehow being paid by Swanson and wanting to harm him. He'd be safer thinking that way.

Slipping the plastic bag with the items he'd bought

over his arm, he put his hand on the outside of his shirt, where his weapon was hidden. But both men just turned and went into the convenience store.

Dane got back into the driver's seat, closed the door and locked them all, since Alexa had gotten in, too. Then he put the bag on the floor in the back and turned to look forward again, eyeing Alexa, who was also watching him.

He merely nodded as if saying hello again, turned the key, backed up and then put the car in Drive.

"So, are we okay?" she asked in her usual lovely female voice.

"Looks like we are," Dane allowed Daniel to grumble as he nodded and glanced at Alexa after pulling onto the road that would take them back to the interstate. He paused and asked, "So who were you talking to on the phone?" It could have been a friend or family member and have nothing to do with him. Maybe even a guy she was dating… Well, he hoped not. And she apparently hadn't been speaking to anyone like that during the earlier part of their trip. Hopefully, there wasn't such a guy, or at least nothing serious.

"It was Cora. She asked our progress and said even if we were close, there was no need for you to be in court today. Tomorrow morning first thing, though? Yes."

"I figured. Did she say anything else useful?"

"We went over the plans."

Dane couldn't help a quick laugh. "Everyone will be protecting each other, too, then."

"Exactly. And I did warn her it was possible that some FBI agents might be there as well, potentially also undercover."

"I wonder if this kind of thing happens a lot at that courthouse." Dane had reached the on-ramp for Interstate 17, and he hesitated only a few seconds to check their surroundings before pulling on to it. He also glanced at Alexa, who nodded her okay.

"I don't know, but we can check with Cora and Moe tomorrow. I suspect this kind of thing is unusual for them, though."

"Me, too." He paused and asked, "Did Cora have anything else to say?"

"Well, yes," Alexa said. "She and I discussed where you and I are going tonight, and I think it might work. There's a downtown hotel, maybe the closest to the courthouse, that Cora said we should head for. The police chief she's been talking to is going to help send in the officers in disguise tomorrow, and he agreed to send two to that hotel tonight dressed that way, too. She'll keep us informed about their progress, and we're to remove parts of our disguise to look more like ourselves, though not entirely, as we check in to the hotel."

"So they're going to be us for the evening, or at least hopefully look that way to anyone who wants to find me. But will our IDs work that way?"

"She said she would have the local authorities give enough info to the hotel reservations staff to ensure we can get in. If we run into any problems, we're to call her."

"That's an excellent assistant DA we're working with," Dane said. Or at least she wanted them to think so.

Well, so far, there'd been no indication Cora was anything but the kind of person she was supposed to be, working hard to ensure that an important witness finally got into court to testify.

Alive and unharmed, if all went well.

And knowing Alexa, and himself, they'd stay safe tonight, even if what had been described didn't work out.

"Okay," Dane said, aiming a quick glance at Alexa. She wasn't exactly grinning or appearing full of relief. Still, she seemed a bit less stressed. Maybe... "So, are you going to give me directions?"

"Absolutely." She started fiddling with her phone again, probably looking for the hotel's address and how to get there.

Should Dane feel relieved? Maybe a little. At least they had a goal in mind, and if it worked out, they'd stay one more night together, at a minimum, before this ordeal ended.

Would it be enjoyable? Maybe, but it would be stressful, too. It would also be the last night Swanson could get someone to kill Dane to keep him from testifying.

Did he have the contacts and means to do that?

Dane definitely hoped not.

He'd never appreciated his protector more than he did this day.

And he intended to feel that way tomorrow morning, after this important night together.

They both had to be doing well, no matter what they did or didn't do that night.

His intent was to do everything in his power to ensure that Swanson paid for what he'd done.

Alexa considered calling Cora again.

The ride from the Cordes Lakes area had been nice and calm.

Even so, Alexa didn't allow herself to pay a lot of attention to the areas off the highway that they went by except to watch for danger. Some areas remained scenic, but as they drew closer to Phoenix there were more buildings of various types around them—offices, retail areas, hotels, even some apartments and residential areas.

For the moment, the voice connected to the map was the only one speaking in the car. Alexa wasn't happy about the silence, but she had nothing to talk about that they hadn't already addressed.

Their future? Any possibility of their being together was so unlikely that she didn't even want to bring it up and heighten her disappointment.

More realistically, she considered discussing some potential scenarios in which Dane got attacked that night, or going to the courthouse tomorrow, and what they would do about them.

Not something Alexa wanted to bring up either, though, at least not right now. Even though all of that remained at the forefront of her mind.

"So what are you thinking about?" Dane interrupted her thoughts.

She wasn't about to tell him. "Just checking out my first views of Phoenix." That was true, even if it wasn't everything.

"Nice town." Dane obviously wasn't starting a conversation, either.

In a short while, the female voice from Alexa's phone told Dane to exit the highway, then the next turn he needed to take. And the next one.

"I'm going to call Cora again," Alexa told Dane. She remembered very well the scenario they'd discussed for her to check in at the hotel for her subject and herself, but she wanted to confirm that nothing had changed.

"Everything okay?" was Cora's greeting when she answered after Alexa put the phone on speaker so Dane could hear.

"You tell me," Alexa responded.

"Yes, as far as I know. I haven't heard from the couple undercover guys, but I figure they'd let me know if there was a problem. I'll contact them now and call you right back."

"Sounds good." As she pressed the phone to hang up, Alexa turned to Dane, who was also looking at her. "Dinner?" she asked.

"We passed a fast-food place a couple of blocks ago."

That, Alexa interpreted as a yes. That way they could just hang out at the hotel until morning, which seemed safest to her.

She hoped.

Dane pulled out of their space and maneuvered around a few blocks till they got to a restaurant that specialized in foot-long sandwiches. Alexa wasn't very hungry but she could always eat just part of a sandwich, and another bottle of water sounded good.

Even better, the place had a drive-through, so they would be in and out of there quickly.

Her phone rang as Dane pulled away after paying for their food with a credit card at the window. It was Cora.

"Everything okay?" Alexa attempted to keep any anxiety out of her voice. After all, she worked in a field in which things could go wrong at any moment. Why worry about them? If there was a problem, she'd simply have to deal with it.

But tonight certainly wouldn't be the best time.

Plus, Dane had stopped driving just before he was about to take the car back onto the road again, and he looked at her, his expression appearing worried, too.

"Far as I could tell, all's fine," Cora said. "Your temporary counterparts were just parking at the hotel when I reached them. They should be heading inside soon to check in as the two of you."

"Lucky them," Alexa said. "We'll be there soon so I can check in as well, in one of my alternate identities as we discussed."

"Good. Keep me posted." Cora said good-bye and hung up.

Alexa considered taking a bite of her meatball sandwich with veggies now, just to keep up her energy, but figured it would be better to wait until they were settled into their room. Dane had handed her the bag before he'd paid, and she'd put it on the floor by her feet.

She wondered what the staff at the sandwich place had thought of old people like they appeared to be ordering full foot-long sandwiches. Well, even oldsters could enjoy eating, or even putting leftovers away for another meal as long as they could find a fridge.

And now her phone began talking again. They were only a few blocks from the hotel. Alexa told Dane to head into the place's official parking lot since, if anyone was after him here and knew they were in disguise, they'd go after the other old men—well, younger undercover cops—instead of them.

"How about if I park here?" Dane said, driving into the parking structure they spotted across from the hotel. The space he chose was near an exit. It made lots of sense to keep it easy for them to run, if necessary.

"Looks good to me."

So did the hotel. It was part of a major chain and appeared to be well kept up. She couldn't tell from here how full it was, but the parking lot they'd entered was only partly full, which suggested there might be plenty of rooms available.

"So now—I'm to get out and find someplace to hang out till you tell me to come back here, right?"

"That's the plan." Alexa was going to check them in, swapping into a different disguise.

She turned and dug into her small suitcase on the back seat. She then took off some of her clothes, whatever made her appear to be an old man. She pulled on a pair of workout leggings with pockets, adding a long vest over the same shirt she'd been wearing.

Then, after removing the hairpiece and makeup that made her look masculine, she put on a wig that hid her short blond hair with longer deep brown wavy locks.

She'd felt Dane's eyes on her as she'd pulled off the clothes. Too bad they didn't have time for her to tease him more.

Not now, at least.

"So who's that beside me?" Dane grumbled, keeping his identity as a geezer for now.

"Your protector, and don't you forget it," Alexa said. "Now let's get going."

They both exited the car. She stayed with him till they located a stairwell, and after Alexa checked to make sure the area was empty, Dane walked down it to wait for her. She ignored her urge to at least hug him as they parted ways, let alone kiss him. Never mind that he wasn't in a sensuous mood at the moment.

"Not many cars on this level," he called up to her after looking.

"Sounds good, but only stay there if there's no one around, got it?"

"You know I do." He chortled a bit as if she'd made a joke. And maybe she had.

He had been in law enforcement, too, after all. And he had a lot of good ideas about how to protect himself, even though he was in official witness protection.

But as she started crossing the walkway to where a valet stood near a kiosk, she heard something off to the side. A grunt? No one was shouting or complaining or anything, but considering who she was and what she was there for, she figured it wouldn't hurt to check it out.

She walked around the corner where a few bushes decorated the side of the building and saw one old geezer sort—maybe—in a fistfight with a tall, muscular man.

Was that one of the guys who'd gone undercover to pretend to be Dane and her? If so, where was the other one? If not, why was someone sparring with an apparent senior citizen?

And why wasn't the guy at the valet stand trying to help?

Alexa turned quickly and headed back to the parking structure, noticing then that someone had exited the hotel lobby and appeared to be heading in her direction.

She grabbed her weapon at the same time she grabbed her phone. She called Dane first.

"Be damned careful," she said as he answered. "And if you don't see anyone coming after you, get in the car and come pick me up right now. Head to the exit at the rear of the first floor of the parking structure, the one that leads to the street."

Chapter 15

Damn.

Not that Dane had thought anything about this situation would be easy. But what was going on?

Why was Alexa demanding that he pick her up? She must not have checked in to the hotel. Why not?

He could guess.

Who was after him, and where were they now?

He had started out the moment Alexa had told him to come, and now he drove out of the parking structure at the exit she'd described.

She opened the passenger door the instant he unlocked it and flung herself inside. She looked mostly like herself now, her lovely self, despite that brown, wavy wig. "Go!" she said.

And he did.

But he couldn't help asking, as he headed onto the nearest street, "What's going on?"

"Not sure, but there was a fight near the hotel entrance between someone at least dressed like a senior, and someone else. I didn't see a second senior. I just figured it was time to go. And I need to call Cora."

She did. She didn't say much additional to the ADA, but she'd put the phone on speaker so Dane heard Cora say, "Glad you're out of there. I'll get some authorities there to check it out. Where are you going now?"

Alexa looked at Dane. He had an idea, fortunately, but he wasn't going to mention it while anyone else was on the phone, even someone who was most likely trustworthy.

Most likely.

"Not sure," Dane said. "Do you have any suggestions?"

"No," Cora said as Alexa held the phone even closer to Dane's mouth. "And even if I did, I wouldn't pass them along. If whatever happened was intended to be an attack on you to prevent you from testifying, I don't have any idea how a third party would have known where you were. Or known that you were in disguise as a senior, which might be why Alexa saw a possible senior, or possible undercover cop, being attacked.

"Have we been hacked? I don't think so but— No, you're unfortunately on your own at least for now. I think getting more cops involved at the moment will only complicate things further—and make it more dangerous for you. I'll make sure the security and protection at the courthouse is ramped up even more than currently planned tomorrow, but right now please just be careful and figure out where to stay the night—in your car, even, if that seems best."

"Got it." Alexa pulled the phone back. "We'll see you tomorrow." She said good-bye and hung up.

It wasn't particularly dark out yet, but Dane nevertheless attempted to drive along the dimmest streets while he, too, observed their surroundings as well as he could.

"Any ideas where to go?" he asked. He actually had an idea, although he knew there were no guarantees it would be safe.

"Not yet, but I'm calling Vince."

"What the—!" the marshal shouted. "Damn. I've got further protection lined up tomorrow at the courthouse but I thought local authorities had things under control tonight, even having a couple undercover guys pretending to be you as you checked in to your hotel."

"I thought so, too," Alexa said. "But at least one of them was probably who I saw fighting."

"Well—I don't really know what's best to tell you now, other than to trust no one. Except each other, of course. And to show up right on time at the courthouse, where you should be well protected. I'll even contact my sources again tonight including the local Phoenix Marshals Service office for any additional resources, maybe even get you to a safe house. But—"

"Please do let them know about us, but I don't want to rely on anyone else we don't know around here right now. We're just going to have to figure out how to spend tonight," Alexa said. "And we will. Thanks, Vince. And good night."

"So now what?" he asked as Alexa hung up on her boss. Maybe she had an idea.

If not, he'd let her know what he had in mind.

Only— He saw a silver SUV driving down the street behind them, from the direction of the hotel they'd left.

Could mean nothing, although the area he'd chosen to hang out in was pretty empty.

Even so… He decided just staying there was a bad idea.

And the silver SUV that had worried him sped up in an apparent attempt to catch up.

"Damn!" Alexa swore. He saw her reach into her pocket, pull out her weapon and hold it in her lap.

"You going to call anyone else here to help out?"

"No," Alexa said. "But I checked before and we're not far from the local Marshals Service headquarters Vince mentioned. Let's go there and hang out in their parking lot if it seems appropriate, and it'll be obvious to anyone following us where we are. I hope it won't be necessary, but I can even call Vince again to get the name and phone number of the local contact he speaks with while we're there to get them to send help if we still see that car or any other that might be a problem. The Marshals Service here might wind up being a better resource than the local police."

"Got it," Dane said.

She gave him directions. The subject vehicle followed at first, but the driver must have realized where they were going. It disappeared, and although Dane drove around the area of the courthouses and even the local police station for a while, they didn't see it again.

"Okay," he finally said, heaving a sigh of relief. "They may be hanging around, waiting us out, but let's get away from this area for now. I've an idea of a different hotel a little farther away to stay the night.

We could just hang out in the car, but if possible I'd like to get at least a little rest to prepare for tomorrow."

He had glanced at Alexa as he'd talked. She looked furious. And determined.

And sexy as hell, somehow.

That wasn't the reason he wanted to spend the night in a hotel with her. Or not the main reason, at least.

He'd do whatever else it took to keep them both safe, even stay in the car as had been mentioned.

But Alexa said, "You're absolutely right. This isn't the way to spend this night. I'm glad you have an idea, at least. I could talk to Cora again and see if she could get local authorities to provide an escort to...somewhere, despite her telling us we were on our own. But that would only make us more obvious again. So— let's be careful, but let's go to whatever hotel you have in mind."

"Will do." Dane once more stopped along the street, this time about a block away from the police station. He saw a couple of patrol cars headed that way, but no silver vehicles or any others.

Were they safe? He could hope, but he doubted it.

But maybe, just maybe, they'd be able to find a hotel room and get a little sleep that night.

Was anyone following them now? Alexa didn't see anyone.

And Dane appeared to know where he was going. Or at least he didn't hesitate when he turned onto one street after another.

Best she could tell, they were going backward on the route they had taken into town earlier but making some additional turns.

She had to ask. "So where are we headed?"

"A motel I noticed when we started driving into town. Couldn't tell for certain, but it appeared to be a bit better than the ones we've been staying at for the last couple nights, especially the first one. And since I knew we needed to be careful, I also looked and thought I saw a parking area in the back that seemed somewhat isolated."

"Which might be a good thing, or a bad thing," Alexa said. Right now she didn't know exactly what was best for them—unless they'd been able to rent a room in the marshals office or even the police station.

And even then, since Dane's enemy used to be a cop, who knew what authorities around here might be on Swanson's side?

Phoenix was a good-sized city. Alexa considered checking the internet on her phone to see where there were theaters, or other hotels, or places that were likely to have people hanging out at this hour on a weekday.

But even in those areas she couldn't be sure that anyone they saw was there for legitimate reasons of their own.

"Hey, we're here," he soon said, and Alexa saw the motel he must have been talking about. It was part of a large chain, like a lot of the places to stay overnight that they'd seen. It was relatively small, taking up only about a third of a city block, and a couple of stories high.

The time was after seven o'clock already. Would they be open to walk-ins? Or run-ins, since Alexa wouldn't want to stay there long.

And at this hour, and after the danger they'd just escaped, she'd bring Dane in with her so she could watch over him as she checked in.

No people visible on the street or in the glow of the illuminated sign. No other vehicles except those already parked there. No movement of any kind that Alexa could see.

Even so, she put her hand over the part of her shirt hiding her weapon. "Let me get out first," she said. "Then I'll want you to come in with me."

"Sounds good." But from what Alexa could see of the expression on the false geezer face beside her, Dane didn't appear thrilled.

She got out of the car and walked up to peer into the reception room. It was lit, and she saw a couple of guys playing cards at a table in the middle of the room.

Bad guys? Well, she wouldn't assume not, but she had no reason to suspect them except that she was worried about everyone around now.

She walked back to the driver's side, opening the door. "Let's go ahead in. But be careful."

"You, too, O Most Revered Protector." That kind of silly address to her again? But his voice was soft and his expression as he looked up at her appeared almost reverent, till he started making faces by lifting his brows.

She couldn't help laughing. "Okay, Not So Revered Protectee, come on."

They were finally out of the car, in a motel room. Now out of his geezer disguise, Dane was pleased.

And concerned, as he stood by the front draperies, pulling them back just slightly. Keeping an eye on this area while Alexa organized her suitcase at the other end of the room. Looking down on the parking lot a bit. He'd decided to keep the car in the front since it was easier to see, easier for them to get to if necessary.

Hiding it in the back could be more dangerous.

He wanted to talk to Alexa, but his mind was racing. This wasn't a good time to start a discussion.

Not any more than it had been when they rented this room for the night.

Geezer Daniel had been with Alexa when, still in disguise as another woman with her wig and different makeup, she had gone into the motel's reception area and talked to the woman behind the front desk.

Alexa had decided on a room on the second floor, as she often did. She didn't ask her companion for his opinion, although she had made a couple of comments that suggested he was her stepfather.

Second floor was fine—again. In any case, they did get a room not far from the wooden stairway to this level. That could make it easier to flee, if necessary.

And easier for someone to sneak up to their room?

Heck, there was no perfect solution, except maybe someplace guarded by real cops not bought off by Swanson.

Assuming they could be certain that any people who were sent were honest.

In any case, tomorrow was coming up fast. This all would soon be over.

Or so Dane hoped.

Would his part of the trial only take a day? If not, tomorrow was Friday. The local authorities would need to ensure Dane remained safe over the weekend, until the trial resumed.

Would Alexa be helping with that security?

And after Dane testified…

Damn, but he would miss the beautiful woman who stood across the room from him now reorganizing things in her suitcase.

The sexy, protective, dedicated individual whom he'd come to know, though not enough, over the past few days.

She appeared to be removing at least some items from his backpack and reorganizing the contents of her bag.

What was she up to?

"Can I help you with that?" he finally asked, wanting to break the silence and figuring she'd say no.

It was something else for which she appeared to be in charge.

"No, thanks." She turned to look at him. She was near the door, using a stand for her suitcase. "I'm just working on ways to get ready for tomorrow, and one of them is to make sure you don't need any luggage to carry into the courthouse. You'll need to go in dressed as you are now, but you'll have to change to look like a former law enforcement officer who's a witness— in other words, put your suit on. I know you have one with you. I checked."

That wasn't a surprise, that she'd violated his privacy and dug into his suitcase.

But he said, "Nosy, aren't you?"

"By career," she said. "And you should be glad."

"Hell yes," he said without thinking. And also without thinking, he found himself strolling across the room.

He took the backpack off the edge of the bed and placed it on the floor.

"Hey," she said. "What are you—?"

She didn't finish as he put his arms around her, pulling her away from the suitcase. And then he began kissing her.

She responded immediately. Her lips on his were torrid and searching, as much as he had suddenly intended to do with her.

The kiss did not last nearly as long as he had hoped. She suddenly pulled away. "Let's check—"

He knew what she meant. She was right. They needed to check everything about the place so they then could hopefully indulge in what he had so carelessly, yet wonderfully, begun.

He was standing tall despite his disguise outfit as he checked their surroundings.

Meanwhile, he noticed Alexa had gone into the bathroom. He doubted she was in there for security reasons. It had a small window, but no one could sneak in there.

Assuming anyone after him could find them now. And he certainly hoped that wasn't the case.

She came back out again. Only—she looked different. Wonderfully different.

She had removed her wig and her clothes down to her underwear.

As he scanned her with his eyes, then looked back up into her face, she said, "I figure we'd better take advantage of this opportunity. It could be our last, you know, and—"

"Oh yeah. I know only too well. But because of that...well, are you sure?" He definitely was. But he owed her a lot. The idea of having sex with her again, quite possibly for the last time, was doing wonderful, hardening things to his body, yet—

"Hey," she said in a soft voice. "I'm the one who just came out here with my clothes off. Doesn't that indicate I'm sure?"

She drew even closer, and Dane reached out to remove those clothes that still remained on her, even as she began unbuttoning his shirt.

Oh yeah, his body was reacting.

And he had every intention of them both enjoying what could be this final night together.

Chapter 16

Was she wise?

Definitely not.

But she was certainly turned on, first by just the idea of having sex again with Dane, and now also because of the reality of his removal of her underwear. His warm, sensual touch on her most sensitive places.

Oh, but two could, and would, play that game. Mostly watching the carnal, heated look in his eyes as he scanned her body, Alexa began undressing him, starting with his hairpiece.

He looked fantastic once his dark brown hair was visible once more. She unbuttoned then removed his shirt next, enjoying the sight of his muscular chest with its smattering of dark hair, too.

But that wasn't enough. Far from it. She stepped away from his hands on her breasts so she could move toward him again and pull his jeans and shorts down.

And maneuver them around the large bulge in front that she wanted so much to see.

And soon did.

She moaned then, both at what she viewed and the feeling of Dane's hands back on her again, maneuvering them toward the bed.

She pulled away long enough, though, to turn out the lights and go stand by the window briefly, but long enough to listen and hear nothing outside, then peek out and also see nothing that made her worry.

This wasn't the first time she'd recognized that tonight could be the last opportunity she would get to have sex with Dane again. Who knew where he'd wind up the next night after at least starting his testimony at the trial? He might even need protective custody by more people than just her, once he had actually gotten into the presence of the murderer he hoped to see incarcerated for life.

Enough. She saw and heard nothing wrong. "Alexa," Dane whispered, looking her straight in the eye as if both challenging and inviting her to join him.

He was now as naked as she was. He'd followed her to the window but now he took her hand, led her away, and, after pulling back the coverlet and top sheet, helped her into bed.

In moments, they were in each other's arms, kissing. Then more. Dane stroked her all over, as she did him.

"Oh, Dane," she said softly against his mouth, and his lips soon encouraged her to be quiet again as he continued their kiss.

He undoubtedly had anticipated this moment, as he had put a condom on the nightstand. She had the pleasure of putting it on him. And that was only the beginning of the amazing pleasure she then experienced as soon as he slid inside. The warmth of his body on hers, his thrusting...

And it continued for a while, each moment making her feel more enthralled, wanting even more, thrilled that it continued, focusing on the pleasure he gave her below.

He reached around to touch her breasts, making her gasp, as he continued his sensual movements that she reacted to with her own. When he touched her buttocks, she did the same with him, enjoying the sounds of his pleasure as well.

And then—

She reached fulfillment, also hearing Dane's gasp as he, too, must have achieved satisfaction.

She lay beside him for a while, listening to his heavy breathing and her own.

Fantastic.

And a touch of hopefulness. This had been so wonderful... Could they ever do it again?

Forever? Would he be the partner she hoped for, for the rest of her life?

Oh, yes, she could hope. But she knew how unlikely it was that they'd ever be like this again.

But she was proud to be on duty. Watching.

"You okay?" Dane asked the first time she rose.

"I'll let you know," she responded.

Covering herself with a towel from the bathroom, she peered out from the drapes first. All seemed fine. She grabbed her weapon next just in case, pulled a long T-shirt on and opened the door slightly, placing herself in front of the opening and hiding her gun behind her.

Surely, if Swanson's fleet of assistants knew where

they were and intended to come after them that night to keep them from court in the morning, they'd have been there by now.

Alexa would remain wary nonetheless.

Still, after locking the door behind her once more, she couldn't resist the enjoyment of getting back into bed with Dane—and the pleasure that again followed.

She didn't count how many times she got up, checked around—and came back to bed to find she'd awakened Dane, and he was ready to make love yet again.

So was she.

But morning arrived, too soon.

Alexa was awakened by her phone ringing. She had it charging on the nightstand on the side of the bed where she slept...when she slept. She glanced first at Dane, who'd also been awakened. Then she grabbed the phone and checked who the caller was.

Vince.

"Good morning," she said, hoping she didn't sound too groggy. It was six fifteen, and she'd set the alarm on her phone for six thirty.

"Good morning." Her boss didn't sound groggy at all. In fact, he sounded like—her boss. "Now, I know you intend to get to the courthouse with Dane before eight, but I want you to get there at seven thirty at the latest. And I want you to tell me exactly where you are now. I've been told there's some unrest around the court, so I'm having an escort sent to accompany you in."

"Unrest? What does that mean?" Alexa was sitting up now, her back against the headboard, and Dane had sat up as well. He was watching her. She hadn't put Vince on speaker before, but she did now.

"Just more people hanging around despite the early

hour. I called DA Francini to ask how things appeared to be going, and he said some of his staff who arrive early for preparation let him know there were more pedestrians around outside than they're used to seeing. No one could say for sure who they were or if they indicated a problem, but I want to make damn sure you get our witness inside safely before the trial begins again today."

"Got it. We'll get on our way soon. And that escort...?"

"Like I said, tell me where you are."

"I assume our phones are safe," Alexa said dryly.

She certainly didn't think Vince was asking while in someone's crosshairs. His voice sounded like Vince in charge. Still—

"Yeah, far as I know. But we'll be damn careful anyway. Now, tell me. And stay there till you've got at least a couple unmarked cop cars accompanying you."

Alexa couldn't help glancing at Dane for his opinion. He nodded. She was the one who knew Vince, but Dane had been under the protection of several of Vince's subordinates besides Alexa over the past months. He apparently trusted Vince, too.

"Okay. Here's our current info." She gave the name of the motel and its general location.

"High class," Vince said dryly. "Sounds good, under the circumstances. I'll call Moe again and he'll get some local cops there right away. Don't leave till they meet up with you, of course."

"Of course."

She soon hung up and then looked at Dane. "You ready for this?"

"I'm more than ready."

Alexa enjoyed the view briefly as Dane got out of

bed naked. He let her shower first, quickly, then took over the bathroom.

Gee, they could have saved some time if they'd showered together, Alexa thought.

Or not. Could they have stayed out of bed after that?

Alexa dressed once more as herself with a wig, while Dane resumed his geezer Daniel appearance.

They both threw things in their respective bags, and Alexa wasn't surprised that Dane confirmed that his suit was now stuffed in the backpack they'd take into court. Alexa had noted before that the fabric was, fortunately, a kind that shouldn't wrinkle.

"Okay," Alexa said. "I'm going out first to check things out, probably wait for our escort. And—"

Her phone rang. She didn't recognize the number. She inhaled deeply as she answered, "Hello?"

"Marshal Colton? This is Officer Len Graben. I'm in one of the unmarked patrol cars that just pulled up to the motel. We were told you're in charge of a man in witness protection that we need to accompany now to the courthouse. Is that correct?"

"Yes, it is but— How can I be certain you're who you say you are?"

"I understand you've spoken with District Attorney Moe Francini and Assistant DA Cora Canfield. You can call them and check us out."

Alexa jotted down what the purported Officer Graben told her, including what his vehicle looked like and its license number, then called Cora's number and verified Graben's information.

"Okay, then," Alexa said after hanging up, turning toward Dane, who stood near the door. "You ready to get to court?"

"After all this time and what we've gone through? Oh yeah."

Alexa called the cop back and said they were coming down, describing their rental car.

She also asked if one of the officers could stop at a fast-food place and grab them breakfast.

"Assuming you have enough other cars to take care of us," she said.

"I believe so," said Officer Graben. "We've got a half dozen. One of the cars can go through a takeout line and get us all a snack and coffee we can eat and drink at the courthouse."

"Sounds good," Alexa said. "We're on our way down."

So far everything that morning sounded good, Dane thought. And last night? Well, he couldn't get it out of his thoughts. Didn't want to. And it was more than sex. He was really falling for Alexa, and he knew it.

Now he did his thing of hobbling down the stairs, though anyone who'd been watching them would know who the frail but overweight senior really was.

He had his backpack over his shoulder as he hung on to the rail and let Alexa handle both carryon bags.

Three plainclothes cops met them at the bottom of the steps. One identified himself as Graben, and another got their room keycards to take into the office so they'd be adequately checked out.

Looked like the cops had thought of everything. Dane hoped so, at least.

He saw a few people apparently leave their rooms in the motel. No one appeared to pay much attention to them.

And fortunately none of them appeared ready to attack him.

Alexa insisted on driving that morning, which was fine.

The cops almost formed a ring around the rental car, one regular-looking vehicle in front, one in back and a couple on each side until Alexa drove off. She drove slowly and insisted that Dane slump in his seat, just in case.

Fine with him. He was, after all, still under witness protection, and this was the day it would most likely matter the most.

Best he could tell, they didn't stop for traffic lights. It took only a few minutes to reach the courthouse.

The cars stopped on the street, and a bunch of people who also must be plainclothes officers, including women, surrounded their vehicle as they exited. Dane grabbed his backpack. Alexa locked the doors.

The officers also surrounded Alexa and him as they ventured up the walkway to a few outside steps. But then a whole lot of other older guys also surrounded them, some getting between them and the plainclothes cops accompanying Dane and Alexa. The officers just glanced at the newcomers and some nodded.

Dane figured they were the additional undercover cops and FBI agents that Alexa had told him about.

The whole group then walked the rest of the way into the tall courthouse building.

He had mixed emotions as they proceeded. He wanted to get his testimony over with and wanted to stay safe. He worried about their surroundings.

He also worried about what it would be like when he potentially had to say goodbye to Alexa. The idea that it might be forever... Well, in addition to all his other swirling emotions, he felt sad.

Dane and Alexa passed through entrance security similar to what Dane had seen in airports.

Apparently, the courtroom where Swanson would be tried was on one of the middle floors. A cop got into the elevator with Alexa and him, and they got out on what he was told was the correct floor.

A lot of uniformed police officers were there, as were some of the geezer-looking law enforcement agents.

And some regular citizens? Looked that way, but some could be part of Swanson's party, so Dane appreciated the protection around them. At least they'd gotten inside safely and would hopefully stay that way.

The cops then ushered Alexa and him down the hall and into one of the courtrooms.

It'd be a lot harder for Dane to appear like anyone but himself there, although he still had to change clothes.

Dane hadn't been in many courtrooms in his career, but he saw the judge's bench, the jury box off to the side, and the area near the other side where witnesses would sit to be questioned by lawyers who had their own tables—the defense and prosecution—beyond the rail that kept the official area from the observers.

Another couple of tables sat just before the bench, and Dane knew they were for court reporters and maybe a clerk or two.

A few people already occupied the room, and Dane figured the couple at a table near the front were the district attorney and his assistant.

But as they approached the rail, Alexa looked at

a person who stood with those two. "Vince!" she exclaimed. "I didn't realize you'd be here."

"I didn't tell you," he said.

A smiling guy approached them. He was large, though not as big as the character Dane now looked like. He was closely shaved and actually bald, and his face had lots of wrinkles.

Dane had learned to trust Vince from a distance. He was glad to finally meet him in person.

"I assume this gentleman is Dane," he said. He held out his hand and Dane shook it.

"We'll be starting soon," Vince continued. "Let's go get you changed into a suit."

"Sounds good," Dane said, and he was soon accompanied to the men's room by Vince and a couple of cops.

Just after they entered, another man who'd been at the table at the front of the courtroom joined them. He was tall and thin, with black hair cut short, a mustache and small beard. "Dane Beaulieu?" he asked. "I'm District Attorney Moe Francini. We need to talk."

"Sounds good to me," Dane said. He went into one of the stalls to change clothes. And when he came out in his suit, holding his backpack, Francini led him to another room down the hall where they sat at a table, with Vince and the cops around them.

Alexa, who'd remained in the hall, joined them.

Another woman walked in. She looked highly professional, undoubtedly a lawyer, slim and tall, in a black suit, lacy white blouse and clipped brown hair. Francini introduced her as Assistant District Attorney Cora Canfield.

In addition to the newcomers, one of the cops who

joined them had the breakfast Alexa had asked for. He even got to sip some lukewarm coffee.

Inside the room, Francini asked questions as if Dane was then on the stand, all about how he'd known Swanson before, as his boss. About how he'd been assigned to look into a prostitution ring—and learned that his boss was the head of it.

And how that had led to Swanson's murder of Dane's partner, Alvin O'Reilly, and the attempted murder of Dane himself.

As they talked, Francini made suggestions now and then about how to address questions, or to counter the likely responses the defense attorney might have on cross-examination.

Cora participated, too, adding suggestions that Francini appeared to approve of.

Neither said anything that would alter Dane's testimony, fortunately. He didn't need to ignore them.

In fact, Dane felt fairly comfortable about the questions and his answers.

He glanced at Alexa now and then. Her wide eyes and pleased smile suggested she was happy with how their planning progressed.

Happy still being with him? If only that was true, and they could still be together in some capacity when all this was over.

And then, finally, it was time. They all rose and, cops surrounding them, headed back to the courtroom.

The hallway was somewhat crowded. Dane recognized that at least some of those hanging around must be from the media, since a few held cameras and others held microphones.

Still others, though, might just be curious members

of the public. They just looked around as they stood there and milled among the plainclothes officers.

All seemed fine, though, as Dane, Alexa at his side and Francini ahead of him, entered the courtroom. Cora seemed to edge Alexa out as she told Dane to follow her past the rail and into the center of the front part of the room near the judge's bench.

"Please sit there," she told Dane.

No judge yet, but there were a couple guys in suits at the table beside theirs, where he assumed the defendant would sit.

The defendant. Where was—?

There. Dane recognized him immediately, despite his appearing a bit older and a lot more unhappy than he'd looked before. Samuel Swanson was escorted by three uniformed cops into the courtroom through a door off to one side of the judge's bench. They ushered him to the table where Dane had assumed he'd sit and gestured for him to be seated.

He did. But not before aiming an infuriated glower toward Dane.

Hell, he should be the one glaring at his former boss, the former chief of police of Tempe. A man who exploited vulnerable people.

The murderer of Dane's partner and friend, and shooter of Dane.

Instead, he decided to taunt Swanson, silently but in a way he figured would annoy the heck out of him.

He simply looked at the hefty guy with the large face and big brown eyes covered with glasses who he was more used to seeing in uniform than the navy blue suit he was wearing now, and smiled smugly, as if the trial was over and Swanson had already been convicted.

That was what Dane hoped, and figured, would soon be the case.

Swanson clenched his fists on the table, still staring at Dane. He showed his teeth as he appeared to snarl even more. Best Dane could tell, he was attempting a silent threat.

Given an opportunity, Dane would send him back a threatening look. Even more, if it was possible. The guy had not only murdered his friend and tried to kill him, but he'd continued to try to do so, and imperiled Alexa, too.

But Dane didn't really need to do anything menacing then.

His presence, and his knowledge, were enough of a threat.

Even so, he turned to look into the rows of onlookers on the other side of the rail.

Alexa was at the end of the front row nearest him. The angry expression on her face suggested she, too, wanted to show Swanson who was in charge.

He doubted she would ever get the opportunity to meet him. It was best that way. But—

He suddenly heard loud pops from outside the back end of the courtroom. Hell! Were those sounds gunshots? Before he ducked, his glance flew toward Alexa, but she was fine, just looking shocked and confused.

He felt scared though. He was undoubtedly the target. Was he about to be killed after all?

He spied a woman he hadn't noticed before at the back of the courtroom. She had a gun in her hand, and was aiming at Dane.

He knew her. She was short and somewhat pretty and dressed in jeans and a tight T-shirt. She'd sometimes come around the Tempe station, apparently flirting with Swanson.

And she wasn't alone. A man, also with a gun, had begun aiming his weapon as he turned one way, then back again, nearing Swanson with each step but apparently approaching Dane.

There was security downstairs. How had they gotten in here with guns?

"No!" Alexa shouted as the cops around Dane tried to shove him to the floor, while other officers burst through another door near the female shooter.

Alexa. The woman was near her now, though still looking toward Dane with her gun pointed—but she started waving it.

And Dane refused to allow Alexa to be hurt. He stood. Ignoring his own fear, he attempted to dodge all the people trying to protect him, but failed, desperately craning his neck to make sure Alexa was okay.

Chapter 17

"No!" Alexa shouted to Dane. "Don't move!"

Fortunately, he had to stay there, under guard by the cops who surrounded him, protected as they grabbed him and thrust him beneath the table where he'd been sitting.

Alexa might not be in charge of his protection now, but she was still going to do her damnedest to ensure he wasn't hurt.

Even though she appreciated he'd probably thought he was going to save her.

She drew her own weapon but didn't have to use it. By then the two assailants had been swarmed by armed and uniformed officers. Alexa recognized some of them, even beneath disguises, as fellow marshals from Blue Larkspur.

The two were subdued immediately, their weapons

seized, and they were taken into custody by some of the local cops.

When Alexa glanced toward the murderer at the center of it all, Samuel Swanson, she saw him glaring from one person to another, shaking his head, clearly furious.

Had he told some of his minions to come here and shoot their way around to get him free? Or had they decided to try it themselves?

How the heck had they gotten inside with their guns?

No matter. Whatever had spurred it, they'd failed.

Swanson had failed.

Dane was safe. And Alexa could hardly feel more relieved, even though she wasn't currently protecting him.

She didn't see him at the moment, not with the crowd of cops around him. She'd seen him thrust down on the floor and he was still there, as far as she could tell. In any case, he was well protected.

And soon the courtroom had been cleared of anyone unnecessary to the trial.

Unfortunately, that included Alexa and the rest of the crowd. She understood, of course. But she would most likely not get to see Dane till the end of the day.

Only... "Well, that was entertaining." Vince had come up to her in the wide, starkly adorned hallway with beige walls and lots of recessed doorways, which was now nearly empty except for more cops and people dressed in security uniforms.

"I guess you could call it that," Alexa said sardonically. Then she said to her boss, "So not only are you here, but so are some other witness protectors in our group. Did you bring them all along?"

"Now what makes you think that?" The grin on his wrinkled face suggested he was holding back a laugh.

She felt like laughing, too. In relief. "Oh, maybe their presence and their jumping in to help protect my subject—our subject—when danger approached."

"Oh, danger more than approached. It jumped in, too. But fortunately, it was immediately caught." He took a few steps until he was right beside the wall, and Alexa joined him.

"A very good thing," she said. "Now...well, I'd love to get back in there to see the trial, but I suspect that won't happen. It's probably safest if they keep everyone who isn't necessary out of there, as long as they consider the cops necessary. But—well, witness protectors, too, couldn't hurt."

"As long as they were definitely witness protectors," Vince agreed. "But the more of us, or purportedly us, they have in there, the more time it'll take to verify who's who. Plus, I'm sure their preference would be locals. So—" He reached into his pocket and pulled out his phone. "I'll check with Cora anyway. I've been in touch with her quite a bit, and gather you were, too. And what I understood now was that she would turn her phone's sound off in the courtroom but check it for texts frequently."

He typed something on his phone, then looked at Alexa and said, "For now, we'll wait. I don't want to start going up and down the elevator. But—"

Alexa was surprised when the door to the courtroom, not far down the hall from them, opened. Cora exited and closed the door behind her.

She joined them. She appeared even more serious than Alexa had seen her before. "I just want to thank both of you, and your additional witness protection staff. The trial is now proceeding, and I feel like our security is good. Really good. But I'm sorry I still can't let you in, even though I know you're part of the solution, not the problem."

"Oh, that's okay," Vince said.

It wasn't necessarily okay with Alexa. She remained worried about Dane and frustrated that she couldn't remain part of his protection. But there was nothing she could think of to say that would change the situation.

"In fact," Vince continued, "it looks to me like you really do have things under control here now. Or if it's not, you've got enough people on the case to take care of any problems."

"Very true," Cora said. "I won't tell you what or where, but we've been talking in great depth with the local authorities and we have not only witness protectors available to take care of Mr. Beaulieu over the weekend, but a safe place to watch over him."

"I take it the trial won't end today," Alexa said, "and neither will Dane's testimony."

"That's right. But the little bit of examination that's gone on so far, with DA Francini in charge, has been going well. Oh, there've been objections on the other side, but nothing that stuck. Still, it's taking a while to get through the interrogation, so we assume we'll have to resume questioning on Monday, then go through cross-examination."

"Got it," Vince said. "Anyway, we're heading back to Colorado this afternoon."

Back to Colorado now? He sounded certain of it, so Alexa was, too. He was her boss. And she had no further obligations here, now that Dane was being taken care of by others. She tried not to let herself feel morose. She had done her duty, gotten him here safely. Dane was now testifying, and the others would ensure his safety from now on.

She hated the idea that she wouldn't have the opportunity to say good-bye to him. But it unfortunately made sense not to put anyone else in his presence now.

Even her.

Damn, but she was going to miss him. A lot. Never mind that it was unprofessional to get involved with one of her protection subjects. She hoped Vince didn't find out about her secret trysts with Dane—she wouldn't want that to come back to jeopardize her career. But she had to admit that Dane was special.

Very special.

If only they could stay in touch somehow. But she knew that wasn't going to happen—and it made her very sad. She just had to ignore it.

She had to say something to Cora now, though. She had to learn how things went at the trial as it continued. She shot a serious glance toward the assistant DA and said, "I hope you'll keep in touch and let us know how it goes."

"Of course." She looked at Alexa then Vince. "And we can work things out so Dane and you can get a chance to talk and catch up after today."

"Sounds good," Alexa said. "But since we're leaving, although Dane does have a backpack with him, he's also got a carryon bag in my rental car. I can bring it up and—"

"Just wait a minute. I'll have someone go get it from you." With that, Cora headed back into the courtroom.

Alexa had little doubt about what would come next. She, and the others, would soon be on their way.

She did appreciate what Cora said, though.

She would at least have one more chance to talk to Dane.

If that worked out.

"So," Vince said, "as I'd hoped, looks like you and I and the rest of our gang can head back to Blue Larkspur this afternoon. We've got a team trying to find the partner of the guy who attacked you on the road, by the way. And we're still attempting to prove Swanson sent the assailants or figure out who did."

"Sounds good to me," Alexa said. "Please keep me informed."

"Will do. And in fact— Well, I've got a couple other possible witnesses in important cases in Colorado who'll be needing protection soon. And, well... I'm looking at giving you a lot of high-profile cases now. You've really showed yourself to be quite a badass."

Alexa laughed. Despite her internal sadness, she couldn't help but be amused. And she was proud. She was delighted at being recognized as skilled in her job. That was a very good thing.

But not so good was that she knew for certain she needed to head home this afternoon. And the fact she wouldn't get a chance to say good-bye to Dane in person kept disturbing her.

Vince and she left a few minutes later, accompanied by an officer in uniform and also followed by three plainclothes agents who had changed out of their disguises.

Others, locals, had apparently taken over everything

necessary to make sure the trial proceeded safely for the witnesses.

Alexa led one cop to her rental car, got the bag out of the trunk and handed it to him. She hoped he was trustworthy, then realized that in her job she trusted no one—or not many people. But this guy certainly appeared to be trusted by the ADA.

She watched him walk off toward the courthouse, wheeling the bag behind him. She figured Dane would get it back sometime that afternoon.

Meanwhile, she knew, Vince was arranging for them to fly back to Colorado that afternoon, so Alexa would meet him at the local airport since her next step would be to return her rental car.

Back to Colorado. Away from Dane. She couldn't do anything to ensure his safety but hoped the local authorities would do it well. *Hoped* being the operative word, but there was nothing she could do about it but worry about him.

And she knew he would remain on her mind a lot. For many reasons.

She had never felt like this before about any man. But she had to leave him behind.

Well, she would soon be on a plane. And there would be no problem getting a ride share to pick her up at the Blue Larkspur airport and take her home once she arrived.

For now, she used her phone's GPS to head toward the rental car office. Vince called while she was on her way and told her he'd been able to get them all on a flight at three that afternoon.

She was going home! She loved her hometown and her family.

She might as well let Dominic know how things had gone.

She pulled over to the curb of the street she was on then and pressed his number, then put the phone on speaker.

"Hey, little sis," he answered quickly. "How's your witness protection going? Do you need some more FBI assistance?"

"I'd wondered if I did, but right now things are just fine."

As she got back on the road again, she described to Dom what had happened since she'd reached Phoenix with her protection subject, the concerns, the danger, even the attack at the courthouse. She naturally told him how well her idea of law enforcement agents in disguise had gone. "It all seemed to work out. I'm on my way back to Blue Larkspur now, but my subject is now on the witness stand in court." She attempted to sound perky, so he'd believe she was thrilled to be heading home.

And she was, mostly.

But she just wished she'd had a chance to see Dane in person one more time...

"Good job!" her bro said.

"Thanks. So how are things with you?"

"Not bad," he said. "But there are some things going on with our buddy Ronald Spence, the drug smuggler."

"Oh yeah. Him again."

"Exactly. He's at it again. I'll tell you about it when you get home. No need to waste your time about it now. So—get home safely, and we'll talk again soon."

"Hope we can see each other again, too. Any chance you and Sami will get to Blue Larkspur anytime soon?"

"Maybe. I'm in Denver now. But I'm open to the idea of heading to Blue Larkspur for a visit."

"I hope so," Alexa said.

It was late afternoon. The trial had adjourned for the day.

Dane felt exhausted. He also felt jubilant. He believed things were going well in his testimony.

DA Francini had asked cogent questions about Dane's work as an investigator for the Tempe PD and his friendly relationship with his partner, Alvin. Their investigation of a solid prostitution ring, as assigned partly by their boss, Police Chief Samuel Swanson.

How Swanson had seemed reluctant to even have any of his detectives look into the criminal enterprise.

How they had discovered Swanson was in charge of that ring.

And what had happened after that.

The questions were phrased well, not leading him to make up answers but allowing him to testify about what he knew and how he knew it.

They hadn't finished by the end of the day, though. Surprisingly, not much yet about the actual murder, and his getting shot, as well as the way he'd been attacked by unknown thugs on his way to testify. That would come the next time court was in session.

He figured, with all the objections and questions raised by Swanson's counsel, that had been planned, so that the most telling information wouldn't be in the minds of the jurors over the weekend. The weekend. Without Alexa around. He knew she was on her way back to Blue Larkspur.

She wouldn't see how the trial progressed, though she could probably follow it in the media.

She wouldn't see him. Nor would he see her. And damn, but he would miss her.

He missed her already...

Dane was accompanied out of the courtroom by Francini and Assistant DA Canfield, along with a number of uniformed cops. His suitcase had been left by the door, presumably brought there from Alexa's car.

So he didn't have to go get it. Or see her to get it, either.

Canfield had introduced him to a couple of plainclothes cops who she said were his next witness protectors. They were taking him to a place where they'd spend the weekend with him. Be in charge.

Protect him.

But neither was Alexa.

No one else could be. Oh yeah, he missed her.

Cora had told him Alexa and her gang, including her boss, Vince, were already on their way back to Colorado.

A couple of phone calls would be set up over the weekend so he could chat with them about how things were going and say good-bye.

He wondered if Alexa had missed saying good-bye to him here the way he missed saying it to her.

"Here we are," said one of the guys who'd accompanied him through the courthouse and out a rear exit. He looked nice and burly and protective, and Dane had no doubt he was armed. His name was John Angelo.

They'd reached a car, and John helped Dane into the rear seat on the passenger side. Officer Len Graben, who'd accompanied Alexa and him before, had now donned street clothes and slid into the other rear seat.

Soon, they were on their way. As they left the parking facility, Dane couldn't help wondering exactly where he'd spend the weekend.

Somewhere safe, he figured.

But though he would probably feel sheltered and secured, he was certain that neither of these guys, or anyone else he might be protected by here, would make him feel as safe—or as pleased—as Alexa had done. Or would light his heart and body on fire the way no other woman had ever done.

Chapter 18

It was nine o'clock on Saturday morning. Alexa was just getting out of bed, quite a bit later than her norm, especially lately.

She had slept reasonably well last night. Surprisingly, her mind had cooperated with what she'd hoped for her body.

After all, she didn't have to try to sleep lightly, in case any danger caught up with her and the man she'd had under witness protection. Or get up several times during the night, to double-check that she hadn't missed hearing anything, also to protect Dane.

Or to make wonderful love with Dane. Multiple times.

Or even just once.

She missed it. A lot. But she missed his wonderful company even more. Even his silly sense of humor.

Dane. She wondered where he had spent the night.

Somewhere in Phoenix obviously, with others now charged with his protection near him.

Not Alexa.

No, she was back home in her quaint ranch-style house in a fairly classic, but generally calm, Blue Larkspur suburb. The other homes around it appeared similar, and she knew most of them were also two-bedroom. A nice neighborhood.

Hey, she was back home now. She'd have to go visit the Gemini.

Get another ride on Reina, with one or both of those sibs along.

She needed someone to talk to, after all. Someone close to her. And—

A good idea occurred to her. Instead of heading straight to the shower, as she'd originally planned after taking off her pj's and throwing on a robe, she went back to where she'd left her cell phone on its charger, on the ornate nightstand beside her comfortable queen-size bed with its fluffy beige coverlet and pillows.

Yes, it was still the burner phone she'd gotten during her adventure over the past few days. She needed to get a new one that she could use forever, or at least for a good long time. In fact, that was one thing she hoped to do today or tomorrow.

She also hoped to be able to go back to her old phone number, since so many relatives and friends had that programmed into their phones. Even if Samuel Swanson wasn't convicted of murder—and she certainly hoped he would be—he would have no reason to look for her while she was no longer protecting his enemy. Not unless he was hell-bent on vengeance in a way she didn't anticipate. And even if he was, it wouldn't be that difficult, phone or not, for him to find her back at her home and back on her job in Blue Larkspur. No matter what, she'd have to be careful.

She pressed her mom's number into the burner phone after unplugging it. It rang a couple of times, then Alexa heard a tentative, "Hello?"

"Hi, Mom," Alexa said. "It's me. I'm using a different phone thanks to work."

"Oh good! I'm so glad to hear from you. I know better than to ask many questions, but I got the impression from Dom that you were working on something important—and in your line of work that can also mean dangerous."

Alexa laughed. "You got it. But the good thing is I'm no longer on that job, and in fact I'm home. Can you join me for lunch today?"

"Absolutely!"

They arranged for a time and place, noon at one of her mother's favorites, Happy Dining, a family restaurant on the south side of Blue Larkspur. It was a place her mom particularly liked, and she was the one who'd suggested it.

Alexa was smiling as she got off the phone and headed for the shower. Would she get to speak to Dane today? That might make her smile even more. A lot more. Maybe he would even tell her one of his corny jokes if they talked.

And just the sound of his voice would cheer her so much...

Oh yeah. She had really fallen for the guy.

She thought she heard her phone ring as she was getting out of the shower in her nice-sized mostly lavender-tiled bathroom and so she grabbed her robe from its hook behind the door and ran back into her bedroom.

She hoped to see a phone number she didn't know, as her mother had. But what she saw was good, too. Dominic's number.

"Hi, Dom," she said.

"Alexa. Hi. Where are you?"

"Home," she said. "I finished my latest assignment, even though the trial isn't over, so here I am."

"Excellent! I hope to come visit soon. Only— Well, I should let you know, as I have with others in the family, that Spence is making more threats against us."

"What? How? And where is he?"

"Wish I knew where he was, but I got the impression from the authorities I've been in touch with over the last few days that he's being more threatening in emails, as well as more discreet about his location. No one's been able to trace him or bring him in, but he's hinted at coming after members of our family since we've remained pretty obvious about wanting to get him arrested again."

"Wonderful. Well, thanks for the warning. But... Well, you be careful, too. Sure, I'm a marshal, and I'd do anything to bring him in, but—"

"But your name is out there like most of the rest of us, as nosing around about where the guy might be so he can be brought in. He'll know it... Plus, he knows a lot of members of the Colton family are after him now. So, yes, you need to be careful."

"Got it." And she did. She knew full well that Coltons and others in law enforcement had to assume there were bad things around, even outside whatever assignment they happened to be on. "Thanks, I guess.

Anyway, I'll look forward to when you get a chance to visit, and Sami, too, if you can bring your fiancée."

Fiancée. Alexa liked Sami but at the moment she felt a tad jealous. Not that she wanted that kind of commitment. But she hadn't really considered getting into any kind of relationship...before.

Oh, dating and having fun, sure. But no one had been interesting enough to spur her to try for anything long-term.

Her time with Dane, though, had made her think about more, especially since all the relationships she'd had before had been brief and never very serious. But Dane? Their bond hadn't exactly been appropriate, given she'd been protecting him. But she realized now that somehow, deep inside, she'd begun hoping that the intensity of the feelings she had developed for him might evolve into something more.

"I'll also look forward to seeing you," Dom said, bringing her back to their conversation. "Anyway, got to get back to work now. Be careful—and I will be, too."

Interesting, Alexa thought after they'd hung up. She had always figured that law enforcement agents could always be in danger. But was that what she wanted for herself for the rest of her life?

Maybe she should consider finding a different, safer career.

Or not.

But if she settled down with someone, got married, had kids, it would be better to have a safer existence.

And if she actually developed a relationship with Dane...

Oh, yes, that sounded wonderful. But impossible.

For now, she headed to the closet in her bedroom to

start looking for what to wear when she met her mom for lunch. She didn't need to get too dressed up, but she didn't want to look like a marshal on duty, either.

Maybe not a dress, but a dressy pants outfit.

She chose a lacy, black, long-sleeved blouse over a pair of sleek black slacks, and decided to wear low-heeled pumps with it. Good. She should look attractive enough for her mom to be proud of her, but not too posh to be at a family restaurant for lunch.

She didn't need to get dressed yet, though. It was only a bit after ten o'clock. She decided to throw on a pair of jeans and a T-shirt, then get on her computer and check any news available from Phoenix, particularly from yesterday.

She doubted any reporters had been permitted into the courtroom, either, but that didn't mean they wouldn't do whatever research they could and relate it in whatever media outlets they represented.

The T-shirt she chose had a logo on it for Blue Larkspur, a representation of the flower for which the town was named—bright blue with a group of attached blossoms.

But before she sat to start her research, her phone rang.

Dominic again? Or Vince, or Cora? Not too many people had this number.

And when she pulled her phone from the pocket of her jeans where she'd placed it, she didn't recognize the number.

Someone else's burner?

A bolt of hope shot through her. The person she knew right now who was most likely to have a burner phone was Dane.

But heck, it could even be a wrong number.

She swiped the screen to answer and lifted the phone to her ear. "Hello?" She kept her voice calm and a bit curious.

"Alexa? Hi. It's the subject of your excellent witness protection."

She smiled as she felt her body grow warm. She moved into her living room and sat on the plush lavender sofa. "Well, you don't sound like any of the women I worked with, so my best guess is that you're Daniel Brennan, although you sound a bit younger than he turned out to be."

A laugh. And then the voice that was clearly Dane said, "Hey, what happened to my protector who had no sense of humor?"

"Oh, *that* witness protector? She's around here somewhere."

Another laugh. "Then put her on the phone."

It was so good to hear his deep, sexy, wonderful voice. But Alexa couldn't tell him that. Instead, she put her professional hat back on and asked, "So how are things in Phoenix? Are you safe?"

"Things are fine and so am I, thanks. I'm sure you know the rules. I can't talk long, and I can't give even a hint of where I am, although your guess about Phoenix or somewhere around there can't be completely wrong since I'll be back in court on Monday. But—"

Dane stopped talking, and Alexa heard a stern voice in the background. Maybe his protector thought he'd gone too far in even mentioning the Phoenix area, no matter that she'd been his protector before, and she was bound to know full well he'd be back on Monday in the Phoenix court where he'd testified on Friday.

"Okay," she said. "Don't tell me anything else. What's important is that you're doing well, you're safe and you'll be back testifying on Monday. Right?"

"You got it. And how about you?"

"I'm fine, back at home in Blue Larkspur, having a good weekend and planning on going back to my office on Monday."

Oh, how she wanted to tell Dane how great it felt to talk with him. To know he was okay.

She also wanted to ask that they keep in touch... somehow. Maybe not get in contact again till he'd fully testified, but after that—

Well, she'd be back doing her job, and Vince had already told her he had people in need of witness protection in mind for her to take on as subjects. And presumably Detective Dane would return to his own job in Tempe as soon as he could.

So—staying in touch might sound like fun, but why bother? It might only make Alexa feel more miserable about not seeing him. Even if she desperately didn't want their association to end.

And so, when they ended their conversation soon thereafter, she said, "I'm sure I can find out on the news next week how the trial goes. I hope you really nail Swanson." But she didn't suggest he call again so they could talk about it.

When he said good-bye, she tried to ignore the stab of pain that went through her.

"Good-bye," she said in return, and hung up.

Good-bye.

It sounded so final to Dane.

He looked around the bedroom where he was hanging out this weekend with his current witness protector, Officer Craig Geraina, a member of the Phoenix PD who'd sneaked Dane into his own home in Gilbert, Arizona, a small suburb of Phoenix.

Dane knew he'd hang out in this compact room—with its single bed, and, fortunately, a TV mounted on a desk across from it and a restroom next door—the entire weekend unless something bad happened here.

Craig had stayed with Dane while he'd made the call on a phone the cop had handed him. Then he'd taken it back and left the room after asking Dane what he wanted to have delivered for lunch from a nearby fast-food joint.

Dane had also been told there'd be a lot of patrol cars going by, though none would appear like a police vehicle. And if he happened to peek out the window in this room—only allowed occasionally, and not at all if Craig told him not to—he might see some civilian-appearing dog walkers going by, accompanied by official K-9s.

Oh yeah. Dane was still being well taken care of. He appreciated it.

He didn't appreciate, though, that he couldn't even talk to Alexa more, let alone see her.

Which hurt, damn it. A lot. He realized now, especially since they were apart and he missed her so much, how much he really cared for her.

Still, if all went well, he'd finish his testimony on Monday or Tuesday. He believed his examination on Friday had gone well, despite lots of objections and interruptions by the defense.

Swanson should get convicted. And when he did, Dane would be released from protective custody—

although he knew he'd have to be damn careful. Swanson's buddies who'd been willing to get arrested for attempting to shoot people in court probably had associates who'd be happy to continually pursue revenge. And whoever the captured would-be killer's ally was remained out there somewhere, although Dane understood the authorities were attempting to track him down, as well as anyone else Swanson had gotten to harm others to help him.

But Dane would soon be able to go home to Tempe. Return to his job as a detective, although it sounded a lot less appealing now, considering all he'd gone through recently.

Well, he'd be alone here in this room a lot this weekend. He had been given yet another burner phone, although he'd been directed to make no calls or texts, darn it, unless told to by his handler. No communication that way with Alexa, either.

But he would look forward to a time that he might be able to get in contact with Alexa again. Sure, they had behaved a bit too intimately, but he had enjoyed it. More than enjoyed it. He'd appreciated Alexa. A lot. Still did.

Okay, he had begun to care for her much too much, maybe even fallen in love with her. Loved how his corny jokes could just about crack her stern façade, how she felt in his arms, how she, like him, was relentless in her pursuit of justice.

He was glad she had left the area and was safe. But oh yeah, he missed her. Would he ever see her again?

He'd at least be able to talk to her again, eventually.

Hopefully soon.

And he definitely hoped that Alexa hadn't really meant good-bye.

Chapter 19

Alexa was delighted that she was going to have some alone time with her mom.

She needed something like that to help her out of what felt a bit like depression. Not that it made sense, but the idea she couldn't see Dane anytime soon was making her feel bad.

But having some time with Isa Colton would certainly help that. Especially just the two of them. With so many siblings, Alexa seldom got to see her mom without additional company.

It was nearly noon. Alexa was in her car now, and she'd reached the particularly nice part of town where Happy Dining was located. Only a couple more blocks, past a few more restaurants on the wide, well-maintained street, as well as some clothing stores and even a wine shop. Driving slowly, she saw her mother walking briskly along the sidewalk toward Happy Dining. Knowing Isa, she'd probably gotten here early and wound up circling the block to find someplace to park.

Fortunately, Alexa saw two curbside spaces in front of a jewelry store and immediately pulled into one. She pushed the button to roll down the window on the passenger side, just as her mother got there.

"Hey," she called. "Would you like a walking companion?"

Her mom stopped, squinted as she looked inside and smiled broadly. "I'd love this particular walking companion."

Alexa quickly got out of the car and pushed the button to lock it. In moments, she, too, was on the sidewalk.

She and her mom hugged. Isa was around Alexa's height. Her hair was shoulder-length, which was longer than Alexa's, but was also blond. She had blue eyes, and her figure was amazing, sleek and attractive, particularly for her age. And she had thrown on a lovely, though not too elegant, pink dress for their meetup.

"So good to see you, dear," her mom said. Despite the other people passing them on the sidewalk, she stepped back and looked Alexa up and down as if assessing her. "You look good. Do you feel good? I heard that the assignment you were just on was dangerous. You didn't get hurt, did you?"

"Not at all," Alexa responded right away, waving her arms out as though wanting her mom to assess her even more. What she'd said was true—physically, at least.

Emotionally, she couldn't help thinking about Dane. About having had to leave him, with the understanding she might never see him again.

"You're sure you're okay, dear?" her mom persisted. "You're acting like—"

"Hey. Well, look at this. Just like I was hoping. Not just one Colton, but two."

Alexa immediately drew herself even farther from her mother and spun around to look at who'd been speaking from behind her in that raspy voice.

Damn. She recognized the guy, of course. Ronald Spence.

What was he doing here?

He looked awful, with his stringy, uneven, un-combed brown hair and rather dead brown eyes that nevertheless stared toward Alexa and her mom. Plus he had a cigarette in his hand and took a puff, causing his cheeks to move, emphasizing his dark, jaggedly cut hair.

"Hello, Ronald," Alexa said coldly. "I'm surprised you're out in public. Why are you here today?"

A few people slipped by them on the sidewalk, but Spence didn't look toward them. His gaze was intently focused on the two women.

"Oh, I've been just sort of wandering around town in areas where I know Coltons sometimes hang out. Don't you like that restaurant down the street? Anyway, there must be something you like around here, since here you are."

"Not for long. We were just leaving." Alexa had placed herself in front of her mom, and she now gestured with her head at her car. They hadn't yet moved away from it, which could be a good thing. "Let's go, Mom." Alexa pulled her key out of her pocket and pressed the button to unlock the doors.

"I don't think so," Spence snarled. "You're both coming with me." Running at them, he yanked a gun from under his denim shirt. Dashing around Alexa, he grabbed her mom. He aimed the gun at Isa, then Alexa, then Isa again.

Damn. Alexa was scared for her mom, and furious. She'd just gone through an ordeal in Arizona as part of her job and more, keeping Dane, and herself, safe. She didn't want to go through anything like that again.

And she would do anything to keep her mom safe.

Barely thinking, Alexa went into protection mode and leaped toward Spence, maneuvering so she could bend enough to kick the gun out of his hand. It flew sideways, toward the street, and Alexa dashed to pick it up, planning to use his own weapon to capture the attacker.

Only—as she grabbed the weapon, Alexa saw her mom gasp, breathe hard, clutch her chest. Oh no.

Alexa knew she had to do what was important: save her mother's life. Isa might be having a heart attack, and Alexa didn't want to leave her by chasing their assailant, who was now running. Someone else would have to catch Spence, much as she wanted to be the one to bring him to justice.

"I've called 9-1-1," said someone on the sidewalk near them, and Alexa glanced that way. A middle-aged woman had approached from the crowd that was now growing around them, and she held her phone up, though she justifiably stayed back.

"Thank you," Alexa said, feeling highly grateful—and frustrated.

Pointing the gun downward and holding on to her mother's arm to help keep her stable, Alexa couldn't help staring through the crowd in the direction Spence had gone.

One of the other women around them said, "Does

she need CPR? I could give it a try," and proceeded to lower her mother to the ground. Not sure, Alexa felt grateful as she watched.

But she also continued to gaze after Spence. If she hadn't needed to stay there to take care of her mother, might she have been able to catch him and bring him in?

Don't go there, she told herself. She'd done what was important. Hopefully, cops would show up as well as an ambulance and—

There. She heard a siren. Apparently so did the rest of the crowd on the sidewalk.

The sirens grew louder. Multiple ones, in fact. In moments, Alexa saw both an ambulance and a police car arrive.

EMTs jumped out, and Alexa explained briefly that there had been some potential danger against her mother, who now appeared to be having a heart attack. As the woman who had been trying to help stepped away, medics began examining Isa. Some uniformed cops got out of the cruiser and also joined them on the sidewalk.

Alexa explained that a person believed to be a major drug smuggler, Ronald Spence, had threatened them. She still had the gun and handed it over to one of the officers by dropping it into a plastic bag he proffered. She also pointed in the direction Spence had fled—as well as getting the officer's ID information, in case she ever had to track down that weapon again.

"I doubt we'll be able to find him, Marshal," said the older of the two cops, "but we'll go see what we can find."

Alexa doubted Spence would be anywhere around

now either, but she hoped the cops—who, after all, reported to her mother's longtime admirer, Chief Theodore Lawson, and he and Isa had been getting closer recently—would get identification of some of the observers still hanging around, as well as their versions of what had happened. Hopefully, the witnesses would describe how Spence's weapon had been aimed at the two Colton women.

She didn't care if anyone mentioned how she'd gotten the weapon from Spence. But she had made it clear, while describing her mother and herself, that she was a US Marshal, and had showed her own ID. That way, her version should be the one to stick, even if they found Spence and he claimed she'd attacked him. She wouldn't let him get away with any more crimes.

One of the EMTs approached and, at her invitation, Alexa got into the ambulance, too. They'd given her mother a preliminary exam. Though Isa appeared in no immediate danger and looked to be breathing more normally, they were still taking her to the hospital.

Once they arrived, med techs immediately wheeled her mother on a gurney to the emergency room, where an ER doctor took over her care. Alexa followed, then stayed in the waiting room nearby.

She sat on one of the stark wooden chairs along the sizeable room's perimeter and pulled her phone from her pocket. She was alone here while she waited, but she needed to let her siblings know what was going on.

It didn't make sense to call her emotionally closest sibling first, though. Naomi wasn't in town, and to learn what was happening would upset her, but she wouldn't be able to dash here to stay with them. Alexa would let her know later.

She instead considered calling Dom first, since she'd been in touch with him over the past few days. Not that what had happened had anything to do with what they'd been discussing. And he wasn't in Blue Larkspur, either.

No, she decided to call Jasper and Aubrey. They were local, and the Gemini Ranch was just out of town.

She called Jasper's number.

"Hi, sis," he said.

"Hi. Look, you need to know this." She quickly told him what had happened, and where she was. "I'd appreciate it if you'd call the rest of our sibs who are local. I don't know how Mom is doing now, but I hope to hear soon."

"Got it. I'll let everyone else know. And Aubrey and I will be there as soon as we can."

Good. That was necessary, though painful. Alexa hated waiting here alone. The idea of Dane being with her telling jokes crept into her head, but she thrust it out since it wasn't going to happen. But she could try to go bother someone here to find out what was going on with Isa.

But as soon as she reached the waiting room door to leave, she was joined by Chief Theodore Lawson. She'd met him before, mostly thanks to his friendship with her mother. He was tall, with silver hair, green eyes and an utterly polite personality.

Right now he stared down at Alexa as they both stood there, those eyes wide and his forehead puckered in obvious concern.

"How's Isa?" he asked immediately.

"Not sure." Alexa let the words out with a sigh, moving her glance so she wouldn't meet his eyes. "They've taken her into the emergency room for a checkup. She had symptoms of a possible heart attack, and—"

"No wonder. I have access to all emergency calls that come into the station, and I heard Spence attacked her. And you, too—right?"

"That's right." Alexa bit her lip. If he knew all the details, would the chief blame her?

But why? She'd done all she could to protect her mother. She hadn't led Spence there. She'd gotten his gun away from him and caused him to flee.

No, she just had a guilty conscience, for no reason except wishing she had done even more to prevent her mother from a possible heart attack.

And the chief? He obviously cared enough to dash right to the hospital when he'd heard Isa had been taken there. Alexa had already wondered if the two of them were in a potential relationship, and now she had more reason to believe it.

Theodore sat in the chair beside the one Alexa had previously occupied, and she slumped back down in that one.

"How long has she been in there?" Theodore asked, leaning forward and clasping his hands together over his knees.

"Not sure. Maybe twenty minutes." Alexa considered checking the time on her phone. How long after noon was it? That was approximately when she'd first seen her mother. But how long had the events with Spence taken? And the aftermath near her car, plus the ambulance ride here?

"Well, that doesn't matter. I'll stay here as long as necessary, and I assume you will, too."

"Absolutely."

Alexa watched Theodore's expression. He had gritted his teeth, and his breathing was fast.

She certainly didn't want him to have a heart attack, too. "Look," she said. "Since you're the police chief, let me tell you the details of what happened."

"Great idea."

And so she did, from the moment she'd heard Spence's voice, to his disappearance beyond the crowd after she'd gotten his gun.

But before Alexa could finish, a nurse in blue scrubs came into the room. Her name tag said Nurse Nelson. She looked older and matronly.

"Mrs. Colton seems to be doing better now," she said, approaching Alexa. "Best we can tell at the moment, she had a panic attack, not a heart attack as originally believed. Someone was threatening the two of you, right, when she started to have symptoms?"

"That's right," Alexa said, feeling somewhat relieved. A panic attack had to be a lot safer than a heart attack, didn't it?

"We want to keep an eye on her for now, though," the nurse continued, "so we're going to move her to one of the rooms down the hall. You can go there, too, to keep her company."

Her eyes moved from Alexa to Theodore, and Alexa said, "This is Chief Lawson. He's a friend of our family, and I'd like him to join us."

"That should be fine," the nurse said.

But there was more. "Oh, and I called some of my family members before," Alexa said, "and they may be joining us." She didn't ask if that was acceptable. She'd let them in a few at a time, if necessary. Anything to keep her mother safe and happy.

"That sounds all right, too," said the nurse. "Your mom will be on monitors, so we'll know if she's getting too stressed. And please don't overdo the number of people keeping her company."

"Of course," Alexa agreed. She followed the nurse out of the waiting room and down the open hall, busy with others mostly in scrubs, to one of the last doors, which she opened. Alexa also heard Theodore's determined footsteps behind her on the tiled floor.

Alexa's mom, in a private room, lay in a light green hospital gown, propped up by the back of her narrow bed. A lot of tubes and things appeared to be attached to her, and there were rhythmic beeping noises.

But she was awake, and called out in a slow, raspy voice, "Oh, Alexa, you're here." And then she stopped and looked beyond Alexa. "And Theodore. Why are you—?"

"Because I heard you were ill, Isa, and I wanted to make sure you were okay." The man who'd been behind Alexa moved quickly forward and bent over when he reached the bed, kissing Isadora's cheek.

Good guy, Alexa thought. So far she'd seen nothing to turn her against it if they had any kind of relationship.

There were chairs at the side of the room, and Alexa and Theodore each took one. "We'll be here with you, Mom," Alexa said. "We don't want to keep you awake or otherwise stir you up, but let us know if you need anything."

"I've got what I need right now with you both here," her mom whispered.

A knock sounded on the door then, and one of the nurses opened it. "Are you okay to have another cou-

ple of family members come in for a visit?" she asked,
looking at Alexa's mom as she walked to the bed.

"Absolutely," Isa said.

Not surprising to Alexa, since she'd called them
first, the visitors were Jasper and Aubrey.

And over the course of the next hour, a few other siblings who lived in or around Blue Larkspur also came
to visit, thanks to Jasper or Audrey getting in touch.
They included Dom, who'd obviously rushed here despite not living in town, as well as Caleb and Morgan.

The rest of her siblings called.

But of those who were there, they all wanted to
hear Alexa's story about what had happened, which
she related to them when they joined her in the waiting room, always leaving Theodore in the room with
their mother. Fortunately, no strangers joined them in
the waiting area.

As Alexa told them how Spence had appeared on
the sidewalk, out of the blue, Caleb stood from where
he'd been seated and growled, "I'll bet he was following Mom. Or maybe you. Or maybe he really was just
hanging out in areas he thought Coltons might appear,
like good areas of town."

"However he did it," Dom said, also appearing furious, "we need to make sure he never does it again."

"I agree," Morgan said. "No matter how he found
them, it's wrong. Very wrong. And—well, I know it's
not our fault, but we should never have used The Truth
Foundation and helped him get free, even though Clay
Houseman copped to his crimes. But we didn't know
that our father had been right this once in getting someone convicted and imprisoned for a long time. Well,
Spence won't be free forever. I'm going to make sure

of it. That's my primary goal right now, bringing Ronald Spence in. I'm working on locating him as fast as I can, and I won't stop."

"You're right," Alexa said, "but that's taking a lot of responsibility on yourself. I'll be looking for the guy, too, and please let me know if there's anything I can do to help."

"I will," Morgan said. "Thanks."

However it occurred, Alexa felt certain her siblings in law enforcement and involved in upholding the law would find the guy and get him arrested—again. She was glad, and proud, that the Colton family wasn't backing down and was out to get Spence.

The conversation slowed down, and Alexa returned to going in and out of their mother's room, trying to ensure there weren't too many people there at the same time. But she didn't even try to get Theodore to leave. Her mother seemed so happy and relaxed when the police chief sat beside her on the bed as they both talked to those of Isa's kids who came to visit.

Alexa was in the room, though, when a doctor in white scrubs, a stethoscope around his neck, came in. "Hi, I'm Dr. Carlo. I checked on Mrs. Colton before and would like to again."

"Do you want us to leave the room?" Alexa asked.

"Yes, please."

In a few minutes, Dr. Carlo came out. "Mrs. Colton is looking pretty good now. We're going to release her to go home, as long as someone can be there with her for the next twenty-four hours or so to make sure she remains stable."

"That would be me," Theodore said immediately. "I'm fine with taking some time off tomorrow."

The next few minutes turned into a bit of a blur after Alexa and a nurse got Isa dressed into her own clothes again, and the rest of them all helped her get ready to leave, while Theodore took a while on the phone to plan his upcoming time off, then left to get his car.

Soon, Isa was wheeled out to the curb in a wheelchair, then helped into Theodore's police SUV. "I'm taking her to her home now and will stay with her there, but any of you can feel free to visit tomorrow, of course, as long as she's left alone tonight to get a good night's sleep."

That sounded good to Alexa, and apparently to her siblings as well. The police chief had taken charge of the situation, and their mother's care, for now. Isa was clearly in good hands.

She had a new man in her life. One who really cared.

Alexa felt happy for her.

But she couldn't help but think about the man who'd entered her own life, thanks to her profession, but was now out of it once more.

She couldn't help feeling sad, thinking of Dane. Maybe even heartbroken. She missed him. Might never see him again. Oh, yes, she had fallen for him, smart or not.

She only hoped all was going well with him now, and would continue to do so in the future, in court and otherwise.

Without her.

Chapter 20

It was almost over. There'd been a pause, though, in the trial this Tuesday morning. For the moment, Dane didn't have to concentrate on anything being said, and so he just sat there behind the rail, looking around at the many people in front of him, near the judge.

Watching the judge have a discussion with both the prosecutor and defense counsel as he leaned down from the bench.

Dane hadn't been permitted to be in the courtroom before he'd testified, which hadn't been surprising. Not that anything he might have heard would affect his testimony.

That had meant he'd been under guard in a small meeting room in the courthouse yesterday morning for a couple of hours. But his testimony had begun around 11:00 a.m. It had continued for the rest of the day.

It had been grueling, but oh so gratifying.

The defense counsel had done her darnedest to attempt to show he was lying or exaggerating, but he couldn't be shaken.

The facts were clear. Months ago, he had been looking into who was running a prostitution ring, thanks to orders from his boss, Police Chief Samuel Swanson—a big mistake on Swanson's part since it soon became clear that the chief was the one they were after. Dane and his partner, Alvin, had started investigating Swanson.

Swanson had unsurprisingly figured it out.

Dane had consequently watched Swanson shoot Alvin. And he'd also watched the gun aim at him and felt the bullet penetrate his arm.

His cross-examination had been even more arduous, but his description was the truth. He hadn't hesitated. He hadn't made even a tiny contradiction.

The defense had clearly not been happy.

And Swanson? He'd glared down at the table in front of him, not directing his fury toward Dane—most likely under orders from his attorney.

From what Dane understood, security in the courthouse had been ramped up enough that he doubted anyone else would show up with guns to attempt to shut him up—even though the authorities apparently hadn't found any of the others Swanson might have hired to come after him. But even while he testified Dane wasn't worried.

That was yesterday. And Dane been permitted to watch the rest of the trial after his testimony, including for a couple of hours this morning.

Not that there'd been much after that, although the defense had managed to bring in a few witnesses. One claimed he'd been with Swanson at the critical time, but his testimony hadn't stood up to cross-examination. And a couple this morning were character witnesses, including a Tempe city councilman. But even acting like a good guy to those he reported to didn't mean Swanson was innocent.

At the moment, the warm courtroom, currently filled with the low sounds of people conversing as they waited for the trial to resume, seemed safe enough.

Dane had thought a lot about Alexa.

What would she have thought about his testimony?

What did she think about him now?

Did she think about him at all?

He hadn't been permitted to get in touch with her again, just in case she was somehow under surveillance by one of Swanson's cronies who were looking for him when he was out of court while the trial continued, such as the rest of the weekend, or last night.

And yeah, he missed her. A lot.

A whole lot. He had to talk to her again soon.

He realized how much he was in love with her.

Right now, he sat behind the railing with a whole crowd of onlookers, including members of the media, watching and listening as the trial got underway.

Good. Time to continue.

Now, Francini gave his closing arguments to the jury. Defense counsel would be next.

Then the jury would be taken to another room to conduct deliberations.

Who knew how long that would take?

No matter. He would be around here, waiting for those results, which he certainly hoped would be correct.

It had seemed fairly short for a murder trial, but the facts seemed pretty clear.

Dane would soon get whatever final backup he could from his protectors, then resume his life.

And would he talk to Alexa again then?

Oh yes.

And more, if possible.

A lot more. He would make sure of that.

Time was passing. It was a Saturday morning, a week after her return home.

Alexa sat at her small kitchen table with her electric stove on one side and refrigerator on the other, all perched on a beige tiled floor. She liked this aspect of her house.

She liked most things about her home.

Even though, at the moment, she was considering how and for where to leave it for the day. She'd at least put on a casual cotton shirt over slim jeans. Nothing professional, but there were plenty of places she could go dressed that way.

Her mind slipped to Dane, as it always did. She missed him terribly.

But somehow she would need to learn to live with it.

No matter how much it hurt.

She was drinking a cup of coffee just brewed in a pot where she could grab seconds or thirds if she wished. She was home for the weekend. Her office was closed, except for emergencies, and so far she hadn't yet been assigned someone else for witness protection, although she'd had some detailed discussions with Vince about procedures she'd been using with Dane and others, as well as several possible assignments coming up soon.

Right now, she was pondering a way to get together with family. Maybe her mother. Or maybe she could even arrange a dinner that night with her mom and Theodore, as well as some of her siblings and their romantic interests...

But that might feel painful, to be there on her own.

Not that Dane was really a romantic interest... Okay, who was she trying to kid? Of course he was. Or had been. But now he was out of her life.

She picked her cup off the table and took another sip. It was getting cold. Should she heat it, or just leave the house and go shopping somewhere?

Alexa had followed the Swanson trial in the media as much as she could from Blue Larkspur. The trial had ended on Tuesday.

The jury had deliberated for a couple of days, and Swanson had been found guilty. No surprise, and definitely a relief.

That meant Dane was most likely out of witness protection, since he was no longer a witness. Swanson was in prison now, or at least on his way.

His sentence had been life, with no chance for parole. Logical. He was guilty of murder.

Of course some of Swanson's colleagues could still be after Dane. But Dane had presumably resumed his job as a vice detective with the Tempe PD. He was in law enforcement. He'd be careful.

And even if Swanson's buddies were unhappy, why place themselves in the position once again of possibly going to prison, too, by harming, or killing, Dane?

No, she figured he was safe. Hoped he was, at least. He had to be back in Tempe. Who was the new police chief there? It didn't matter to Alexa, but she certainly hoped it was someone honest and straightforward, a good superior officer for Dane.

They had spoken once since Dane's testimony. He had called Alexa the next day, on Wednesday, but she'd been at work and hadn't been able to do much but trade hellos and a few good wishes. She'd appreciated hearing from him.

He'd sounded so sweet. Made her laugh a few times. Made her really miss him like she'd never missed another man. So— Well, it didn't matter. If what they'd said to one another before hadn't truly been good-bye, maybe that conversation was.

Even so, she'd pondered later that day, and after, if she dared call him back and talk more, maybe even about getting together again someday. They no longer had professional reasons to stay apart, after all. And he was constantly on her mind, in her thoughts, populating her dreams...

With that once more filling her mind, she slammed the cup back on the table, though not hard enough to break it. Time to do...something.

She rose, ready to go grab her purse and get in her car.

Except—the doorbell rang. Interesting. She wasn't expecting anyone, or even any deliveries. She pushed her chair back and left the kitchen, heading for the hallway leading to the carved wooden front door.

She peered out the side window—and gasped.

Dane stood there, and he clearly saw her.

He was grinning.

She pulled the door open. "Come in," she exclaimed and moved out of the way so he could.

What was he doing there?

And why did it make her feel so ecstatic? As if she didn't know. She had fallen for this jokester.

He brushed gently against her as he stepped into the wide hall. He was just as she remembered—not that they'd been apart very long. But he was tall, his dark hair combed perfectly to frame his angular, handsome, smooth-shaven face. He wore a nice blue buttoned shirt tucked into dark pants; he looked somewhat dressed up.

Why? Was he in Blue Larkspur for business?

Whatever his reason, she was delighted to see him.

She closed the door behind him. "Hey, it's early," she said. "When did you get here? How did you get here? And why—?"

"Why? Because I really wanted to see you, Alexa."

"Oh," she said. What were the answers to her other questions? Did they matter?

Should she tell him how happy she was to see him? Should she tell him how she really felt about him? Maybe… But not yet.

"Hey, have you had breakfast?" she asked. "Or how about some coffee? I have some fresh brewed in my kitchen. And—hey, how did you know where I lived?" The smile she'd been aiming at him turned into a frown. "You've never been here before, and I don't recall ever telling you."

"Hey, I'm in law enforcement, like you are. Your address wasn't hard for me to find, though I kept it as secure as possible on the source I used. Of course I didn't know for certain you'd be home, but I'm delighted you are." He put his arm around her, still grinning. "And yes, I'd love some coffee."

Good. A distraction of sorts. She could ponder what to say, what to do, while they spent a little downtime in the kitchen.

"Great. This way," she said, feeling a bit sorry as she pulled away but nevertheless led him down the hall.

She grabbed another empty cup from the wall cabinet near the sink and poured him some coffee, also refreshing her own.

She handed his to him.

Then she demanded, "Why haven't I heard from you since the one time we talked after your part of the trial?"

She almost wished she could take the question back, but he didn't look upset or offended.

"Because I was concerned about you. I wanted to make sure no one appeared to be after me in retribution to my helping to put Swanson away for life, since they might also go after my witness protector. I assume you know no one else has been caught."

"Yes, I'm aware of it."

He was still standing, but he put his coffee down on the table, and so did she.

They were suddenly in each other's arms.

"I'd do anything in the world to protect you, Alexa. Even stay away from you. I really care about you. A lot. In fact, I—"

Alexa put her finger over his mouth.

She'd been shocked just now, when he showed up on her doorstep. And now he admitted he'd stayed away from her for her protection.

Because he really cared about her.

Her mind pulsed with emotion already.

Was he now going to say he loved her?

If so, did she want to hear it?

Did she love him?

Oh yeah. But they couldn't be in each other's lives. She didn't want to move to Tempe. And him, near Blue Larkspur? And it was too soon for the "L" word—they'd only spent a few days on the move together. Or was it? After all, the heart wanted what the heart wanted.

She couldn't help it. She'd already put her coffee back on the table. Now she threw her arms around him again and pulled his head down toward hers.

Their kiss made her want to forget all her questions and just live in the moment.

With Dane.

Okay, he had to tell her why he was really here right now.

But not immediately. Not while he was enjoying, loving, their kiss.

Loving her.

He basked in their closeness a while longer. He drew out their kiss, using his tongue to tease her, his arms to keep her tight against him.

But then— Well, they had to talk. He pulled back, gave her another quick kiss on her gorgeous, inviting lips, then smiled and sat at her table.

He gestured to the chair across from him. Her lovely face appeared confused for an instant, but she did as he'd suggested.

"Okay," he said, taking a sip of coffee before digging into what he had to say. "How would you feel about seeing me more often here, in Blue Larkspur?"

Her expression grew even more puzzled. "You're kidding, aren't you? What about your job with the Tempe police?"

"Well, I've enjoyed it—sort of. Until my superior turned out to be a murderer. And until my partner was killed. Oh, I could have taken on more and different responsibilities there now, but—"

He'd already considered different ways to approach

this. One thing he hadn't said was that he had been in Blue Larkspur for a day, driving up here after the trial was over.

For a good reason. One that had made him delay attempting to see her.

Since, if it worked out, he would potentially get to see her a lot.

And it had.

"But what?" she encouraged him, her brow furrowed over those beautiful blue eyes.

"Well, I've just accepted a job with the Blue Larkspur PD, also as a vice detective—or I'm close to accepting it. The offer is hanging there for a few days. And I intend to accept it as long as you don't mind seeing me while I'm here. Maybe even entering into a relationship, particularly when things have calmed down after a while and our adrenaline isn't pumping any longer over me being a witness and you protecting me. Or my worrying about protecting you. What do you think?"

"I think— I'm not sure." She still looked confused, although was that hope he saw there, too? "But I believe I'd like to try it. Only, if it doesn't work out, you could be stuck here with a new job and all. How do you feel about that?"

He rose once more and put out his hand. She took it, and again stood in front of him. Close to him. Tempting him.

"I think I love you, Alexa," he said, clasping her hand even more tightly.

"And I think I love you, Dane. But—"

Wow. That was certainly hoped for. And to hear it so soon...

"Hey," he said, "you know me. I can be serious—

or not. This time, I'm serious. Only... Look. If I stay here and take this job, I may just have to arrest you."

"What? What are you talking about?"

"Well, I'm a cop. You know that. And I'll be here spending time with you. Sure, I'm a vice detective, but I can arrest people who commit crimes. And you're doing just that."

He'd been trying to keep his expression serious. But, heck, he was a jokester from way back. She knew that, even though they'd gone through some pretty nasty situations together.

And now? Well, if she went along with this joke, he'd feel even more in love with her.

"Tell me what you mean." She tried to pull her hand away, but he didn't let her. "Why would you possibly arrest me? What crime am I committing, or have I done something already, with my witness protection? Or—"

"Hey, I can arrest people for theft, you know. And you're in the process of stealing my heart."

"What! For a moment there, I thought you really were serious. But I should have known better." She started to laugh. Hard. So hard, he saw tears in her eyes.

Her giant smile was clearly driven by amusement.

"You law enforcement clown," she said, gasping as her laughter slowed down. She tightened her grip on his hand this time. "Now kiss me."

And Dane knew he had won her over. Forever.

He took her into his arms and obeyed her command.

* * * * *

The whole desperate plan began simply as a last-ditch attempt to save his life. He never intended for anyone to get hurt. That day, not long after Thanksgiving, he walked into the bank full of hope. It was the first time he'd ever asked for a loan. It was also the first time he'd ever seen executive loan officer Carla Richmond.

When he tapped at her open doorway, she looked up from that big desk of hers. He thought she was too young and pretty with her big blue eyes and all that curly chestnut-brown hair to make the decision as to whether he lived or died.

She had a great smile as she got to her feet to offer him a seat.

He felt so out of place in her plush office that he stood in the doorway nervously kneading the brim of his worn baseball cap for a moment before stepping in. As he did, her blue-eyed gaze took in his ill-fitting clothing hanging on his rangy body, his bad haircut, his large, weathered hands.

He told himself that she'd already made up her mind before he even sat down. She didn't give men like him a second look—let alone money. Like his father always said, bankers never gave dough to poor people who actually needed it. They just helped their rich friends.

Right away Carla Richmond made him feel small with her questions about his employment record, what he had for collateral, why he needed the money and how he planned to repay it. He'd recently lost one crappy job and was in the process of starting another temporary one, and all he had to show for the years he'd worked hard labor since high school was an old pickup and a pile of bills.

He took the forms she handed him and thanked her, knowing he wasn't going to bother filling them in. On the way out of her office, he balled them up and dropped them in the trash. All the way to his pickup, he mentally kicked himself for being such a fool. What had he expected?

No one was going to give him money, even to save his life—especially some woman in a suit behind a big desk in an air-conditioned office. It didn't matter that she didn't have a clue how desperate he really was. All she'd seen when she'd looked at him was a loser. To think that he'd bought a new pair of jeans with the last of his cash and borrowed a too-large button-up shirt from a former coworker for this meeting.

After climbing into his truck, he sat for a moment, too scared and sick at heart to start the engine. The worst part was the thought of going home and telling Jesse. The way his luck was going, she would walk out on him. Not that he could blame her, since his gambling had gotten them into this mess.

He thought about blowing off work, since his new job was only temporary anyway, and going straight to the bar. Then he reminded himself that he'd spent the last of his money on the jeans. He couldn't even afford a beer. His own fault, he reminded himself. He'd only made things worse when he'd gone to a loan shark for cash and then stupidly gambled the money, thinking he could make back what he owed and then some when he won. He'd been so sure his luck had changed for the better when he'd met Jesse.

Last time the two thugs had come to collect the interest on the loan, they'd left him bleeding in the dirt outside his rented house. They would be back any day.

With a curse, he started the pickup. A cloud of exhaust blew out the back as he headed home to face Jesse with the bad news. Asking for a loan had been a long shot, but still he couldn't help thinking about the disappointment he'd see in her eyes when he told her. They'd planned to go out tonight for an expensive dinner with the loan money to celebrate.

As he drove home, his humiliation began to fester like a sore that just wouldn't heal. Had he known even then how this was going to end? Or was he still telling himself he was just a nice guy who'd made some mistakes, had some bad luck and gotten involved with the wrong people?

Don't miss
Christmas Ransom *by B.J. Daniels,*
available December 2022 wherever
Harlequin books and ebooks are sold.

Harlequin.com

HIEXP0922

HARLEQUIN
PLUS

Announcing a **BRAND-NEW**
multimedia subscription service
for romance fans like you!

Read, Watch and Play.

Experience the easiest way to get
the romance content you crave.

Start your **FREE 7 DAY TRIAL** at
<u>www.harlequinplus.com/freetrial</u>.